"What do you think you're doing?" Bronwyn demanded

and pushed her hands against William's chest. It felt like a brick wall.

"Stop that, or I'll drop you," he answered calmly. "I'm taking you home."

"I can walk!"

She knew that his shirt was half undone. He could catch his death. But by now they were nearly halfway across the yard, so it would be useless to protest any more.

William's foot slipped. Bronwyn's arms tightened around his neck as he quickly righted himself. "You are an awkward burden."

His words should have angered her. But she scarcely heard them. She was too aware of her arms about him.

He stopped in front of the cabin. Her breath caught in her throat as he let her down. Her legs slipped slowly past his hips. When her toes touched the ground, her thighs brushed against him.

Neither of them moved....

Dear Reader,

Harlequin's WEDDINGS, INC. is a continuity series that revolves around a wedding chapel in Eternity, Massachusetts. Margaret Moore's *Vows* is the seventh book in the series and the story of how the legend of Eternity began. America is a new setting for the author, whose previous novels have been medievals, and readers are in for a treat with this tale that *Affaire de Coeur* describes as "fast-paced and gloriously romantic." It's the story of a Welsh immigrant who finds herself involved with the Underground Railway. We hope you enjoy it.

Our other titles this month include *Desire My Love* from Miranda Jarrett, the next book in the continuing saga of the irrepressible Sparhawk family of Rhode Island; *Betrayed*, another wonderful Regency from author Judith McWilliams about an American heiress forced to spy on her British relatives; and *Roarke's Folly*, the third book in Claire Delacroix's ROSE SERIES, which began with *Romance of the Rose*.

Keep an eye out for all four titles, wherever Harlequin Historicals are sold.

Sincerely,

Tracy Farrell
Senior Editor

Please address questions and book requests to:
Harlequin Reader Service
U.S.: 3010 Walden Ave., P.O. Box 1325, Buffalo, NY 14269
Canadian: P.O. Box 609, Fort Erie, Ont. L2A 5X3

MARGARET MOORE

Vows

Harlequin Books

TORONTO • NEW YORK • LONDON
AMSTERDAM • PARIS • SYDNEY • HAMBURG
STOCKHOLM • ATHENS • TOKYO • MILAN
MADRID • WARSAW • BUDAPEST • AUCKLAND

To my husband, Bill, who is not William,
and to Steven and Amy,
who will always remember Boston

ISBN 0-373-28848-4

VOWS

Copyright © 1994 by Margaret Wilkins.

Weddings, Inc.

Join us every month
in Eternity, Massachusetts...where love lasts forever.

A Note from the Author

Being asked to be part of a new continuity series was very exciting. It was a pleasant challenge to create the ancestors of the contemporary citizens of Eternity, Massachusetts.

In the name of research, I decided that a trip to Massachusetts was in order. My family and I were able to enjoy the New England countryside, learn about the Salem witch trials and go whale watching. Unfortunately, we also managed to get completely, hopelessly lost trying to drive in downtown Boston. About all we saw of that beautiful, historic city was Boston Commons, because we were concentrating on street signs and the map, which had the one-way streets incorrectly marked.

Nonetheless, Boston has already become part of our family's collection of shared memories, and we can even laugh about our unexpected adventure. We just won't ever try to drive there again!

Chapter One

Eternity, Massachusetts, 1855

"I am still not convinced this was the wisest course," the clergyman whispered to his tall, lean and broad-shouldered companion as they waited in the shadows of the dockside alley.

"Perhaps not," his friend agreed in a low, deep voice. "Yet we couldn't risk hiding him much longer. Tinkham's offer of a reward for information about runaway slaves is obviously having some effect."

The older man nodded, then both fell silent and watched the activity on the piers, apparently undisturbed by the scents of fish, hemp, tar, salt water and cargo from ports scattered around the world. Seamen called to each other in a variety of languages. Heavy casks of water, molasses and ale thumped rhythmically as they were pushed along the wooden piers. Hawsers creaked in the breeze, and water lapped against the wooden hulls of the vessels. A small crowd gathered on the deck of the nearest sloop, preparing to disembark.

The two men did not appear interested in the bales of cotton and wooden crates of cargo rising like small mountains close by, either—except for one crate, in one particular pile, near the sloop that belonged to the wealthy, influential and notably abolitionist Falconer family.

The clergyman sighed. "It pains me to have to agree with you, William, but I cannot deny the obvious. I thought the Fugitive Slave Law was the worst to face us. Now that Tinkham's a marshal, I fear there may be more trouble to come."

"He must have powerful friends to be made a federal marshal. Certainly no one in the town expected it."

"No. Or at least they pretended to be shocked."

"If the North goes to war with the South, we must be prepared for even more hypocrisy," William Powell replied.

Many of the people of Eternity were outspoken in their abhorrence of the Fugitive Slave Law, which permitted slaves who had reached free states to be captured and returned to their masters.

Some had joined Reverend Bowman, who was a conductor of the Underground Railroad, a network of abolitionists and free blacks who conspired to lead slaves north to Canada. As for the others, talk was cheap and free of danger, at least in Massachusetts.

Then there was William Powell, who said nothing and did his utmost. William was second to Reverend Bowman in the organization of the Railroad in their area, yet only the reverend and his wife knew that

William was involved and that he was the most zealous abolitionist among them.

"Have you seen your brother yet?" Reverend Bowman asked quietly.

"No. I thought I would wait until the package was safely loaded. There will still be time to say my farewells before the *Demelza Jane* sails."

"He will gone for some time, I believe."

"Yes."

"If war comes, perhaps it is just as well he will be far away. I'm sure John would enlist at once."

William's face remained impassive.

"Let us hope cooler heads will prevail."

"I hope so, Reverend." Despite William's calm tone, no one in America wished more fervently than he that an armed struggle be avoided, at almost any cost, because he knew the price of rebellion all too well. Not simply for those who fought, but for their families, too.

"Did John repay you for your last loan?"

"No."

Reverend Bowman eyed his companion compassionately. "William, you must tell him the truth about your financial situation. And you simply must stop lending him money you can ill afford to lose."

"He is my brother."

"I'm not saying abandon him. First mates are well paid, and you've got your father and Constance to look after."

"I can handle my own affairs."

The minister heard the hard edge to William's voice and realized he was intruding on William's personal business. He continued anyway. "I wish you had told me about the mortgage. I certainly applaud your motive. However, I could have—"

"Josiah will repay me."

"Unless he gets taken by a slave hunter, or decides he must flee to Canada."

"He won't until he has his whole family. With the five hundred I've loaned him, he needs only a little more to buy his son, and then he can go."

"William, I appreciate your intentions—"

"I will pay the mortgage, Reverend."

There was no mistaking the absolute finality of William's tone. The minister sighed and said, "How is your father these days?"

"Good."

"I'm happy to hear it."

William nodded toward the end of the docks.

Ed Tinkham, followed by his son, Frank, and five other men, sauntered along the pier. All of the men were armed and, with the exception of Frank, looked as hard-bitten and callous as a man could be. Eighteen-year-old Frank looked as if he would rather be anywhere else.

Tinkham smiled at the people, who moved out of the big man's way, until he stopped beside the crate that had been the object of William and Reverend Bowman's scrutiny.

William stepped forward. The reverend laid a detaining hand on his arm. "Let James handle this."

William inclined his head in agreement. James Falconer, whose family owned the sloop and several other small ships, would have more influence with Tinkham.

"We know there's a runaway in this box," Tinkham announced.

The people on the deck of the sloop drew closer to the gangplank and watched. A lone crewman, obviously unsure of what he should do, muttered something in response.

"I don't need a damned piece of paper! There's a runaway slave in that crate and I'm going to get him."

The crewman mumbled again.

"I don't give a damn if Falconer's not here. Stand out of the way, or I'll shoot you right there. Frank, open the damned lid."

After a dubious glance at his father and an apologetic one to the seaman, the round-faced youth started to pry open the top of the wooden crate.

"Fetch my wagon," William ordered quietly. He ignored the minister's protestation and marched onto the pier just as the marshal gave a shout of triumph—which was cut short when a black youth shoved the crate lid off from inside, forcing all the men back. He climbed out quickly, horror and panic on his face. His eyes squinted in the bright sunlight.

Suddenly a shrill shriek pierced the air.

A young woman ran down the gangplank of the sloop and paused dramatically. A stiff autumn breeze blew back her woolen cloak and made her blond hair stream out behind her like a flag of battle.

William Powell did not usually notice young women. However, no man on the pier could have ignored this woman, with her blond hair and blue eyes, flawless complexion and astonishingly shapely figure garbed in a plain blue gown.

The slave hunters recovered first and surrounded the fugitive. William cursed and rushed forward.

Before he was able to reach them, the young woman cried, "Uncle Ennion!" and launched herself from the gangplank. She landed on Tinkham's broad back, knocking him to the ground.

"Get the hell off of me!" the marshal yelled, struggling in the young woman's fierce embrace. "Get *off!*"

Seeing his chance, the fugitive bolted through the gap made by the fallen marshal. He spotted William, who gave a slight nod in the direction of the alley while he continued to advance purposefully on the slave hunters. The runaway dashed toward the narrow lane as William elbowed the closest of the marshal's men into the water.

"I can't swim!" the hunter yelled, his arms flailing helplessly.

Frank hesitated as the runaway disappeared into the shadows. He looked at his father, then dispatched the other men after their quarry before he reached down to fish the man out of the cold salt water.

William went toward the woman, who still gripped the struggling Tinkham. "Excuse me, miss. I believe you have made a mistake," he said, taking hold of her slender arm. He felt sinewy muscle beneath his fingers. She was probably a servant or a lady's maid. Not that it mattered to him who she was, or what she did, or to what class she belonged.

Relieved of his burden, Tinkham got up. "I'll have you put in jail!" he cried.

"I don't think that would be wise," William remarked.

"Not my Uncle Ennion, after all," she said mournfully, her countenance the picture of innocence while she straightened her straw bonnet. "Sorry, I am."

William doubted anybody, and certainly no woman from the location identified by her musical accent, could be so innocent.

Tinkham glared at William, glanced dismissively at the woman and leaned over to pick up his battered hat. "Damn right I'm not your uncle Onion."

"Tinkham, you are addressing a lady." .

"The hell . . ." The marshal caught William's eye. "You've made a big mistake," he said gruffly. "You've prevented a federal marshal from doing his job."

"Please forgive me," she pleaded contritely. She smiled coyly. "I see how wrong I was. Much handsomer than Uncle Ennion you are."

Marshal Tinkham appeared to be slightly mollified. Obviously the woman knew exactly the effect her beauty had on men.

"Is your friend hurt?" Her troubled gaze went to the man standing on the pier who looked like a half-drowned hound dog.

"He'll be fine," the marshal growled. "Come on," he said to his men. "We have to find that boy. He's worth a lot of money."

"Good day to you, sir, and sorry I am I thought you were related to me," the young woman said sweetly.

The marshal grunted and strode away, trailed by his son and the soaking man.

When Tinkham was out of earshot, William faced the young woman. "You really didn't believe he was your uncle, did you," he charged sternly.

Although she frowned, her eyes twinkled merrily in the shadow of her bonnet. "Oh, but I did, or I would be breaking the law, wouldn't I, stopping that man from taking the poor lad back into slavery."

"You might have been hurt."

"Seven brothers, me. I know how to wrestle. I had a good grip on him, too. I'm sorry I have no time to chat. We are to be getting off here. Good day to you, sir, and thank you for your concern. However misplaced."

"Are you Welsh?"

"Aye. From Aberfan. Have you been there?"

"No," he lied.

"A pity. There was that about your voice made me think I'd found a Welshman."

"I'm an American," William said. He struggled to hide his surprise. He had been in Massachusetts fourteen years, more than half his life. He had been determined to lose any trace of Wales in his voice, and he was convinced he had—until this moment, when a Welshwoman stared at him with a boldness he remembered well. And hated.

Her eyes narrowed slightly. "As I said, a pity. We are here to work at Miss Pembrook's School for Young Ladies."

"We?" He had no reason to stay and talk—except that Tinkham might return to question the crew regarding the origin of the crate. It would be wise to remain on the pier awhile yet.

"My brother and sisters and me."

She scrutinized his deliberately impassive face.

"What is it?" she asked suddenly, disconcerting him again. "Is there something wrong with the school?"

"Nothing at all. My sister attends it."

"Mr. Powell!" A voice like the screech of an ungreased axle cut across the pier.

"That is Miss Pembrook," William said, pointing toward the schoolmistress and his half sister, Constance, seated in the buggy.

As he approached them, he quickly surveyed the docks. He saw no sign of Reverend Bowman or Tinkham and his men, although he noticed his horse and wagon waiting near the alley. Obviously Reverend Bowman had thought of another way to help the slave escape.

"I hope I'm not too late to say goodbye to John," Constance said shyly. She smiled prettily and, as always, reminded William of his stepmother, who had died giving her life.

William lifted Constance down. "Thank you for bringing her, Miss Pembrook."

"Miss Powell was really most insistent," Miss Pembrook said through thin, colorless lips. She scanned the pier and the deck of the sloop. "Since we are expecting a new cook today, I agreed. The young woman is to arrive on the Falconers' vessel. I trust James will be able to point her out to me."

William twisted and gestured at the young woman making her way down the gangplank carrying a valise and a large basket. A boy of about twelve and two little girls followed her as she came toward them. "I think she is the person you are expecting."

If it had been possible for the pale-faced Miss Pembrook to go any whiter, she would have. As it was, her lips grew even narrower and her mousy brown brows lowered ominously.

"*You* are Bronwyn Davies?" she demanded rudely when the young woman drew near. "Well, fortunately I arrived in time to see your outrageous, barbaric and *most unladylike* behavior. Any sensible person would agree that your presence would not be appropriate at a school whose aim is to educate young ladies of quality. Therefore, I must inform you I cannot give you employment."

The beautiful stranger reddened and took a deep breath. "I brought my sisters and brother all the way from Boston..."

"You should have thought of them before your shocking display."

"Who are you to speak to me like this?" the newcomer said defiantly. "As if I give a fig for what you think! I'd do it again this moment. I could never work for such a rude, uncaring person, anyway. Good day!" She whirled around and marched toward her siblings, leaving Miss Pembrook staring in surprise.

William watched while the now unemployed cook spoke in hushed and angry Welsh to her brother and sisters. What a temper she had! Almost as bad as his Irish housekeeper.

He was torn between a desire to upbraid Miss Pembrook for her discourtesy and the woman for her outburst. But what else could he expect from a young woman so obviously at the mercy of her passions? People like her meant trouble, and he should have nothing more to do with her.

"Well!" Miss Pembrook said after a moment's silence. She grabbed her buggy whip. "Well! I don't know what this country is coming to, letting people like *that* come here! Good day, Mr. Powell. Constance."

Miss Pembrook cracked her whip and the buggy whirled down Wharf Street in a cloud of dust.

Constance tugged on William's sleeve. "I think she's pretty, Willy. You need a cook, don't you?"

"We've got to say farewell to John," he reminded Constance curtly.

Constance looked so contrite he was immediately sorry for his harsh tone.

He took her hand. "I don't think we can afford to hire—"

"But what will they do, Willy? We can't leave them here. It wouldn't be right."

Without waiting for William to give another excuse, Constance darted forward. "My brother will hire you," she announced.

The woman looked at Constance, then William, surveying him dispassionately from head to foot.

"Is there anyone in Eternity who could help you?" he asked noncommittally.

She rose. "No. We only came to this town because of the job."

"You're Welsh, aren't you? I heard you talking," Constance said brightly. "My father is from Wales. He's been sick. Perhaps Welsh food will bring back his appetite. My brother says all he needs is a few decent meals."

"Is that so?"

This woman made him decidedly uncomfortable. He wasn't used to being so blatantly examined by anyone. "Are you a good cook?" he asked.

"Very."

"Modest, too, I see," he answered without a hint of humor.

"Please say yes," Constance entreated. "Dada will be so happy. He's always saying he misses Welsh cooking."

"How many would I be cooking for?"

"There's Dada, my brother, Mrs. Murphy and Sam. I live at school most of the time, but I come for visits."

The woman gazed suspiciously at William. No doubt, with her figure and beauty, she had been the recipient of any number of dubious offers and illicit proposals. "I am not alone. I have my brother and sisters to think of."

"Oh, they can come, too, of course," Constance said.

William crossed his arms and let his sister do the talking, although he suspected the cook was attempting to ascertain if her virtue would be at risk.

As if a pretty unmarried Welshwoman her age would have any virtue left.

"Perhaps your brother's sweetheart wouldn't want me in the house."

"Oh, don't worry about that! He doesn't have any sweethearts. He says he doesn't have time for such things."

"Do you want the job?" William demanded, quite sure he didn't wish to have his whole life discussed on the Eternity wharf, even though he had decided that Constance's suggestion did have some merit. Dr. Reed had said his father needed to maintain his appetite. For his father's sake, he would hire this woman—but he would avoid the kitchen.

"How much will you pay?" the woman asked.

"It depends on how well you cook."

He's a perplexing fellow, Bronwyn Davies thought, with eyes she couldn't read, a grip like the iron made in the works at home, and features no one would call handsome.

At first, when he had come to her aid, Bronwyn had wondered if he was going to join the fight. Yet all he had done was pull her off that fat lawman. She was used to loud, talkative men who argued for hours, sang like angels and fought at the drop of a hat.

Her brother, Owen, fidgeted behind her impatiently. He probably wondered why she spoke to this stranger. She didn't want to explain now. Besides, Owen was younger and would have to do what she said.

"We'll live in your house, I suppose?" she asked, keeping her tone light. Just because he didn't have any lust in his eyes and the little girl was sweet and kind didn't mean the man didn't have some ulterior motive.

"There is a cabin on my farm," he replied after a moment's hesitation. "It's near the house. You and your brother and sisters will live there."

She lowered her arms. Then she crossed them. "Would I have to do housework?"

"No, I have a housekeeper."

"Oh. Good." She hated dusting and washing, which required no imagination or skill at all. "I will cook for you, and with thanks." She held out her hand in the American way. "My name in Bronwyn Davies."

He didn't touch her.

"Introduce me," Constance whispered.

"I am William Powell and this is my sister, Miss Constance Powell."

"Ah, Gwilym Pool, is it?" she said, using the Welsh version and pronunciation.

"In America it's Pow-ell. My name is William Powell."

She felt a sting of disappointment in his blunt rejoinder. Was he ashamed of his heritage? Or perhaps the Americans couldn't pronounce the names properly. Yet somehow she didn't think a man with the stern gaze of William Powell would care which was the *easiest* way. He would surely care which was the *right* way. "This is my brother, Owen, and my sisters, Mair and Ula."

Constance curtsied. Bronwyn, suitably grave, did the same. Owen bowed slightly. The little girls unabashedly stared at Constance until Bronwyn nudged them. They tried a curtsy.

Bronwyn gave the man a warm, friendly smile—which apparently had absolutely no effect on this tall, dour fellow.

"Follow me," William Powell ordered. He hoisted the largest basket as easily as if it was empty and walked away.

"Come on, Owen," Bronwyn said. She forced herself to ignore the man's coldness and her own slight dread at making a decision so quickly. "I've already got another job! America truly is marvelous—and didn't I say it would be?"

Bronwyn and Owen picked up the rest of their baggage and shepherded Mair and Ula toward a wagon, trailing the tall man. When they reached it, she prepared to hoist Mair up. Before she could do so, Mr. Powell took the eight-year-old and put her in the wagon. He did the same for the younger Ula. Owen needed no assistance and helped to stow the rest of the baggage.

Constance glanced at her brother with a thoughtful expression. "I suppose they can visit some shops while we say our goodbyes to John."

"Yes, of course," Mr. Powell replied with a slightly guilty start.

"John sails today for the Orient. Fancy, going to China!" Constance explained.

Despite the pleading in her sisters' faces, Bronwyn said, "We shall wait here." Mair and Ula were good girls, but they had a weakness for sweets and pretty ribbons. Owen's vice was licorice. She would like to indulge them, but they had little money to waste on such things.

"Aren't you going to introduce me, too?"

Bronwyn turned around and encountered merry blue eyes that had to belong to a relative of William Powell.

"John!" Constance cried happily.

The two men stood side by side, making a comparison easy. They were both the same height and build, and had dark hair and faces tanned from a life spent out-of-doors. But the second man was good-looking and apparently good-humored. William Powell's face was lean and hawklike, and his iron-gray eyes serious.

"This is my brother, John, the first mate on the *Demelza Jane*," her new employer said.

Decidely attractive, John Powell pushed his hat well back on his forehead and leaned negligently on the side of the wagon. Bronwyn didn't appreciate his impertinent scrutiny. He was probably a charming, irresponsible rogue who thought himself quite the ladies' man.

Still, the Welsh was obvious in him, and she wondered if he would try to deny his heritage. "Who is your lovely companion, William?" he asked, continuing to stare at her boldly.

"The new cook." William Powell shifted impatiently.

"Maybe I have time for one last meal at home."

"Oh, please, John!" Constance said.

"You're always welcome, John. Father would be glad to see you once more." Although William Powell's countenance remained unchanged, his tone was distinctly chilly.

John Powell gave his brother a surprised look. "Well, I had better not. The weather might turn for the worse if we linger." He tipped his hat to Bronwyn, smiling as before, but now his expression was curious and speculative, as if he considered her some kind of unusual creature. "A pleasure to meet you."

She inclined her head.

"I should return in the early spring," the younger Powell said, turning his attention to his brother.

"Safe journey, John." The brothers shook hands.

Suddenly Bronwyn had the strange sensation that the two men had exchanged personalities. William Powell smiled with genuine affection and warmth. His whole appearance altered. He seemed younger and gentler. John Powell became solemn and anxious. "Take care of Da," he said quietly.

"I will."

In the next instant, John once again became the charming young seaman, and William the dour farmer.

John faced Constance. "Give me a farewell kiss," he said pleasantly. She complied and he hoisted her onto the wagon seat. "Safe journey," the little girl said softly.

John nodded and turned away, then glanced back at his brother. "Oh, my new suit wasn't finished yet. I told Borden you'd collect it next week. I haven't settled the bill. I'll pay you when I return."

"I'll remember."

John Powell waved and headed toward a tender for the *Demelza Jane*, whistling merrily.

"Miss Davies, you must sit on the seat with me," Constance commanded, "or your dress will be ruined."

"Thank you," Bronwyn said solemnly. She obeyed what was undisputably an order. In some ways, this little girl was much like her older brother. Her serious expression and demeanor suggested she was years older than her actual age.

In one way she was very different. Her clothes were extremely good, from the top of her velvet pillbox hat to the soles of her buttoned kid shoes. Her dress and matching jacket were made of silk and decorated with ribbons and flounces. Clearly whatever strictures Miss Pembrook placed on the students at her school, plainness of dress was not one of them.

Bronwyn hesitated. She wasn't sure of the proprieties in America. Perhaps she should stay in the back with her family.

Mr. Powell said, "Sit on the seat."

She put her hands on the side to pull herself up, but Mr. Powell took hold of her elbow to assist her. Once again she was impressed by his strength. He was taller and thinner than the miners and ironworkers she had known. Obviously he had inconspicuous muscles. And surely it was the unexpectedness of his strength that made her so aware of his body next to hers when he joined her on the seat.

William Powell clucked his tongue, but before the horse moved, James Falconer seized the horse's bridle. "Leaving without saying goodbye, Bronwyn?" he asked, smiling pleasantly.

Chapter Two

The shipowner's son had a warm smile on his handsome face, and James Falconer's fine clothes fit his slim body to perfection. He glanced dismissively at Mr. Powell. "Giving her a ride to Miss Pembrook's school?"

"No."

"She decided not to give me the job," Bronwyn said.

"Whyever not?"

"She didn't approve of my behavior."

"Ah! Were you the woman involved in the business here a few minutes ago?"

"Business? A fight, it was."

"I hope you were not injured," Mr. Falconer said anxiously.

"Not a bit," she replied pleasantly. Bronwyn hadn't known a wealthy young man before. She had heard it said many times that Americans were not so rigid with regard to class. During the short voyage from Boston, she had come to believe that, for he had been most concerned about the welfare of her family.

"I am happy to hear that. It was most unfortunate I was detained elsewhere, because I assure you, had I been present, there would have been no need for you to interfere." He surveyed the wagon and gave her a questioning look. "But this is a regrettable turn of events for you."

"I've hired her," Mr. Powell said quietly.

There was a current of emotion between the two men that made Bronwyn uneasy. On the one hand, she sensed animosity. On the other, she couldn't be sure if her employer's taciturn nature merely made Mr. Falconer uncomfortable.

Constance wriggled impatiently. Mr. Falconer ignored the little girl. "How convenient. Has he told you about his father?"

"Enough," Mr. Powell replied for her. "We should be on our way." He slapped the reins on the horse's back.

Mr. Falconer stepped away from the wagon. "Good day, then, Bronwyn. And good luck. Please remember, if this situation doesn't work out, I will be happy to help you in any way I can."

Bronwyn didn't even have a chance to wave a farewell, for the horse moved in such a stop-and-start fashion she had to hold tight to the sides. She feared that otherwise she would find herself on the ground.

"Isn't this cozy?" Constance said. She shifted daintily on her side of the seat. Her movement forced Bronwyn closer to Mr. Powell and more than once she was pushed against him. He felt as hard as a marble statue. And he was as friendly, too. "Just wait until

Mrs. Murphy meets Miss Davies, Willy. She'll be happy she doesn't have to cook!''

Willy? Bronwyn sensed that any outburst of laughter would meet with disapproval so she desperately tried to stifle the urge to giggle.

The nag proceeded along the road, which wound through the prosperous town. Several businesses lined the street, including a tailor's, a dry-goods store, a livery stable and what appeared to be a newspaper office.

People stared at them, in particular a rather large woman in a very ugly, very elaborately decorated bonnet. She also wore a gown composed of an astonishingly bad combination of stripes and checks. Another woman, also plump and dressed in an outfit of snuff-colored fabric with a hat that seemed an attempt to emulate the other woman's, whispered to her confederate as they went past, although the woman smiled and nodded a greeting.

Bronwyn wondered if she had done something improper by sitting beside Mr. Powell. She told herself that if they thought something amiss, surely they would frown or turn away. After all, most people in Massachusetts were descendants of Puritans, or so they had told her in school. Probably Mr. Powell didn't often drive through the town with a family of strangers.

As if he could read Bronwyn's thoughts, Mr. Powell said, "We are an unusual sight for Eternity. Mrs. Sawyer and Mrs. Wormley will be talking of this for days."

Bronwyn, normally never at a loss for words, could only say, "Oh?" Mr. Powell didn't seem particularly disturbed by the prospect of gossip, and she hoped he would comment further. He did not.

Likely his brother would have told her more about the women, or given some explanation for why their gossip was of no consequence.

The brothers were a strange contrast for close relations, one so jovial, the other so solemn. Despite Constance's constant stream of chatter about the town, the shops and the people, Bronwyn found herself trying to decipher the inscrutable features of the man next to her.

Mr. Powell had not been pleased by his brother's request to pick up his new clothes and, incidently, to pay the bill. She noticed, now that she sat so close to him, his own clothes were not new and hadn't been for some time.

"There's the millinery shop," Constance announced. "Jane Webster owns it and she's a relative of mine. Tell them about Sarah Webster, Willy."

"I don't think—"

"Please," Constance pleaded.

"No."

Constance seemed so disappointed that Bronwyn spoke, even though she could think of nothing more boring than listening to a man who was as expressive as a fence post try to tell a tale. "Please, Mr. Powell. It must be a fascinating story."

He looked as if he would refuse, until he saw his sister's face. His features softened, and he sighed. "Very well."

"You'll like this," Constance said to Owen and the girls. "Willy tells it so well! And it's about my ancestors, too." She gazed at him adoringly. "Go ahead, Willy."

Bronwyn suppressed a sigh when William Powell began. "Over one hundred and fifty years ago—"

"What is he saying?" Mair interrupted in Welsh.

Mr. Powell paused. "Mair and Ula don't understand much English," Bronwyn explained.

"They don't?" Constance asked.

"No. They are learning English, though. Perhaps you could help them?"

"I would be happy to!" Constance exclaimed eagerly. "And they could teach me Welsh so I could talk better to Dada."

"No," Mr. Powell said harshly.

"Why not?" Bronwyn demanded. "It is only right she speak her father's language."

"She has no need. Da speaks English."

His tone made it obvious that further protestations would be useless. Bronwyn turned to Owen. "Explain to them." Owen nodded, and as William proceeded to tell the story, he quietly translated for the girls.

"Over one hundred and fifty years ago, terror swept through the villages of Massachusetts," William Powell began solemnly. "A group of girls in Salem became strangely sick, had weird fits and unusual symptoms. They eventually confessed to knowledge of witches, covens and secret supernatural gatherings. They had been bewitched, they said.

"Eventually others told equally bizarre tales of midnight revels, supernatural visitations, sinful invitations. The leaders of Salem and the nearby towns feared that the Devil was at work among them. Men, women, children—it appeared no one could be certain who the Devil might choose for a disciple.

"Many people were imprisoned—cast into dank, dark cells in jails, yet obliged to pay for their dismal food and lodging. Trials were held. Witnesses testified. Many were hanged.

"Some communities seemed full of witches. Others apparently escaped. Not Eternity. One person, one young woman, was cried out as a witch. Sarah Webster."

"My great-great-great-great-aunt," Constance interrupted proudly. "She lived on our farm."

"Shall I continue?"

It was apparent Mr. Powell didn't appreciate interruptions once he had started. Constance reddened, but Bronwyn thought the child wasn't upset. Indeed, she was surprised at how annoyed *she* felt at the interruption. While William Powell's face remained unexpressive, his voice rose and fell dramatically, lending color and fire to the tale.

"Sarah was only seventeen the summer the rumors of witch-hunts in Salem reached the people of Eternity," William went on. "Sarah had been to stay with friends in Salem the previous year and knew some of the unfortunate women accused.

"Then Sarah herself was cried out by the girls who were thought to know such things. At first, the townspeople were aghast—until they recalled how curiously Sarah had acted the past winter.

"She had become solitary. Aloof. And given to singing to herself as she wandered through the woods on the hill by her house—"

"Where the chapel is now," Constance added. Again, William looked at her, and again she reddened and appeared contrite. Bronwyn decided this was some kind of a game between them.

William Powell playing a game. It was nearly as incomprehensible as William Powell telling a story, and so far, telling it well, with just the right amount of gravity and drama.

"Perhaps worst of all, sometimes she wasn't walking alone. A tall, dark stranger dressed all in black was with her.

"Sarah was arrested and put in prison where it was cold and damp and dark." His voice lowered as he spoke, sending chills down Bronwyn's spine. "She was kept there all alone until she was brought before the judges, to confront them, all alone."

"Judge Falconer, Judge Tamblyn and Judge Bowman," Constance added quietly.

"These learned men had known Sarah all her life, yet now their words were harsh, their faces grim." The volume of his voice increased. "If there was a witch among them, she must be rooted out and *destroyed*.

"Three young men were brought into the room. They told the judges how Sarah had entered their bedchambers at night, sat on their chests and tried to entice them to join her in sinful revels."

In the back of the wagon, the children's eyes grew wide with amazement.

"Of course they were lying," Constance said firmly. "Each one wanted to marry Sarah, and she refused them all."

William frowned. "Maybe you would like to tell the story?"

Constance shook her head.

"Very well. I will go on. That is just what Sarah told the judges. Not making any such offers, said the men.

"They were sent from the room. Judge Falconer asked her about the tall man. Sarah said nothing.

"The judges each pressed her to tell them about the mysterious stranger and to explain her songs. Were they a means to summon this possibly supernatural stranger?

"Sarah's only answer was a scornful expression.

"A witness was brought in who claimed to have seen Sarah and the stranger together often." William's voice became that of an old man with a pronounced English accent. "'Yes, I saw 'em,' David Borden told the judges, 'whisperin' and talkin'. A tall, handsome fellow he was, all in black, wrapped in a big black cloak. One time he knew I seen 'em. Such a look he gave me—and that same day my pigs took sick and died, every one. Cursed 'em, he did, as sure as I'm standin' before you.'

"Now, this David Borden had been a member of the settlement since it was founded, so paying attention to his words were the judges.

"Again, they asked Sarah to identify the stranger and to explain what they had been doing together.

"And again Sarah remained silent. Sarah's family begged her to speak. Whatever she had done, whoever this man was, all would be forgiven, her father pleaded.

"Still she didn't answer." William's face grew stern, inexorable. "The judges said they had no choice but to pronounce Sarah Webster guilty of witchcraft based on the evidence they had heard.

"She was condemned to be hanged by the neck until she was *dead*.

"The day of her execution dawned. Clad only in a white shift, Sarah was led to a large tree at the edge of town.

"Pale she was, and ill and small in her thin shift surrounded by the judges in their black garments.

"Once more they asked her if she had anything to say in her defense. Once more she shook her head." His voice dropped. "They placed the noose around her neck.

"Then a man, dressed in black, his cloak flying in the wind, rode down the street on a horse as dark as a moonless night. He drew a sword and with one mighty stroke cut the rope from Sarah's neck. He pulled her onto his stallion and they galloped away."

William hesitated a moment. "Sarah Webster was never seen in Eternity again. Some said the man in black was a sea captain whose vessel had docked in Salem the year before, a man reputed to be a drunkard, and married, too. Many chose to think so after the hysteria ceased.

"But there were those who were convinced Sarah Webster had been saved only to be claimed—" he paused dramatically "—by the Devil himself!"

Bronwyn let out her breath slowly. "A story it is. To be sure, it was only a *man*," she said, as much to herself as the children.

"Doesn't Willy tell it well?" Constance asked brightly.

"Yes, he does. A poet in there, I think." She thought of the way he had spoken and the arrangement of some of his words. "Or a Welshman."

His only response was a scowl. Bronwyn didn't care. He couldn't fool her. Under his cold, implacable exterior lurked a man with the blood of bards in his veins and the songs of the men of the mountains in his voice.

"They shouldn't be scared," Constance said. "It wasn't the Devil—it was the sea captain. He was supposed to come in the spring, and he couldn't. His ship was wrecked. His wife had died before he set sail, so he was planning to marry Sarah. He didn't drink too much—that was just gossip.

"Anyway, he married Sarah. She wouldn't ever come back to Eternity because of the way she'd been treated. She and her husband moved to Halifax, in Canada. Her family would go visit her there."

Bronwyn repeated the information to the children. Owen appeared disappointed by the real ending, but Mair and Ula were clearly relieved.

The journey proceeded in silence for several minutes. The children grew sleepy.

"Your other brothers—are they in Boston?" Mr. Powell asked suddenly.

"The rest of my family is dead," Bronwyn said flatly.

"My sympathies."

There was a hint of true compassion in the simple words, so she said, "Gareth and Ivor died of influenza. Davy died at the ironworks. Iowerth, Ianto and Morgan in an explosion in a mine."

"Is that why you left Aberfan?"

"Yes, and other things."

He said nothing more, and Bronwyn's thoughts strayed to her happy memories of home when Dada, Mam and the boys were alive, sitting around the big table in the kitchen, singing in the chapel, following the boys when they went out walking with their girls— until they caught her. They got angry and threatened to tell Dada, but they wouldn't dare. She had seen them walking their girls up the mountain. If the girls' fathers or brothers heard *that*, well, there would have been trouble. Young couples often did things there best left for their wedding nights.

Bronwyn wondered if her reticent companion had ever been married or had a sweetheart. She didn't think so. He wasn't handsome, or even pleasant. If he was so determined to become an American, maybe he had become a sort of adopted Puritan.

She had wanted to come to America for a different reason.

Wales was not the land it had been. Once the Welsh had been bold, rebellious fighters. They waged wars against encroaching enemies and then against the injustice of the landowners, many of whom had made their money in the slave trade before it had been made illegal. Now, though, with prosperity, her people were content to waste their lives in other men's factories and mines, and to spend their earnings in the pubs.

They had forgotten what it meant to be Welsh, nearly as much as had the man beside her.

So she had left them to come a land where there were still people ready to fight for justice and freedom. When they were settled and the children a little older, she would find out how she could help in the abolitionist cause.

The sun began to set behind a low hill and the air grew chilly as William Powell turned the wagon into a narrow, tree-lined lane. "This is my farm," he said simply.

She caught the scent of apples as they drove along the lane to the farmyard. On one side was a huge white frame house. Nearby stood an even bigger barn, and behind it she could see fields marked by rail fences. There were conspicuous gaps in the fence distinctly at odds with the well-kept appearance of the rest of the grounds.

A flock of ducks ambled across the road. Mr. Powell halted the wagon. That awakened the girls, who sat and rubbed the sleep from their blue eyes. "Are we there yet?" Mair asked in Welsh.

"Yes," Bronwyn replied.

Mr. Powell jumped lightly from the wagon and held out his hand to help her down. Warm, his hand was, and callused. His fingers closed around hers.

A door at the rear of the house flew open, and a large woman appeared. Her hair was flaming red, her cheeks nearly the same color, her apron voluminous, and she had a pipe clenched between her teeth. "Jesus, Mary and Joseph, what's this?" she bellowed in an Irish accent so thick that if Bronwyn hadn't have lived near the dwellings of the poor Irish in her valley, it would have been unintelligible. "And what are those brats doing here?"

Bronwyn frowned, her lips tight. Ignoring Mr. Powell, she walked toward the woman and said in passable Gaelic, "Show me the kitchen, you old hag. Touch a hair on the head of any of my family, you'll regret it."

William Powell stared. The woman's mouth dropped open and her pipe promptly fell on the ground. "Who the hell is this?" she asked incredulously.

Bronwyn braced herself for a harsh rebuke from Mr. Powell, ready to defend her words, but he merely said, "Mrs. Murphy, this is Miss Bronwyn Davies. The new cook."

"Come, Owen. Come, girls. This woman will show me the kitchen now," Bronwyn said, unable to keep a note of triumph out of her voice. She faced William Powell. "Getting supper now, if it is not too early."

"You must be tired. I'm sure Mrs. Murphy—"

"—must see I can work hard," Bronwyn interrupted. "So, supper tonight, is it?"

His only response was a shrug, so she went into the house.

On the threshold of the kitchen, Bronwyn sighed for
sheer joy. The room was twice the size of any kitchen
she had even seen, and spotlessly clean. Hams and
strings of onions and herbs hung from the rafters,
creating a marvelous smell. She could see a well-
stocked pantry, a huge cast-iron stove, well blacked
where necessary, its nickel plating shining, and a large
table.

She hurried to remove her bonnet and cloak, and
hung them on a convenient peg near the door. She
handed Owen a bucket and gestured toward a pump
near the door. "Filled, please," she said, and off he
went.

She helped Mair and Ula remove their bonnets and
cloaks. "Go you to the pantry there. Tell me if you can
find potatoes, oats, apples and the flour. Be quick,
now, girls." They went about their tasks.

Mrs. Murphy entered the room. "Wonderfully
clean, Mrs. Murphy," Bronwyn said in English while
she rolled up her sleeves. She had no wish to make an
enemy in the house of her employer. However, she had
wanted to show Mrs. Murphy she would not be bul-
lied. "Can you show me the pots?"

Mrs. Murphy's eyebrow arched. "Not talking in the
Gaelic now?"

Bronwyn decided it would be wise to be honest.
"Not knowing much."

Mrs. Murphy didn't respond except for a loud, de-
cisive sniff and a nod in the direction of the pantry.
Then she settled her large body into a chair near a
window beside a basket of what appeared to be the

remains of socks. Mrs. Murphy took out a large round stone and darned.

Mr. Powell did not come inside. Bronwyn tried not to feel abandoned when she realized that or to wonder when she would get to meet the elder Mr. Powell. She had a meal to prepare, and she wanted to impress the Powells and Mrs. Murphy. To do that, she would have to concentrate on the food.

William strode through the farmyard toward the barn. It was nearly time for the evening milking, so Sam would probably be there. He himself would finish the milking and have his hired man clean out the cabin for the Davies family.

He looked up the hill to the chapel and wondered where Reverend Bowman had taken the runaway. They wouldn't be able to use the chapel again soon. Either Tinkham was having too much luck finding the refuges of the Railroad or the rewards were proving very successful.

No matter how risky it became to help slaves fly to freedom, William would not stop. He could not.

He did not merely sympathize. He had to help them because he knew exactly how they felt. Trapped. Afraid. Alone.

And he would, although in his own way. Not like James Falconer, with his meetings and his speeches, or the men who wrote articles and pamphlets.

Not like his father, who fought first and with no thought of the danger. Who left his young son to take care of his even younger brother, paying no heed to their fears and worries. He had returned whenever it

suited him and told stories of brave adventures out-
witting the British around countless unfamiliar hearths
to admiring women.

In much the same manner as his son told the story
of Sarah Webster. William halted on the threshold of
the barn and muttered a curse. He had never been
more disgusted with himself, because he had told the
story to impress Bronwyn Davies.

He shouldn't have, by God. He had no need to impress a Welshwoman. He knew—too well—what they
were like. They had thought nothing of using a boy to
send messages of undying love and devotion, or pain
and heartache when another woman took their place.

How many had his father bedded? All of them. And
why not, if they were foolish enough to throw themselves at him?

Fortunately, things had been different in America
when his father had finally had to flee Wales before
the British imprisoned him. In America his father had
been simply another immigrant with two sons to care
for.

But a miracle had happened. His father had fallen
in love with Charity Webster, and she with him.

The Websters had been farmers in Massachusetts
for two hundred years, and when Gwilym Powell
married Charity, he took over the family farm and
started a new career, while William's gentle, loving
stepmother had provided them with their first real
home in a very long time.

Maybe Bronwyn Davies was different, but he
doubted it.

"Sam?" he called when he didn't see his hired man anywhere in the barn. A bucket of milk stood outside one of the cows' stalls.

No answer. William went out the back way and shouted.

"Here!" came a barely audible cry from the farthest end of the orchard.

William quickened his pace until he could see Sam. The stocky Irishman hurried to meet him. "It's your father," he said, puffing. "Seemed quiet enough, so I brought him out to the barn. He hoofed it!"

William swiftly ascertained where Sam had already looked, then started to search himself. Unfortunately, whatever was wrong with Gwilym Powell's mind, it certainly did not dim the cleverness that had enabled him to escape countless parties of British soldiers. They probably wouldn't be able to find him until he smashed a fence. Usually it was difficult to subdue him, and often they had to wait until the wooden fence was nearly pulverized and his father stopped of his own accord.

William hoped he found him first. He was in no great hurry to have to explain the nature of his father's illness to strangers. Most of the time, Gwilym Powell was fine, although quite frail. Then, for reasons no one could figure out, he would imagine himself in Wales. He would don a dress, which had been used both as a disguise and a badge of belonging to the Rebecca rebels, who were so named because of their concealing garments. The fences became the detested gates the British government had built to collect tolls for the use of a road.

Suddenly there came an enormous bellow and the sound of smashing wood. William and Sam took off at a run. They careened around the side of the barn to see the elder Mr. Powell, wearing a faded calico dress over his shirt and trousers, bashing the fence with his cane.

Bronwyn Davies appeared at the door.

William continued to approach his father, ignoring her. Until she began to sing.

The old man halted, his cane in the air. Then he lowered his cane and walked meekly toward the house.

"Blessed saints in heaven!" Sam exclaimed. "Will you take a look at that! If we'd known a song was all it took, we could have tried it long ago."

William didn't respond as he marched toward the house. Nor did he wait for Sam, who hurried along behind. He recognized the song. He had listened to his father and his friends sing it while they marched.

He hated it. Nevertheless, William marveled at the calm way Bronwyn handled the situation. He had feared that when she observed one of his father's spells, she would grab her cloak, gather her siblings and leave, like most of the servants he'd hired.

"I've never heard a voice like hers, neither. Where'd you find such a beauty with so much brains and courage, William? My God, if she was to say she was the illegitimate daughter of Queen Victoria, I'd believe it."

"She's the new cook."

"Oh."

William entered the kitchen and halted as the scents of his childhood struck him like a blow. The bread. The stew.

Home. A dream. A memory. An anguish of sorrow for what had been that was gone.

With a great effort he forced himself to show nothing and to say nothing as he joined his father seated at the large wooden table. The three children also sat, chattering in Welsh as if they were in a house in Cardiff. Mrs. Murphy and Sam spoke in Gaelic or English to Constance.

"Gwilym!" his father said jovially. "Where is Evan?"

William caught Bronwyn's eye at the name, but he replied to his father in English. "John is on his ship."

"Well, that is too bad. Look you, here is stew like your mother used to make. And oat bread! I feel like a man been starving for years. A pity it is Evan is not here to share."

William sat. Bronwyn hovered uncertainly near the stove until his father said, "Sit, you, and eat."

She took the only spot available, across from William, who had ample opportunity to see the way she looked at his father. How many other Welshwomen had regarded Gwilym Powell with respect and admiration bordering on adoration simply because he would sooner knock a man on the head than try to reason with him?

The rest of the meal passed in a swift babble of Welsh that William didn't bother to try to follow.

He did appreciate seeing his father so much like his former self. And despite his efforts not to, he enjoyed watching Bronwyn. When she thought the children were misbehaving, a little wrinkle of disapproval appeared between her brows. Her eyes grew bright with laughter when his father made a joke.

For once William even wished he was a little like his brother. John could charm women as easily as he could eat.

He reminded himself he had no need to have bevies of young women practically on the verge of swooning when he walked into a room. Infatuation was not what he wanted. To find a woman you could love with your whole heart and have her return the feeling—that would be different.

"Willy, may I have some bread?"

He tried not to wince as he passed the food. He had never cared for the nickname, although Constance always called him that. It had been her first word, and he had been proud of that when he was thirteen. Now, though, he wondered if he should ask her to stop.

Especially when it struck others as funny, despite their best efforts to hide it.

His father commenced the tale of their journey to America. He painted it as a great adventure full of the romance of flight and pursuit, and narrow escapes that were a marvel of the brotherhood of the rebels and the support of the people.

William, however, remembered it all differently. He could only recall the terror and the fear of what would happen to his father and his younger brother if they were caught. Would his father be sent to prison, or worse? Would he and his brother be separated? Who would take care of them? Could he take care of John by himself, if necessary?

He remembered the hushed voices and concern on the adults' faces. The hiding in the confines of cellars and boxes. The anxiety that John would sneeze or somehow reveal their whereabouts. And the one riotous battle he had witnessed. The screams, the shouts, the anguished cries of the wounded. The blood.

Then, leaving behind the land where he was born and the grave of the mother he had loved.

No, it had been no glorious adventure for him.

He stood up so fast his chair fell over. He righted it quickly.

"There is rude, boy!" his father exclaimed. He rose nearly as swiftly as his son. With an abrupt motion, the older man's hand went to his chest and the color drained from his face. He sat heavily.

Dismayed, William hurried to his father. "Como, Da, a rest is what you need," he said, and helped him to stand.

As they went slowly from the room, William gave Bronwyn a quick, accusatory glance. "No more storytelling."

Chapter Three

Bronwyn dressed swiftly in the silence of the cabin. The sun was just beginning to peep above the rounded hills, and already she feared she had slept too late. She would have asked the younger Mr. Powell when he wanted his breakfast, but after his abrupt departure last evening, he hadn't returned to the house. Or at least, not while she was still there.

Surprisingly no one had commented on William Powell's action. Mrs. Murphy had looked a bit concerned, but soon she was deep in Gaelic conversation and singing mournful ballads with Sam Muldoon while Bronwyn cleared away the dishes.

So the evening passed until Bronwyn had finished tidying the kitchen. Mrs. Murphy suggested it was time they all went to bed, rose from the table and ordered Sam to show Bronwyn and the children to their cabin.

The cabin had been another pleasant surprise. It was small and divided into two rooms. The larger one had a stone hearth where someone—perhaps William Powell—had kindled a fire. The other room was a bedroom, containing a large iron bedstead she had shared with Mair and Ula, and a much smaller bed where Owen now lay. There were plenty of quilts and sheets, and everything was scrupulously clean.

When she was completely dressed, Bronwyn gently shook Owen. "I am going to the house," she whispered when he opened his dark brown eyes. "Go back to sleep if you can and let the girls sleep as long as they like. Very tired they were last night. When they are awake and dressed and washed, bring them to the kitchen."

Owen nodded gravely and Bronwyn hurried outside. She had little doubt that Owen would not sleep, no matter how tired he was, for he was a responsible lad. He was probably already building up the fire so the cabin would be warmer when the girls awoke, and he would be dressed and have water ready for them to wash.

A part of the sun appeared on the eastern horizon. The sky glowed pink and orange and set the heavy dew to sparkling like bits of glass. Bronwyn took a deep breath of the clear air, scented with the tang of the sea. How different from the valley where she was born! For the past few years, the sky there had glowed pink and orange, but not from the sun. From the ironworks.

And the grass was dead, the water murky.

When she drew nearer to the spacious farmhouse, she paused and looked at the nearby wood. The trees were beginning to change color. She had heard about autumn in New England and was anxious to see the brilliant shades the leaves would turn.

She spotted a small stone building, almost invisible among the trees and rocks. And yet familiar it was, like many of the buildings of her valley. This must be the very place Sarah Webster had walked and waited for her lover to come back. She started toward the structure, wondering about the songs Sarah had sung to herself and what it would be like to be so much in love you would be ready to die for your beloved.

She, of course, did not want to fall in love. Not yet. That meant marriage, and marriage meant babies, and more ties. She wanted to be free awhile yet. Free to find some excitement in this new land.

When she was still a ways from the chapel, she realized William Powell was behind her. She stopped so abruptly she nearly fell over. "Am I late for getting the breakfast?" she asked anxiously.

"No. I usually eat after milking."

"You do that yourself?"

"I do much of the work around the farm." He began walking toward the farmhouse and she had to trot to keep up with his long strides. Apparently he planned to accompany her to the kitchen.

This morning his clothes were even older and more patched than the ones he had worn yesterday, his shirt faded and open at the neck, his hat one of straw. Yet he seemed surprisingly dignified in them, as if a prince had tried to disguise himself as a beggar and not quite succeeded.

"You didn't go inside the chapel, did you?" he asked.

She decided to be as reticent as he. "No."

"Good. There are bats."

"I am not afraid of them."

"No, I don't imagine you are." He frowned a little more deeply.

"How did a Welsh chapel come to be here? Did your father build it?" she asked breathlessly.

"Yes."

"Wonderful, it is. Like a bit of home."

"I suppose."

"He must be lonely for the valleys sometimes. He said he wants to go back someday."

"I know."

"Will you, too?"

"Never." The vehemence in his tone shocked her and she halted abruptly. What on earth had happened to make him react like that? And what kind of man could unleash such venom in a word, and then keep walking along as if nothing out of the ordinary had occurred?

He was certainly an unusual man, her employer. Most of the time he was stoic and even cold, his face grim and his eyes serious. But he was a Welshman, and for them, everything was passionate, whether love or hate or singing or working. To try to control that... well, it would be like trying to rein in a gale at sea.

She hurried to catch up to him. "You should have told me your father was one of the Rebecca rebels."

"That was long ago."

She remembered James Falconer's strange question about William Powell's father. "Does anybody around here understand what he was part of?" she asked. "What he fought for?"

"They think he is mad."

"People said the same thing about my uncle Dafydd, him always going on about the way the houses were being thrown together too quick. He warned them of pestilence and death. After the cholera epidemic in 1849, nobody called him mad again."

"My father *is* ill. Dr. Reed blames it on too many blows to his head, fighting in his glorious rebellion."

She heard the scorn in his voice and stopped, this time waiting for him to halt, also. "Are you ashamed of him, then? He stood up for his beliefs and tried to make things better for his people."

"Yes, he cared very much about 'his people.'" And little for his family, William thought bitterly. But that was past and now his father was simply a sick old man who needed to be cared for. William intended to do a better job than his father had done for his sons.

"I will come for breakfast soon," he said matter-of-factly. He strode off toward the barn.

He saw that Sam had already commenced milking, so he wordlessly got a clean milk bucket and started to work.

He hoped Bronwyn Davies hadn't gone inside the chapel. The chapel's main use for the past few years had been as a secret sanctuary for runaways. Jacob's specially built pews, which William had told people were modeled on those found in Wales, provided an extra, if tight, refuge. However, Bronwyn Davies would know there were no such benches in Wales. He would have to make sure she stayed away from the chapel.

At least she was a good cook. His father had eaten more yesterday than he had in a week.

Nor did she find his father's behavior cause for alarm, which was a relief. He was no cook, and neither was Mrs. Murphy.

On the other hand, she seemed just as excitable and hotheaded as his father and John, eager to fight physically, rather than with reason and discussion.

To be sure, no man could go through life without some measure of disagreement. William had fought the few times he considered it absolutely necessary. Usually, however, calm discussion was the way he won his arguments.

Bronwyn Davies obviously didn't feel that way. She had literally jumped into the fray on the pier, regardless of her own safety, and probably without stopping to think of the possible consequences—like the men who were always advocating war with the South without considering the men who would die and the families that would be destroyed.

Unthinking, unreasoning passion was a dangerous thing.

He straightened with a weary sigh and wondered when he could find out the fate of the runaway from the pier. To do that, he would have to go to Reverend Bowman, for he knew only two others directly involved in the Underground Railroad. Jacob Kent had made the crate, so William was quite certain the reverend would not use the Kents' hiding place so soon after the unfortunate discovery. The only person William could ask, then, was Reverend Bowman himself.

And he had plenty of personal troubles to think about. His father had not had a quiet night. This morning he seemed far from well. Maybe he would be better after a good breakfast. There wasn't much money to pay for another visit from Dr. Reed.

As William carried the bucket of milk to the root cellar, he decided he would insist that his father stay in bed for the rest of the morning and ask Mrs. Murphy to keep an eye on him. If his father grew worse, the doctor would have to be summoned.

He had eleven men coming to help get in the fields of corn and tobacco, and they would all have to be fed at noon.

Miss Pembrook had hinted that the cost of tuition at her school might have to be raised, and Constance's education had already caused a serious depletion of his funds.

The payment of the next installment of the mortgage on the farm was due soon.

As if all this weren't enough, he had stupidly hired the most fascinating, passionate, beautiful Welshwoman he had ever met in his life.

He wiped his hands on a rag and called to Sam to join him. While they crossed the yard, the stocky, black-haired Irishman sang, his voice rising and falling with the joyful melody.

Sam was about the closest thing William had to a friend, even though their relationship had none of the easy camaraderie usually associated with the term. Sam had been the one to teach William about farming, patiently instructing a shy lad in a way that made even the most mundane task interesting.

When they arrived in the kitchen, William saw everyone except his father seated at the big table, and although he had to sit across from Bronwyn Davies again, he ignored her. That might be difficult for many men, but not him. After all, he was used to difficult tasks.

So he did not notice how her face flushed from activity and the heat of the stove. He did not see her blond hair tied in a low knot at the nape of her slender neck and the tendrils that escaped to brush her silky cheeks. Nor was he aroused by the tantalizing glimpse of the swell of her breasts made possible because she had undone the first few buttons of her bodice. Instead, he listened to Mrs. Murphy and Sam as they talked about the chickens.

His housekeeper and his hired hand ought to be married by now, he thought, telling himself it was the sight of them together that brought marriage to his mind. They made no secret of their mutual affection.

Mrs. Murphy always protested that she wasn't ready for another husband the rare times he asked her about her relationship with Sam. He knew that wasn't the truth. Mrs. Murphy wouldn't wed as long as the stepson of her beloved Charity Webster Powell remained unmarried, not just from a sense of duty, but because he had loved his stepmother nearly as much as Mary Murphy did. To Mary Murphy, Charity Powell would have been a saint if she had been fortunate enough to be Catholic.

Years before his father had married Charity, she had found Mary Murphy standing on the streets of Boston clinging to her son's hand. They had been the only members of their family to survive a horrendous crossing from Ireland. Charity had offered her a job, and so had earned Mary's undying devotion. With the death of her benefactress, Mary had transferred her devotion to the family, for which William supposed he should be grateful. It was just that he didn't want his state to prevent Mrs. Murphy from finding her own happiness.

Despite Sam's affection for the housekeeper, he stared unabashedly at Bronwyn's pretty face and form as she flitted about the kitchen. However, Sam quickly turned his full attention to the food when it was set before him—and when he caught Mary Murphy's censorious eye. Indeed, Mrs. Murphy cast so many black looks at Bronwyn Davies that William began to fear his housekeeper was going to cause trouble there.

All William wanted from life was peace and a small measure of comfort. If Mrs. Murphy didn't get along with Bronwyn Davies, the young woman would have to go.

Mercifully, Bronwyn's brother and sisters sat quietly and waited until the others had been served before eating. Mrs. Murphy would appreciate that. And when Bronwyn finally sat, she was only there for a few moments before she was jumping up to cut more bread or fetch more bacon or cheese.

Eventually the huge meal of oatmeal, bacon, eggs, cheese and bread was nearly finished. William noted with some satisfaction that Mrs. Murphy had nothing to say about the quality of the food.

He reached for the large coffeepot and poured himself a steaming mug. The aroma was strong, rising above even the bacon and he scrutinized the dark green liquid uncertainly.

"*She* made it," Mrs. Murphy whispered loudly. She nodded at Bronwyn, who suddenly seemed to find cutting bread a most interesting pastime.

Sam took one look at the contents of the mug and said, "I'll go feed the pigs." He grabbed his coat from the peg near the door and left.

William added his usual amount of thick cream to his coffee. The color did not change very much. He added more until it appeared almost normal. Then he took a sip.

It tasted like nothing that had ever passed his lips before, and certainly nothing like coffee. His eyes started to water and he had to fight the urge to choke.

Mrs. Murphy regarded him with concern as he managed to swallow. "She already had the pot going by the time I came in," she explained. "She told me she needed no help."

The housekeeper poured herself a mug, took a gulp, made a face, then hurried to the door, where she spat out the coffee with great force. "By the saints, that's *awful!*" she cried. She wiped her mouth with the back of her fleshy hand. The little girls giggled, and Owen looked horrified. Constance was clearly shocked.

William lifted the lid to the pot. A handful of unground coffee beans lay in the bottom like strange aquatic creatures.

Mrs. Murphy cast a scornful glance at Bronwyn. "Never going to catch an American husband if you can't make coffee, girl!"

Bronwyn glared at her. "Not coming here to find a husband," she retorted boldly. "If that was all I wanted in life, I would have stayed in Aberfan."

"Huh!" Mrs. Murphy snorted skeptically.

"Besides, if you had not come late to the kitchen, I might have had time to ask you, but the breakfast had to be made and so I did my best."

Mrs. Murphy's jaw was slack with surprise.

Although his throat still felt as if someone had poured coals down it, William had an almost overpowering urge to smile. For once in Mrs. Murphy's life she had encountered someone who had just as volatile a temper.

But showing his amusement would only make matters worse, so he made himself appear suitably stern. He slowly rose to his feet. "Miss Davies should be instructed in the correct method of brewing coffee. I am sure she will learn quickly. Otherwise, the food was excellent. Please prepare some breakfast—" he nodded toward a wooden tray on a shelf near the stove "—for my father. I will take it up to him. Then, Constance, I have to get you back to school."

Bronwyn looked as if she had something else to say, but with more wisdom than he credited her for, she remained silent and readied the food for his father.

"Can't I stay a little longer?" Constance asked. She glanced at Owen, who did not look at her.

"No. Go upstairs to say goodbye to Da and then we must be leaving."

His sister frowned, but did as she was told. Mrs. Murphy went upstairs with her. Mair and Ula helped tidy up, their faces serious as they carefully carried dishes toward the tin sink. Once the table was cleared, they asked to go to the barn to search for kittens. Bronwyn agreed after a questioning glance at William Powell that met with no response. Owen wanted to help Sam, and Bronwyn told him he could after he filled the stove's reservoir with water for washing.

There was a knock at the door and William Powell moved to open it. A tall black man stood on the step, his hat in one hand and a small bundle tied in a bandanna in the other.

"We'll be in the far field today," her employer said to him. "I have to take Constance to school, then I'll be there to help."

The visitor turned and left. "They'll be ten more men for lunch," William Powell said flatly.

Ten more men! Bronwyn stood motionless for a moment, trying to calculate how much food ten hungry American men could eat.

"Is he one of the ten?" she asked when Mr. Powell didn't show any signs of leaving the room.

"Yes."

"I've never seen a black man before. Was he a slave?"

"Was—and is, according to the law."

"A terrible, inhuman law it is."

"It will be changed."

"Not fast enough."

He didn't reply. How could he, when she was right? "Has anybody tried to capture him?" she asked after a moment.

"Once."

Bronwyn nodded. The man was big and muscular. No doubt he was quite capable of killing an opponent with his bare hands. "Why doesn't he go to Canada?"

"He won't until he has bought the rest of his children."

"The rest?"

"He purchased the youngest ones first because they were cheapest. His son is fourteen. His owner wants a thousand dollars for him."

Bronwyn stared, aghast at the huge sum.

"Josiah needs another hundred dollars."

"What about Mr. Mathews' wife? Where is she?"

William Powell looked toward the window and spoke in an emotionless voice. "Dead. Her master beat her to death when she refused to take another husband after Josiah ran away."

"Terrible," Bronwyn whispered.

She thought of the young fugitive on the pier and what he had seen and survived in his young life. All at once the hardship of her life in the Welsh valleys and the voyage across the ocean seemed like minor inconveniences.

Mr. Powell stepped to the table and picked up the coffeepot. He went out the door and she heard him pour the contents on the ground.

When he returned, she wondered if he was going to say anything more about her coffee, but he did not. He put the pot with the rest of the dirty dishes, then went to a cupboard and retrieved a strange device. It was a wooden box with what appeared to be a funnel on top and a handle at the side. He picked up the small burlap bag that contained the coffee beans, took out a handful and put them in the funnel on the box. With slow, deliberate motions, he turned the handle.

"Ah," she exclaimed, going closer as the aroma of coffee filled the air. "You grind the beans!"

"Yes."

She peered over his shoulder. "Sorry I am I didn't do it right. Tea I can make, and ale and wassail and brandy broth—"

His hand stopped. "My mother used to make brandy broth," he said softly, his gaze still fastened on the grinder.

Suddenly she realized how close to him she was. And how frustrated she was that he wasn't looking at her. "Were you very old when she died?"

"Six."

"Lonely it must have been for you and your brother."

"Yes."

"And your father."

He looked at her, and she almost wished he hadn't. "There were plenty of other women wanting to take her place," he said coldly, recommencing his slow, methodical grinding, "with or without benefit of marriage."

Speechless, she felt as if he had slapped her. But why did she feel so ashamed?

Because of the accusation in his eyes, as if she had been one of the women tempting his father away from his young motherless boys?

She glanced at William Powell. Lonely he was and embittered and full of resentment for the women of his homeland. Welshwomen. Like her.

If he was ready to judge her by those others, perhaps such a prejudice would be impossible to overcome. Maybe it would be useless to try.

"Is the tray ready?" he asked.

"Aye."

Without another word or even a glance in her direction, he took it and left the room.

Bronwyn started to wash the dishes and reflected that she should be used to silent men who didn't wear their feelings on their faces. All the males in her family were quiet for Welshmen, with the exception of the uncle for whom Owen was named. Uncle Owen was a preacher and known as Davies the Thunder because of the booming sound of his voice, which carried outside the stone walls of the chapel. Her brother Owen could have a voice like thunder if he chose, but he rarely did.

"I hope I am not disturbing you."

She turned to see James Falconer leaning against the frame of the open door. He wore a fine riding jacket and breeches, and his boots shone with polish. His hat was in one hand, a short riding crop in the other.

What had brought him to the Powell farm today? Her?

She quickly tucked some stray strands of hair behind her ear and wondered if she looked as hot and disheveled as she felt. And here she was up to her elbows in soapy water, too.

Maybe Mr. Falconer was simply paying a call on her employer. "Mr. Powell is upstairs with his father."

"I came to inquire after you, Bronwyn. I wanted to make sure you suffered no ill effects from that unfortunate incident with Marshal Tinkham."

She flushed hot to the roots of her hair. This rich young gentleman had ridden all the way here to ask after her health. "I am well, thank you."

"I'm glad to hear it."

Owen came in with the bucket. "Water, Bron," he said unnecessarily. He gave the briefest of nods toward Mr. Falconer. It had been clear through the whole of the journey from Boston that Owen did not like Mr. Falconer, although he could never be made to say why. He had been protective of her since their parents had died, just as her other brothers had always been.

Well, she was tired of having other people judge her actions, and certainly her younger brother had no business doing so. "Thank you, Owen," she said. "You can go."

Her brother gave her a strange, searching look, then went outside.

"Where is Mrs. Murphy?" Mr. Falconer asked.

"Upstairs."

Bronwyn twisted her apron in her damp hands as he came farther into the room. She told herself she had no reason to feel so nervous. He was simply smiling at her approvingly, wasn't he? She should like him.

"How is old Mr. Powell?"

Bronwyn's brow creased with slight disapproval. There was something about the way Mr. Falconer asked his questions—too curious for courtesy, as if he were interrogating her. "He is not very well," she answered.

"You are not frightened of him?"

She shook her head. He smiled at her again.

She wondered what was taking Mr. Powell and Mrs. Murphy so long upstairs.

"Perhaps I could trouble you for some tea. It is a long dusty ride from town."

"Certainly, Mr. Falconer," she said, glad to have a task to take her to the pantry. Once there, she drew a deep breath and chided herself for being a fool.

James Falconer was a gentleman. A rich gentleman. True, he had stood a little close for comfort, but surely she was just being silly. And what of his appraisal? Most men looked at her like that at least once. Even William Powell.

"I will be happy to make you some scones to have with your tea," she called out.

When she returned to the kitchen, Mr. Falconer's smile was charm personified. "No, thank you, although I'm sure they would be excellent. It is warm enough in here without making you bake." His gaze rested on her unbuttoned bodice and she turned away swiftly. Through the window she saw a magnificent black stallion tethered near the house.

"Is he yours?" she asked, hurrying toward the window and away from Mr. Falconer.

"Yes," he replied with pride in his voice. He came to stand beside her.

"Wonderful, he is. I have never seen a horse so fine in all my life."

"I've been told I'm a good judge of animals," Mr. Falconer said.

Once she had seen a fox creeping toward a hen-house, and that image came to her mind now.

Which was ridiculous. Mr. Falconer had always acted the gentleman.

"Do you enjoy riding?" he asked, stepping a little closer.

She tried to smile. "I don't know how."

"It would be my pleasure to teach you." He moved closer still. "You are an extremely beautiful woman, Bronwyn."

She wasn't sure what to do. His attention was surely flattering, but...

He reached out and put his hands on her shoulders, then drew her toward him, a hungry gleam in his eyes. "Very beautiful."

"Good afternoon, James. What brings you here today?" William Powell said.

Bronwyn pulled away from Mr. Falconer to see William Powell standing at the hall door.

She glanced at both men uncertainly. What did he think, seeing Mr. Falconer's hands on her in such a way? His tone had been calm, as always, and she could find no answers in his dark, inscrutable eyes.

She told herself it didn't matter what William Powell thought as she went over to remove the kettle from the stove. He wasn't her father or her brother, after all. And he already had a low opinion of Welsh-women.

Which she might have looked to be confirming.

She poured the water into the teapot, spilling some on the table. She wiped it up quickly with trembling fingers.

William Powell sauntered into the kitchen. "I would invite you into the parlor, James, but I don't think Mrs. Murphy would appreciate the dirt. Please, sit down. Miss Davies, if you will excuse us?"

Bronwyn picked up a bowl of peas she planned to shell for dinner. Once outside on the veranda, she sat in a chair that happened to be near an open window.

"I was riding by and decided to pay a call," Mr. Falconer said. "I was concerned about Bronwyn."

"I assumed you were here about the mortgage." A chair scraped across the floor. "I will get a check."

"Oh, no. I was simply being neighborly. If it's a problem . . ."

"It is no trouble."

William Powell's footsteps crossed the kitchen and became quite faint. They returned quickly.

"You really don't have to do this," Mr. Falconer protested.

"I want to pay my debt as soon as I can."

"Very well. If you insist." There was a moment of silence, then Mr. Falconer said, "Miss Webster said to say hello."

Miss Webster? The relative of Constance's, Bronwyn recalled. Was she a friend of William Powell's? A matronly spinster? Or something rather more special? Bronwyn shifted her chair slightly closer to the window, her hands deftly shelling peas all the while.

"Bronwyn is a satisfactory cook?" Mr. Falconer asked.

"Yes."

Just satisfactory?

"I suppose she can cook all the English dishes. She offered to make me scones."

"She is Welsh."

"Same thing."

"No, it is not."

Bronwyn had to smile. So, he had not lost all his pride in being Welsh.

"I had a devil of a time with Tinkham yesterday," Mr. Falconer went on. "He insisted on checking most of the other crates for escaping slaves."

"Did he find any?"

"Of course not. That would be breaking the damnable law."

"The law will be changed," Mr. Powell replied calmly.

"William, you must agree it's time to take action against the South. They want to extend slavery even further west—it's all part of their conspiracy to take over the entire country!" Mr. Falconer's tone was fervent and excited. "Come to the next abolitionist meeting. You may be surprised by what we know."

"I don't believe every white man in the South hopes to see the country dominated by the slave-owning class. Most Southerners don't even own any slaves." Mr. Powell's voice was quiet and reasonable. "Nor do I think fighting is going to accomplish anything except destruction and death."

"But you must agree that slavery is evil!"

"Yes."

Bronwyn frowned skeptically. In theory he might agree, but she had no respect for a man who wouldn't fight for what he believed in.

"Will we see you at the meeting?" Mr. Falconer demanded.

"I don't think so," Mr. Powell replied. "My father has taken a turn for the worse."

"I'm sorry to hear that," Mr. Falconer said. He sighed and stood up. "I suppose I shall have to be content with your answer. I can see I have interrupted you on a busy day, so I will be on my way. First, though, I will take my leave of Bronwyn, if you don't mind."

"Please do."

Bronwyn hurriedly shifted her chair to where it had been and bent her head over the bowl of peas like a nun at devotions.

So, William Powell wasn't going to try to dictate who could or could not speak with her. That was good. She didn't want him acting like her relatives. Or anything at all. Except her employer, which he was.

But that didn't explain why she felt so disturbed he apparently didn't care.

Mr. Falconer's boots appeared in her limited line of vision. "Good day, Bronwyn. I hope I see you again soon."

She rose to her feet and curtsied slightly. "Good day, Mr. Falconer."

He smiled at her, and she decided she had been mistaken about his intentions. At least he was a man prepared to fight for his beliefs.

As Mr. Falconer walked to his fine horse and mounted, she realized William Powell was standing on the threshold to the kitchen, looking at her. Just... looking.

"I usually take Mrs. Murphy into Eternity every second Saturday morning. Her son works for the Tamblyns and she stays there to visit and to attend mass on Sunday," he said after Mr. Falconer had ridden off.

"I'm chapel."

"I suspected as much. If you would like to go to town to do some shopping, I will take you, and to the Methodist church on Sunday."

"That would be good of you," she said sincerely. "Who will look after your father?"

"Sam."

She picked up the bowl and went toward him. She waited for him to move out of the way.

"Excuse me, Miss Davies," he muttered, stepping aside.

It suddenly occurred to her that William Powell always addressed her as Miss Davies in a formal way that really was discomforting. "Please, call me Bronwyn."

To her great surprise, William Powell's face actually registered a change of expression—but it was not one to please her. He gave her a look that could only be called scornful. "Good afternoon... Miss Davies."

Bronwyn hurried past him into the kitchen, vowing that from now on, she would think of this puzzling man as her employer. And only that.

Chapter Four

William marched to the field, his stoic expression belying his churning emotions.

Call her Bronwyn? The way James Falconer did, he supposed. The way several other men probably had.

Damn her, he didn't want to call her by her first name. He didn't want to think about her. Or about how different he and James must look to her. James was every inch the well-to-do gentleman and he looked no better than a farmhand. He undoubtedly smelled like one, too.

Bronwyn. It meant white breast. How many men had seen her no doubt pale, smooth, perfect breasts? Caressed them with rough hands? Kissed them with heated lips as a prelude to making feverish love?

Welshwomen didn't have any restraint when it came to making love. Maybe even James Falconer had...

Jealousy was an emotion for fools, and to be jealous of a woman like her was especially stupid.

What was wrong with him that a woman he had known less than twenty-four hours could upset his life like this?

He should be more anxious about his mortgage. He really had not wanted to pay James yet. It was a week before the usual payment date, but there was no way under heaven he wanted James to think he was anything but prosperous.

Damn James Falconer, too, with his fine clothes and manners. The fellow had been born into wealth, a prosperity that came from generation after generation living and working in this town.

His father had been more concerned with rebelling against the exorbitant sum charged for the use of roads than with amassing personal wealth. No doubt if Gwilym Powell had used his energy to earn money, instead of fighting the British or enjoying the attentions lavished on him by his women, his family would have been much better off. *He* would be wearing a fine tailor-made suit and having Bronwyn looking at him as if he were the lord of the manor...

That was not important. She was not important. The mortgage *was* important—the mortgage he had taken out to lend Josiah Mathews the money to buy back his son.

William knew Josiah was good for the money, of course. However, he would have to be rather careful with his finances until the debt was paid off.

And he had just hired a cook with three young children to support. A cook with eyes the color of the sky in springtime and hair like ripening wheat.

He swore softly, unmindfully using the Welsh words he had heard his father utter countless times when trouble was upon them.

* * *

Bronwyn wondered if William Powell would say anything more to her about Mr. Falconer's visit.

While it might have looked to William Powell as if he had interrupted an intimate moment, she had been grateful for the interruption. She had realized James Falconer was too self-confident, as if he expected her to be overwhelmed by his flattery and delighted by his impudence. She would also show William Powell her morals were just as pure as his, despite the swiftness with which he cast judgment upon her simply because she was Welsh. That did not seem impossible as the next week passed, because he continued to address her respectfully, the rare times he spoke to her.

Most of the time he wasn't even on the farm. He left Sam to look after the daily chores while he took his oxen and helped his neighbors get in their harvests.

When he was at home, he never lingered in the kitchen after a meal or when he returned with the tray that had held his father's meal.

Indeed, William Powell never seemed to speak very much to anybody, although she heard him discussing things about the farm and livestock with Sam Muldoon, and household matters with Mrs. Murphy.

Sam Muldoon was a good and kindhearted man. Bronwyn appreciated his patience as he showed Owen how to do the chores. He liked to sing, too. Not so fine as a Welshman, of course, but it was good to have music.

The senior Mr. Powell remained in bed. Mrs. Murphy thought he simply needed rest, and Bronwyn hoped she was right. William Powell said little about it, except to remark that if his father didn't improve soon, the doctor would have to be called. Surely part of his serious silence had to be concern for his father.

She enjoyed the autumn weather, which stayed clear and not too cold. The leaves of the trees were even lovelier than she had imagined, like something out of a painting. The children, too, seemed happy with their new life in Massachusetts, which was a great relief to her. So many of their friends and relatives in Wales had tried to convince her to leave the children with them. She had informed every one of them that Owen, Mair and Ula were her responsibility and she would not abandon them to anyone, no matter how well-meaning the offer.

Sam had asked if she intended to send Mair to school. Bronwyn decided she was too young. Also, Mair's English was still not very good, and Bronwyn didn't want her to have any trouble. She remembered her own English schoolteacher all too well, and the board she made the girls wear around their necks if they forgot where they were and used Welsh. Even if things were not so bad as that here, children could tease newcomers who spoke different from them mercilessly, and she would not risk the hurt to Mair's feelings.

On the following Friday evening, when she had finished cleaning the kitchen and while the children were on their way to the cabin, she realized William Powell remained in the kitchen. He set the tray down on the table, but this time, instead of leaving at once, he simply watched her.

She gave him a sidelong glance. He had been harvesting on a farm a few miles off and gotten back late.

He still wore his working clothes: a faded homespun shirt open at the neck, old trousers that hugged his muscular thighs and boots that he carefully scraped every time he entered the house.

What would he be like if he ever got too excited to take his time? she wondered. And she wished he would stop staring at her.

"Yes, sir?" she asked while she rolled down her sleeves.

"I want to talk about your wages, Miss Davies. Please, sit."

She doubted a man who kept such a pantry as William Powell would be tight with pay to her. Besides, what would she do if she thought it insufficient? She was not anxious to have to move on again, and she had no idea how plentiful jobs for cooks might be in this place.

She sat across from him, with the wide wooden table in between. "Is my work satisfactory?"

"Yes." He gazed at the table, and his long, lean fingers brushed across the scarred top. "I am afraid I cannot pay you as much as you might expect."

"Oh?"

"I . . ." He cleared his throat. "I have had some expenses."

She thought he was simply making his opening bargaining foray, but to her surprise, he blushed. "I regret I can only offer you five dollars a month. I hope it is enough to compel you to stay." He said the last words like a challenge.

Bronwyn's gaze traveled to the man's hands on the table. Five dollars? What was that in pounds and shillings? Was that good for a wage in Massachusetts, or was he simply taking advantage of her ignorance? She had no idea.

The passage to Boston had taken nearly every penny she had. Although she had managed to earn some extra money on the ship by mending for some of the wealthier ladies, she was still very short of funds. Any money would be very welcome indeed.

She regarded him steadily, willing him to look up at her. He raised his dark eyes questioningly.

Now there was no scorn in them. All she saw was a inquiring expression that seemed to burn into her soul and a hopefulness in his usually inscrutable face. What for? Was he hoping she would agree to the amount because it was a low wage?

No. It was another kind of hopefulness that made her heart race like it never had before. "I accept."

"Good." He stood up and pulled out a worn leather wallet. Slowly he removed two dollar bills and placed them on the table. "I will pay you the rest at the end of the month."

"Thank you."

The sun was nearly gone now, and the kitchen quite dark. Shadows surrounded them in a blanket of intimacy.

Still he didn't leave.

She rose and went a little closer to him, trying to see more of his eyes. "If I am to be staying, you should call me Bronwyn."

He hesitated a moment before answering. "It wouldn't be right."

"You could speak Welsh when we are alone."

"I've forgotten how," he replied softly.

"I don't believe that," she answered in Welsh.

"I don't want to." English, cold and harsh. "Do you want to know why I forbid Constance to speak Welsh?"

"No."

"Because Welsh reminds me of nothing but fear and uncertainty," he said, his face hard and cynical. "When my father was off on his glorious rebellions, he left me to look after John. I had to listen to others talk about what was happening, and to wonder whether my father would be home that night, or killed, or taken prisoner. Or if he was with a woman.

"Then my father decided to come to America. He took me away from Wales. So be it—now I am an American. I will be one—and so will Constance." He abruptly turned on his heel and strode out of the house.

Bronwyn tore off her apron and threw it on the table. What kind of man was she working for? He confused her so much she didn't know if she should like him or hate him or pity him or all three at once.

The only thing she knew for certain was that he was the most intriguing man she had even known, and she wished he wasn't. He wouldn't fight for what was right. He was ashamed of his heritage.

And she had absolutely no idea how he really felt about her.

Reverend Ephram Bowman sat in his study. To anyone who happened to walk past the room, it would appear the learned gentleman was deep in preparation for his sermon on Sunday. In fact, Reverend Bowman was memorizing a poorly written copy of the shipping schedule for small vessels leaving Eternity made by one of the clerks of Falconer Shipping who was sympathetic to the abolitionist cause. When he had committed it to memory, he would destroy it.

He could have asked James Falconer for a list, or Azariah Tamblyn before he sailed. Both men were active in the Railroad, but like most of his agents, he used them sparingly. Nor did his many agents know all those involved. It was safer that way. The fewer to have knowledge, the fewer who could reveal it.

A brief knock interrupted him. Quickly he slipped the list into his desk drawer. He knew he could trust his wife; unfortunately, he had no such firm belief in the servants. It was known that Marshal Tinkham was offering to pay, and pay well, for information that would lead to the capture of runaway slaves, and servants were, after all, fallible human beings. When the list was safely hidden, he called out, "Yes?"

"It's James Falconer to see you, sir."

"Come in, James, come in." The reverend smiled as the young gentleman entered the room. "How may I help you today?"

"I was wondering if the package so regrettably discovered in one of my crates has been safely shipped elsewhere?" James asked.

Like all of those committed to helping fugitive slaves, James spoke in allusions as an extra precaution.

Reverend Bowman nodded. "Shipped and delivered safely, I am happy to say," he replied.

"That is a relief," James said. He sat in one of the reverend's overstuffed wing chairs. "I felt badly I wasn't able to offer any assistance."

"Perhaps it was just as well, with you so outspoken in the abolitionist cause."

"Disapproving, Reverend?" James inquired with a charming smile. "I simply cannot remain quiet, like some people in this town."

Reverend Bowman knew James Falconer referred to William Powell, but he said nothing. William wanted his involvement kept secret because he thought it safer for the runaways after that incident with the previous marshal.

"Have you heard any gossip about William Powell, Reverend?" James asked, his handsome countenance full of concern.

The minister frowned. "Gossip? What do you mean?"

"About William and his new cook? She's a very pretty girl, Reverend, and some people are...well, you know the type of thing people are likely to say about a bachelor who has a pretty young spinster for a cook."

"That's the young woman Miss Pembrook refused to take on as cook because she participated in the brawl on the pier?"

James nodded.

"If it were any other man, I might see cause for a little fatherly chat, even if William is a Methodist. However, William is a very fine, moral man. Besides, Mrs. Murphy and his father are there, too. I'm sure people in this town have better things to do than worry about William Powell, of all people—or they should have."

"Yes, I'm sure you're right, Reverend Bowman. I'll do everything I can to insure these rumors are stopped at once. I know several of the townspeople are still hopeful William will agree to run for a selectman. I would hate to think his chances might be ruined because he helped a young woman in distress."

"So would I. I'm certain, though, that William is behaving in a most proper way."

"Are there any more packages coming soon?"

"I have not been informed of any."

James rose to his feet. "Well, if I can be of any help with delivery or storage, please let me know."

"I'll do that, James, and thank you."

Jane Webster lifted her plain, friendly face to look at the people entering her small dressmaking establishment on Saturday morning. The leader of the familial group was a beautiful young woman with quite a remarkable figure garbed in a simple dress and cloak. She was followed by a boy in baggy cotton trousers, short jacket and cap, and two little girls with plain dark dresses, white aprons and cloaks.

Jane made a quick estimate of the worth of the garments the woman was wearing. Trim, neat, not expensive, but she had obviously done the best she could with limited funds. Given the woman's figure, that was enough.

Jane glanced down self-consciously at her pretty, pink patterned chintz dress. It was a lovely creation with creamy lace about the bodice, a silk sash, long bell sleeves, and several flounces and intricate tucks. None of which, unfortunately, could disguise her less-than-perfect figure. She suppressed a sigh. At least she wasn't as fat as her brother, Theodore. Teddy had recently sold his saddle horse because, he declared, a carriage was more dignified, not because he found it too much of a struggle to climb onto a horse's back.

"How may I help you?" she asked, pleased to have a customer so early in the day. The women who lived in the town generally did their shopping during the week. The farm wives and daughters usually spent their mornings at the market and left their purchases until later in the day after they had sold their produce.

"I will be needing some white broadcloth," the young woman said, by her accent obviously not from the United States.

Jane went to the shelves where she kept her plain cloth. Keeping in mind the woman's garments, she selected a variety of quality, starting with the lowest priced and going to midprice.

"This is quite nice," she said. She unrolled some of the cheapest from its bolt.

The young woman scrutinized the fabric, then glanced at the children. "Girls, touch nothing! Owen, watch them."

Jane smiled at her client. She appreciated that the young woman realized small fingers were often dirty fingers. She wished more of her customers thought of that!

"How much is this, then?"

The talk turned to the material before them, and Jane had quite an enjoyable time talking with the young woman, who seemed to know rather a surprising amount about sewing and fabric in general. She was more concerned about the durability and texture of the fabric than the price, which was also a most pleasant change from her usual patrons.

The woman purchased a few yards of the broadcloth, some soft flannel and a length of wool for trousers for the boy. She also bought some ribbon for the little girls, who behaved themselves admirably, despite the tempting display of threads most children managed to rearrange.

The door to the shop opened, and this time Jane was even more surprised to see William Powell standing on the threshold. He carried a large box from the tailor's. "Good day, William!" she called out. "A new suit?" She hoped he had finally allowed himself the luxury of some new clothes.

William shook his head. "It's John's. It wasn't finished before his ship sailed."

Jane frowned. "So of course he asked you to pick it up for him and probably pay the bill, too."

William didn't reply. He didn't have to. Jane had known the Powells since they had settled here, and as much as she admired William, she saw John for the irresponsible rogue he was. Not that she would ever dare say so to William.

William sauntered into the shop, his tall, manly figure out of place among the lace and silks and calicos.

He glanced at the young woman. "Are you ready to leave, Miss Davies?" he asked coolly.

Jane sucked in her breath. She had been so slow-witted! She had heard about William's new cook, the pretty young woman from Wales. People had been talking of her, and the escape of the slave, for several days. She'd had no idea the young woman was so pretty, and she should have recalled the accent from when William first arrived in Eternity, although he had spoken rarely even then.

"Ready now, after I pay," Miss Davies said, her manner curiously stiff compared to what it had been before William's arrival.

Jane let out her breath with something of a smile. After all, this woman worked for William. That was all. To be sure, she was pretty, but James Falconer—who had never really liked William since the day William had made his nose bleed all those years ago—had taken to publicly declaring that if any man could be trusted in such a situation, it was William.

She *was* very pretty, though.

Nonetheless, the way Miss Davies paid her money swiftly and swept out of the store, gesturing briefly for the children to follow her, would seem to indicate she didn't even particularly *like* William.

James Falconer also made no secret of his attraction to the woman. He had apparently said more than once, in the tavern and coffeehouse, that if he had known the girl was a cook, he would have fired his father's at once to hire her. Maybe the girl had hopes for James. With her blond hair and rosy cheeks, she was so lovely she might indeed have some chance. Still, old Mr. Falconer would certainly try to stop any such match. He had made it clear for years he expected James to marry nothing less than a Boston heiress.

Jane came out from behind the counter and walked with William toward the door, speaking to him of his father, how the harvesting was coming along and other small matters pertaining to the farm.

Bronwyn, seated on the wagon, tried not to stare. So, this was Jane Webster. She was a nice woman. Quiet and presentable. She and Mr. Powell would make a well-matched couple. Of course, anybody coming to visit would find their house as silent as a tomb. . . .

Their conversation continued. Bronwyn gave the children the sticks of candy she had been saving for the ride home to keep them quiet and from jostling the wagon. Not so she could listen better.

Jane Webster was talking to Mr. Powell about his mortgage. They must be on fairly intimate terms if they were discussing his financial situation.

"You might have come to me, William, for that extra five hundred," Jane said. "I would gladly have given it to you."

"Falconer can more easily spare the money, Jane," William replied.

Jane wondered how much it had cost him to pay for the suit. "Promise me you won't hesitate to ask me if you need some help with a payment. Or anything at all."

"I will, Jane. Thank you and good day."

"Good day."

William climbed aboard the wagon. As they drove away, Jane went into her empty shop and headed for the back room where she did the sewing. The young woman who worked as a seamstress for her lifted her dark, wistful eyes. "Any mail today?" she asked, her Portuguese accent heavy and her tone filled with hope.

Jane shook her head sorrowfully. "Not today, Emmanuella."

Emmanuella's husband, Miguel, had come to America without his wife. He promised to send for her when he had enough money. For a time, he had worked for Theodore in the bank.

Tired of waiting and worried about him, Emmanuella followed him to Eternity. Unfortunately, by the time she arrived, Miguel had moved on. Neither Teddy nor Jane had any real idea where he had gone, but they both agreed it would not be safe for Emmanuella to try to find him alone. Jane offered Emmanuella the room over the store and board in exchange for the woman's obvious skills with a needle. Then they started sending out letters to other banks, to newspapers, to land offices, anyplace that might be able to provide information on Miguel Silva's whereabouts. So far, no one had heard of him, yet Emmanuella never gave up hope.

Jane opened a tall, dark cupboard and looked at the bridal gown hanging inside. It was of white satin, with several flounces and yards of lace, and had taken Jane many hours to make with delicate stitches and her finest embroidery.

With a deep sigh, she closed the doors. At least Emmanuella had married the man she loved.

Chapter Five

"She got out of the city passin' for a white woman," Ed Tinkham said as he read the letter in his hand. He held it closer to the dim light that illuminated the back room of the dockside tavern. "She wore a veil, too. Says here she can read and write. They figure she might come by this way, since she knew some of the other runaways came through this town."

The informer nodded understandingly. "I have heard nothing of her, but perhaps it's too early."

"She's worth a lot of money." Tinkham squinted at the drawing that accompanied the letter. "Pretty thing she is, too. Tempt a man to buy her hisself, if I wasn't saving my money to buy a nice little piece of property."

James Falconer looked carefully at the picture, which depicted a very beautiful young woman who apparently had more than a little white blood in her ancestry. "The conductor is extremely cautious."

"He oughtta be, breaking the law."

Falconer scowled. "And you made too much of a fuss on the wharf. Otherwise, I might have been able to prevent the slave's escape."

"It wasn't our fault. It was that foreign girl's. She got a hold on me—"

"I should have thought that would have been an unusually enjoyable experience for you."

"What the hell are you talking about?"

"I merely mean to suggest you've probably never had a woman as beautiful as she grabbing you for any reason."

"Huh! I should have arrested her."

"For what? Bad judgment? I only wish she had jumped onto me."

Tinkham's mouth twisted into a feral grin. "I just bet you do."

"Back to business," Falconer said coldly. "How much will you pay for information about this woman?"

"Two hundred dollars."

"It says here she is worth five thousand. I would think five hundred would be a fair sum."

"Two fifty. I got expenses."

Falconer smiled scornfully. "Beer does not come cheap, I see. I will take four hundred for information."

"*If* you get any."

"If she comes within a hundred miles of here, I will."

"All right—provided we catch her."

"I cannot be responsible if you're unsuccessful. You either pay me for the information when I give it to you, or you will not get it."

Tinkham sighed. "How be two hundred when you tell us, the rest when we catch her?"

"No. I believe some people are getting suspicious. I want the whole amount."

"Well, all right. This time, since she's a valuable commodity. But next time..."

"I'm not sure there'll be a next time. As I said, some people are beginning to suspect."

"But they wouldn't suspect *you*," Tinkham said with a sly grin. "Not James Falconer."

The shadows on James' face made him look faintly demonic. "My reputation remains unsullied, and I intend to see it stays that way. I am upholding the law—"

"—and getting paid pretty well for it, too."

"Unfortunately, there are too many people in Eternity who don't agree. Now I must be on my way. I can't tolerate the stench. Oh, not you, Marshal. The tavern."

James paused at the door. "I would like to suggest you leave Frank behind the next time you go chasing runaways."

"What for?"

"I don't think his heart is in his work."

"He's just mooning over Geraldine Gibson. I can handle him."

Falconer's expression became hard and cruel. "See that you do, Tinkham, or one of these days, Frank might wind up dead."

Bronwyn made a final check of the children's faces and hands and surveyed them critically to see if they were ready for church. The girls wore their best dresses in a simple style and dark wool under covering cloaks and plain straw bonnets. Their white pantalettes showed beneath the hems and above their buttoned boots. Owen, quite conscious of his new trousers, adjusted his cap and straightened his short jacket.

She heard the sound of a horse and the creak of the wagon. She hurried to open the door to the cabin. The morning was warm for autumn, although clouds obscured sunlight. Puddles dotted the farmyard. Delighted with the mud, the pigs moved lazily in their pen outside the barn.

William Powell waited on the seat of his wagon. Bronwyn bid him a brief good-morning, but she didn't look at him as the children clambered aboard the vehicle. She lifted her skirt and prepared to join them in the back.

"Your dress would fare better if you sat up here," Mr. Powell observed.

She *was* wearing her very best dress of dark green wool crepe, and although her cloak was long, the seat would not be as dusty as the back of the wagon. She went around the side of the wagon and climbed aboard.

They rode in silence until Owen asked a question about the Indians who had once lived in this part of the country. Mr. Powell didn't reply in a monosyllable, nor did he begin to tell a story like the one about Sarah Webster. He simply and succinctly related parts of the history of the area.

Owen moved forward to hear, and Bronwyn had to smile when she saw his keen expression. She knew he had great dreams of seeing a real live savage. He was disappointed to learn that the Indians were long gone from here.

"Destroyed by men who thought they were in the right," Mr. Powell remarked coolly.

"History does not always change what is right," she said forcefully. "But if you try to *force* people to change..."

Owen and the girls shifted impatiently in the back of wagon.

"It doesn't matter," he replied. "Too many people think the way you do."

By now they had reached the town proper. The wagon rolled over the stone bridge and along the main street to a large green. Wagons, buggies and carriages were parked around the green, and horses grazed on the grass.

He gestured at the white frame structure at the end of the green. "That's the Methodist church," he said.

Bronwyn's only response was an affirmative nod as she got down from the seat and led the children toward the building.

She realized some people nearby had stopped to look at them. There was that woman—Mrs. Sawyer, she thought—and her apparent shadow. Mrs. Wormwood? Wormley? Again Mrs. Sawyer had on a millinery creation of unsurpassed ugliness and a gown that was certainly colorful. Mrs. Wormley obviously took her sartorial cue from her friend, for her dress and hat were garish imitations of Mrs. Sawyer's.

When they were nearly at the church, Bronwyn spotted James Falconer advancing toward her. He wore the latest fashion, his jacket fitting his slender torso to perfection. Beneath the jacket was a fine white shirt and collar, with a dark tie knotted about his neck. His face was smoothly shaven, his hair oiled, and the odor of bay rum drifted to Bronwyn's nostrils.

"What a pleasure it is to see you this morning, Bronwyn," he said warmly.

She dropped a slight curtsy. "Good morning, Mr. Falconer."

Out of the corner of her eye, Bronwyn saw William Powell. His face remained impassive, but she thought she saw a slight tensing in his jaw.

So, he was not pleased James Falconer spoke to her, despite his offhand remark the other day. The knowledge made her happy, although she didn't care to examine why.

"You are on your way to church, I suppose?" Mr. Falconer inquired.

"Yes."

"I am almost tempted to become a Methodist."

"You are not?"

"No. Episcopalian."

William Powell came to stand beside James Falconer. Compared to that well-to-do gentleman, his jacket was nearly shapeless, his white shirt poorly pressed, his tie knotted as if he had been in a great hurry and his trousers too baggy at the knee. Yet his innate dignity gave him something fine clothes could not provide nor poor ones disguise.

"The service will be starting soon," he announced.

"Good day, William," Mr. Falconer said politely.

"Good morning, James. Come, Miss Davies. We'll be late."

Mr. Falconer smiled blandly and tipped his beaver hat to Bronwyn. "Good day to you again, Bronwyn." He sauntered across the green.

An enormous woman suddenly strode into view, trailed by a stream of children. "How do, William!" she bellowed. She planted her hands on her ample hips. One of the children caught her eye. "Alvin! Stop bitin' your nails or I'll cut that finger off ya!" she chided good-naturedly. "Geraldine, take his finger out, fer Gawd's sake!"

Bronwyn looked at the hapless Alvin, who appeared to be in the middle of the throng of children. A young woman Bronwyn guessed to be about her own age gently removed a digit from the boy's mouth. The other children waited silently, and Bronwyn noticed that although their clothes were not new—indeed, parts of the youngest's garments had probably been worn by every sibling before him—they were spotlessly clean.

"Is this here your cook I been hearin' about?" the woman demanded in her deep, yet surprisingly friendly voice. "Looks kinda skinny to me." She winked at Bronwyn, then grinned.

What could one do but grin back?

"This is Mrs. Gibson," William said. "Mrs. Gibson, Miss Bronwyn Davies."

"Call me Ma. Anybody calls me Mrs. Gibson I start lookin' for my mother-in-law." She guffawed at her joke. "Geraldine, the baby's headin' for a puddle!"

The "baby," a youngster of nearly two, was indeed tottering toward a puddle. Geraldine, with a patient smile, neatly intercepted the escapee.

"Land sakes, I don't know what I'd do without that girl," Ma said with a nod to her daughter. She gave Bronwyn a conspiratorial nudge. "Had hopes of marrying her off to William here, but she didn't take to the idea. Silly gal!"

Bronwyn glanced at William. He was staring off toward the church as if contemplating the divine—but he was beet red. She desperately wanted to laugh, yet she didn't know how Ma Gibson would react, except that it was sure to be conspicuous.

"Before we go in," Ma Gibson said to William while she began burrowing in the largest reticule Bronwyn had ever seen, "I heared your pa's feelin' poorly these days, so I brung him some of my tonic. This'll clean 'im out." She handed William a bottle of thin brown liquid. "It's powerful, so don't use too much at a time or the poor fellow'll probably explode."

"Thank you," William said solemnly, but Bronwyn noticed that his lips were twitching.

"Ain't nothing. Come on, kids! Myron, touch your sister again, I'll tan your hide!"

Ma Gibson and her children, which Bronwyn had numbered an astounding fifteen, marched off toward the church, Ma admonishing all the while.

William pocketed the explosive tonic and walked toward the church, leaving Bronwyn and the children to follow along behind.

He stopped when he reached the steps of the building. Miss Pembrook and Constance were there, and Mr. Powell joined them.

Bronwyn hesitated. She wanted to have absolutely nothing to do with Miss Pembrook after that embarrassing episode on the wharf. Still, she wasn't going to let the woman's presence prevent her from doing anything. She grabbed Mair's hand, gave Constance a nod of greeting and a brief hello, then swept into the church, nearly dragging the children along behind her.

Once inside the main doors, they were in a small anteroom. Opposite them, another set of doors led inside.

"Miss Davies!"

Jane Webster stood beside the inner door. "How good to see you again," she said kindly. "I suppose William brought you?"

Her gaze went past Bronwyn toward the outer door. Like a woman searching for her sweetheart, Bronwyn thought.

"Yes, he did," she replied.

Mr. Powell, with Miss Pembrook on his arm and his sister holding his other hand, appeared in the doorway. Miss Webster hurried toward them.

Bronwyn ignored them and led the children into the church. She chose the first pew with space for four people, which was close to the back. She got the children seated in time to watch Miss Pembrook walk grandly up to the front pew. The schoolmistress sat beside some white-haired gentlemen who appeared to be prosperous merchants. William Powell and Constance entered a little later and took their places about halfway down the church. Miss Webster sat on the other side of the building beside a very plump young gentleman who was clearly a relative.

Although it really didn't matter to her, Bronwyn was pleased that Miss Webster was in another pew.

As the minister droned on, she recalled the intimacy of the evening in the kitchen when William Powell had discussed her wages. He had been close enough to touch. To kiss.

She wished she *had* kissed him. Just to see what he would have done, of course. He probably would have acted as if a kiss was a terrible sin. Or perhaps—she watched him bend to listen to something Constance said, the barest hint of a smile on his lips—perhaps he would have smiled slowly, his face lighting with pleasure when he leaned close to return her kiss....

She could almost feel his body against hers, hard and strong and full of warmth. His kiss would be firm, and also tender, seeking, asking, demanding, and she would have answered—

The pump organ wheezed into life. With a guilty start, Bronwyn opened her eyes and reached for a hymnal.

Owen closed the book even though the hymn had only begun and stifled a discontented sigh. He had hoped chapel in America would be more exciting than it was in Wales, but he supposed he might have known better. Church was church.

At least Mr. Falconer wasn't here. He didn't like the impertinent way the man looked at Bron, or the way he oiled his hair, like English gentry. He certainly didn't trust him, and he couldn't understand why Bron didn't tell him to go to the devil. She had said as much to plenty of other fellows who looked at her the way Falconer did.

He glanced at Bron. He didn't think she would be swayed by handsome features and good manners or Falconer's money. She was the one always saying what was in a man's heart was more important than what was in his pocketbook.

He also knew better than to ask her, or there would be a temper from her.

As the hymn continued, Owen wondered what was wrong with Bron. She had a golden voice that could set the rafters to ringing. Yet after the first few notes at the beginning of church, she sang as if she had a cold in her throat. He nudged her. "Are you well?" he asked in Welsh.

"Fine, now hush."

"Then why aren't you singing?"

"Not to be embarrassed."

"Why embarrassed? You've sung in the festivals."

"I know that, boy. But everybody here sings like opening the lungs would be a sin, so I am thinking we had best be soft."

"Oh." It wasn't like Bron to worry about what other people thought or did. Or at least it hadn't been before they arrived in America.

Maybe leaving Wales was not proving to be the wonderful thing she had claimed it would be if Bron was not willing to sing out loud.

His gaze followed hers. She stared at the back of Mr. Powell's head with the little frown on her face she always wore when she was thinking and not wanting to be disturbed.

He hoped she wasn't unhappy. For so long she had woven pleasant dreams around coming to America. She had worked long and hard to pay for their passage, in spite of the friends, relatives and young men who tried to convince her to stay.

The voyage had not been easy, either. Nonetheless, her dreams hadn't seemed so fanciful when they arrived at Boston and Bronwyn quickly got the cooking job.

Owen looked at Miss Pembrook, with her sour expression and hostile eyes. He was certain it was a blessing she had not taken Bron, after all.

For himself, he liked the farm, he liked Sam and he liked Mr. Powell, who seemed a man you could trust. In fact, he had even come to hope William Powell would marry his sister. Although Bron would never agree, Owen knew it was his duty to find her a good husband, or at least make sure she didn't marry badly. He was the oldest male of her immediate family, and that did not change with their location.

He wondered how William Powell felt about Bron. Bron was very pretty, but maybe William didn't want a pretty wife. He didn't seem to take any notice of her temper, good or bad. That was a favorable sign. Unless it meant he wasn't noticing her at all. Owen decided to keep his eyes open when his sister and William were together—and he would make sure Falconer knew Bron was not alone in the world with no male to protect her.

"Listen to the sermon now," Bron scolded quietly.

"I cannot understand the man," he protested in a whisper.

"You'll learn."

William regarded the minister steadily and tried to concentrate on what was left of the service without much success.

He was too aware of Bronwyn behind him, because Constance kept turning around to smile at her and her family. Not because Bronwyn Davies was a vision of pious beauty, her blond hair in a plain bun framing her angelic face. And certainly not because his thoughts were tending toward the decidedly earthy.

He tried not to let his mind wander to the night in the kitchen. He was ashamed at how close he had come to kissing her then—until she had asked him to speak the detestable tongue of his childhood.

He must never forget where she was from. That was reason enough to have little to do with her.

At last the service was over. Jane Webster waved to Constance and seemed about to head their way, but Ma Gibson asked her loudly about the price of wool. Jane's brother, Teddy, monopolized the Kents with questions about the relative merits of oak versus maple for a writing desk. Miss Pembrook engaged Reverend Hale in severe and earnest conversation about what sounded like one of the more obscure points in his sermon. So William made his way to the back of the church without having to talk to anyone.

The forgotten bottle of tonic bumped against his hip. He was grateful for Ma Gibson's concern, but he would never let his father touch a drop of her potion, even if all her children were alive and well and the woman swore the medicine she concocted was the reason.

Had it been a mistake to assure John there was no need for him to stay home this winter? John had suggested that, and with as much sincerity as he had ever displayed.

However, that would have been like putting an eagle in a cage. John would have been content for about two days; then he would have started chasing skirts or getting into drunken brawls. None of which would have disturbed their father, of course, but it would be *his* job to listen to the complaints and gossip, while his father lay in bed or in the dream world of the past.

Neither of them seemed to know or care about responsibility and William resented John's even asking. John was twenty-four years old. Surely he could decide for himself whether to go or stay. How long was John going to compel his older brother to make his decisions for him?

It had been obvious John wanted to sail, so of course William told him to leave. Only now, as he tried not to stare at Bronwyn Davies gliding gracefully across the green, did he admit that he might have had another motive entirely. A selfish motive.

Perhaps he was nothing but a Powell, after all.

Mair and Ula scrutinized Miss Powell much as a missionary might a cannibal chief. Bronwyn had told them during the journey home they might play until it was time for the noon meal, and Constance had asked to join them. Unfortunately, language was proving to be a difficulty.

"Her clothes are pretty," Mair whispered in Welsh.

"And her shoes. Somebody has done her hair up nice."

Constance said something. Mair wasn't quite sure what it meant. Since Constance had no Welsh, they stared at each other blankly for another few moments.

"I want to see the piglets," Ula said quietly. "Maybe *she* would like to see them, too."

Mair nodded and said, "Come" in English. She took Ula's hand and walked toward the barn. Constance hesitated a moment, mindful she had on her very best dress. But Owen had gone with Sam to the barn, so she followed along behind.

"Your father seems to be feeling better these past few days," Sam told William while Bronwyn prepared the supper. "He'll be up and smashing the fence before you know it. And down to the kitchen to see what's going on in his house."

"There is nothing to see," William snapped.

Sam's response was a slightly suspicious look.

William realized he might have reacted too quickly to an imagined notion that there was something unusual for his father to see, such as his son's paying too much attention to a pretty young woman, so he calmly started to discuss oxen, despite the distracting presence of Bronwyn.

How completely competent she was. She had probably been getting breakfast for a houseful of people since she was little more than Constance's age. Surely it wasn't so surprising she didn't want a husband and the resulting brood of children.

Dear Lord, why did he have to think such things?

"Those sausages are burning," he noted. He rose from the table, went to the stove, and he unthinkingly grabbed hold of the pan's handle.

"O'r annwyl!" he yelped, the Welsh words flying from his lips. He dropped the pan, which sent sausages skidding across the floor, and ran to the tin sink. There was a bucket of cold water there and he plunged his hand inside.

Bronwyn hurried over to him. "Is it bad?" she asked.

"Not much," he lied.

Bronwyn pulled his hand from the bucket and examined the red mark on his palm. "That's not much to worry about. The handle was turned out, or it would have been hotter." She went to the pantry and returned with a jar. "I'll put lard on it to soothe it."

She took hold of his hand again, her smaller one holding his like a vise. He stared at the top of her head and did his best not to notice the variety of tints in her bountiful hair. Her eyes were downcast, and he could almost count her dusky lashes. She ran her tongue over her bottom lip while she concentrated, and it was almost more than he could stand.

Ignore her, he commanded himself as her fingers stroked his palm, spreading the soft substance.

Fortunately—and before he totally embarrassed himself by taking her in his arms—she stopped. "Your hand should feel better soon."

"But you won't be able to work hard today, Will," Sam observed. "And you wasted all them sausages, too."

William didn't reply.

"I'll fetch something for you to wrap around your hand," Bronwyn said.

"It must be terrible to have to be nursed like that, Will, me boy," Sam said gravely, "to judge from the expression on your face. I'm glad it wasn't me burnt me hand and having to have a pretty girl hold it."

William scowled as Sam chuckled.

"Come on, Owen," Sam said. "Let's feed the pigs."

William didn't bother to wait for Bronwyn to come back, but followed Sam out the door. He decided to leave the care of the pigs to Sam and Owen. Sam was a wonderful companion for a boy—a patient teacher, a pleasant workmate. He had raised his son, who now worked as a singing waiter in Boston, by himself, and done a fine job.

"I'll take care of the buggy," he called to them.

"Right," Sam replied. He led the way across the yard and sang his favorite song. William had always liked that ballad, with its beautiful, haunting tune and promise of steadfast love.

As he entered the barn and prepared to push the buggy back into its place, he softly sang the words Sam had taught him years ago when William had asked what the Gaelic meant.

For there are truths that I must learn,
Roads that take a different turn,

Tides that call me, sails that swell,
And I must rove, to love you well.

But when my soul has drunk its fill,
When the tide has lost its pull,
Then, my love, I'll turn for shore,
Safe in your arms forevermore.

He sighed softly, then caught sight of Bronwyn standing in the doorway, her body silhouetted in the sunlight. William stood as still as a block of wood.

"There is a lovely voice you have. A bard there was in your family for sure, with the story-telling and the voice. The Welsh is in you, man, as much as the color of your eyes," she said, clearly expecting him to deny it.

Before he could reply, a series of shrieks came from the back of the barn. He sprinted toward the pigpen and knew Bronwyn ran behind him. Together they rounded the corner.

Constance sat in the pen covered in muck and manure, shrieking as if pursued by demons. "They're going to step on me!" she wailed.

William swiftly jumped over the fence and scooped up the sobbing, dirty, odoriferous child. He shoved the pigs out of his way and went to the gate. Sam and Owen ineffectually tried to guide the pigs into the barn. The other girls stood nearby, their hands pressed to their mouths and their eyes full of laughter.

"We were trying to pet the piglets," Constance managed to say between gulps for air when he set her down. "My pretty dress!"

William stalked up to Bronwyn. "Look what they've done!" he all but shouted.

"Who?" she dared to answer.

"Don't be angry, Willy," Constance cried.

"Those brats probably pushed her in!"

"If any relative of mine made such a noise over a dress, ashamed I would be!"

"She leaned too far, Bron," Mair explained, starting to cry, too.

Ula, not understanding much except that Mr. Powell and Bron were arguing and everything was somehow their fault, began to weep.

Bronwyn put her arms around them, pulling them close to her. "Now see what *you've* done!"

William pressed his lips together. Somehow or other these Welsh hoydens were responsible for Constance's state, because she had never before ventured anywhere near the pigpen. They probably shoved her in, thinking it good sport until she raised a hue and cry.

"We will discuss this later," he growled, keeping the anger from his voice as best he could. "Please take Constance to the kitchen to be cleaned up."

"You clean her up. I've got dinner to cook."

William glared at her, but his voice assumed an overly polite tone. "I have no wish to trouble you, Miss Davies, but since you are the only woman on the farm at present, I must ask that you oblige me in this."

Bronwyn looked at the disheveled child, whose face was streaked with tears. Constance had calmed down somewhat, but it didn't take a lot of perception to see that the argument going on before her was more cause for upset than falling in the pigpen.

She ran her gaze over Mr. Powell. His shirt and trousers had suffered from carrying Constance, and he was none too fragrant.

"Very well," she said sullenly as she took hold of Constance's hand.

He flushed bright red. "I'm going to the pond."

When Bronwyn and Constance, followed by a subdued Mair and Ula, arrived back at the house, they heard the elder Mr. Powell shouting for an explanation of all the noise. She called out that it was nothing serious, but in a few minutes, while Owen fetched the water for the bath, they heard slow footsteps coming down the stairs.

"Dada!" Constance cried happily when he entered the room.

Bronwyn hadn't seen Mr. Powell since that first day, and she was surprised by the change in him. Before, he had looked like a biblical prophet smashing an idol, with his shoulder-length iron-gray hair and long beard. Now he was a pale, frail elderly man.

"Fell in the pigpen, is it?" he asked in English. His eyes twinkled merrily in his gaunt face.

Constance nodded, her face serious. "Willy got angry."

Bronwyn busied herself finding linens and heating the bathwater, as well as keeping watch on the cooking food.

"Not surprised, me."

"He shouted at Miss Davies."

Mr. Powell sighed heavily and sat down. He looked at Bronwyn. "You must forgive my son," he said. "He has no chivalry with the ladies."

Bronwyn was about to agree when it occurred to her that most of the times a man referred to chivalry, it meant the man doing and the lady waiting. Better, perhaps, to have an honest face-to-face shouting match. At least you could be sure how your opponent felt.

Mr. Powell stood up. "I will be making sure the pigs were not frightened out of their fat," he said with a wink, "while you women have your gossip."

"Perhaps you should rest...."

The old man's face became the stern image of his son's. "Not in my grave yet." Then his irritation seemed to disappear before her eyes, for he smiled. "Or is it you cannot bear to part with me?" he asked innocently.

Bronwyn could understand why women liked Gwilym Powell. Would that his son could learn to let go of his annoyance so swiftly and with so much grace.

"Then I will go," Mr. Powell said, "but I promise only for a little while."

When he had gone, Bronwyn handed Constance a blanket for modesty. The little girl started to remove her soiled clothes, another frown on her face.

"What is it?" Bronwyn asked while she inspected the garments as they fell on the floor. "The underclothes will probably be fine with a good wash."

Constance sat on the bench still wrapped in the blanket. Her gaze strayed to the other girls, subdued and watchful in the corner. "I'm sorry, Miss Davies," she murmured. "It was my fault. I tried to pet the piglets and fell. Then I got scared."

"I know, dear," Bronwyn said gently. Indeed, she wasn't angry at Constance. She was angry at William Powell for his unfounded accusations of her sisters. Or at least she had been. "I am thinking of what you can wear. I'm afraid your pretty dress is ruined."

She waited for more tears, but Constance merely shrugged. "Uncle John won't mind too much. It *was* very pretty, though." She brightened. "He'll probably bring me home another one. He always does. I hope you're not cross anymore," she added. She looked at the girls again.

Bronwyn shook her head. "No, I'm not angry at them." Mair and Ula could get into mischief, which was to be expected of children. If it had been Mair to fall in the pen, they would have shared a good laugh and no one would have accused them of a willful act of spite.

The girls grinned at each other. "Much," Bronwyn added in Welsh. The grins disappeared.

Owen carried in two more buckets of water. Constance blushed and pulled the blanket closer around her. She needn't have bothered. Owen never glanced in her direction.

"That's plenty, Owen, thank you. Fetch some more kindling, please."

He nodded wordlessly and left without acknowledging anyone's presence. It was obvious Constance didn't know whether or not to look relieved that Owen had ignored her. And wouldn't it bother William Powell to think his coddled half sister might be interested in attracting the notice of a Welsh lad newly arrived from the country he professed to hate? She smiled grimly. "Mair, fetch a pair of your new drawers."

Mair seemed about to protest, saw the look in Bronwyn's eye and wisely left without a word.

By now there was enough hot water for a bath. Constance went over to the tin tub Bronwyn had brought from the cellar.

Constance glanced at Ula, still sitting silently in the corner. "I would like privacy, please."

"I've still got to watch the dinner," Bronwyn reminded her.

"Very well. *You* may stay," Constance replied regally.

Bron wondered if the Powells' manner of giving orders was in their blood. Nonetheless, she shooed Ula out, and when Mair returned with the drawers, she took them and told Mair to go with Ula to the cabin until it was time to eat.

Bronwyn busied herself with the dinner preparations. The scent of soap filled the air.

"It's too bad Willy couldn't have a tub, too," Constance remarked. "The pond will be cold."

Bronwyn uncharitably hoped the water would be freezing. She opened the oven, ready to put in a cake.

"Is that cake?"

"Yes."

"Willy likes cake. Did he ask you to make it?"

"No."

"He'll have a nice surprise, then."

Bronwyn scowled. She was in no mood to give William Powell anything nice.

"We're not gossiping," Constance observed. "Dada said we should gossip."

"No, he said we would. Men think women don't do much else when they're together."

"Miss Pembrook gossips," Constance said with an air of conspiracy.

"Does she now?" Bronwyn eyed the potatoes critically.

"Yes. She knows a lot about everybody, and tells it all, too."

"You shouldn't listen," Bronwyn admonished her. Perhaps Constance was merely indulging in some fanciful speculation.

"Oh, she doesn't gossip with *us*. She gossips with the mothers. She doesn't know we can hear her."

Bronwyn stopped stirring the vegetables. "You eavesdrop?"

"No," Constance said. She shifted around in the soapy water. "My room is right over the parlor and the voices come up the chimney when there's no fire. I can't help but hear."

"I see."

"I'm finished."

As Constance got out of the tub, Bronwyn wondered what the child could wear in addition to the drawers. She spied one of Mrs. Murphy's voluminous aprons hanging near the door and took it from its place. Constance stood patiently while Bronwyn contrived to make a garment that satisfied the dictates of modesty, if not fashion.

Constance surveyed her strange dress and giggled. "I hope Mrs. Murphy doesn't get angry."

"She'll understand, I'm sure."

Bronwyn glanced at the stove. All that remained to do for dinner was to serve it.

"I had better call everyone," she said. She went to the door and shouted that dinner was ready. Bronwyn's voice could be very loud, so in a few moments she saw Mair and Ula come from the cabin, and Owen, Sam and the older Mr. Powell walk around the side of the barn.

William Powell did not make an appearance.

"If he's at the pond, he won't hear you," Constance said.

"Does it take the man all day to wash?" Bronwyn muttered as everyone took their places.

When William Powell had still not arrived several minutes later, with the food on the table growing cold and the children impatient, his father took matters into his own hands. "We won't wait," he said. "Eat."

"Shouldn't someone see where he is?" Bronwyn asked. Perhaps he would be angry if they didn't wait, even if it was his father who gave the order to begin.

Sam looked up from the food laid before him with a pained expression. Owen stared at the meat as if he had never seen meat before.

"I will go," she said at last. She peevishly reflected that as far as men were concerned, the world could stop spinning as long as there was good food to be had.

"If he's not at the pond, don't search for him. Maybe he took a walk," Mr. Powell said.

The image of William Powell enjoying a leisurely stroll down a country lane was enough to make Bronwyn smile skeptically as she hurried outside and toward the pond.

The air was cool after the heat of the kitchen, and fragrant with the smell of burning wood. The ripe apples in the orchard scented the breeze.

She followed a path through the small stand of trees that surrounded the pond and looked around. She saw William Powell's shirt hanging on a bush to dry, then his trousers on the ground under a tree.

But he was wearing them and only them, and he was lying on his back asleep, with his face shadowed by the branches that moved in the slight wind.

Asleep, he appeared much younger than he did when he was awake, with the cares of life on his brow. His tanned, naked chest moved slowly. Her first impulse was to let him stay sleeping in the warmth of this sheltered spot.

Her gaze traveled over his lean belly to the white skin that marked the line where his trousers usually ended. He must remove his shirt when he worked outside.

But there was the dinner hot on the table and he had called her sisters "brats." She crouched and nudged him. "Mr. Powell!"

"What?" Staring at her with his dark eyes, he sat up with a suddenness that shocked her speechless.

"Getting cold," she finally managed to say.

He glanced at his naked chest, but it was Bronwyn who blushed. She rose quickly. "I meant the dinner."

He stood up and grabbed his shirt from the bush. "I fell asleep."

"I know."

"You're still angry." He pulled on his shirt.

"You accused my sisters of pushing Constance in the pen deliberately," she reminded him. She looked away from his still all-too-visible chest. "Come, your father is waiting."

"He came downstairs?"

"Yes."

Lines of worry creased his brow. Bronwyn hurried after him as he marched along the path. "He seemed well enough."

"I'm sure he does. He would make an effort to hide his weakness from a beautiful woman."

"I don't think—"

William spun around and glared at her. "I know my own father. If he thought a woman watching, he would do nearly anything to impress her. I have seen him."

"I was going to say I don't think I'm beautiful."

He stared at her. "I don't believe you." His gaze faltered. "You are the most beautiful woman I have ever seen in my life."

Before she could reply, his expression changed. "I wish you were not. It would be better. For my father's sake." He strode away and left Bronwyn alone on the path.

She watched him go, then followed slowly. At first she was unexpectedly elated to discover he thought her beautiful. Men had told her so before, and she knew she was prettier than some, but it was only now, when *he* said it, that she believed it. A man like William Powell would not flatter.

Then dismay crept into her heart. She didn't want any man to find her beautiful or fall in love with her. He would only be disappointed because she would not reciprocate his feelings. She could not fall in love.

She had come to America to be free, and she was going to be.

Chapter Six

Bronwyn sighed while she made more coffee. Once again, the laborers had made short work of the huge lunch she had prepared, and once again, William Powell ate nearly the whole meal without looking at her.

Perhaps he blamed her for his father's relapse, although she hoped he did not. Gwilym Powell had become ill during the meal after Constance's fall into the pigpen, and he hadn't been able to come downstairs again.

She glanced at William as she poured his coffee. Maybe he repented telling her that he thought her beautiful. It could be he feared she would now be waiting for him to make a proposal of marriage.

She wished she could ignore him as he so effectively ignored her. She couldn't decide if the difficulty arose because he thought her beautiful or from his quiet dignity or his dutifulness. Or because she was convinced he would be a noble addition to the cause of freedom for slaves if only he would join the fight.

At the moment, all she was sure of was that William Powell disturbed her as no man ever had.

Bronwyn sighed with exasperation—although whether at herself or William she would have been hard-pressed to choose—and looked out the window. Josiah Mathews sat on the veranda. He didn't come inside the kitchen with the rest of the men. He never did. He simply sat on the porch and ate food that had been wrapped in his bandanna.

Today, this reminder of William's acquiesence to the accepted status quo annoyed her. To think a man whose own father had fought oppression should countenance such a treatment of others! Well, today she would speak.

In spite of her resolution, she didn't have a chance to say anything for some time. The men inside kept her busy ladling more soup and cutting more bread.

Finally she set another loaf of bread right in front of William. "Why is Mr. Mathews outside?" she demanded.

Apparently sopping up the last of his soup with a piece of bread was more important than whatever she had to say. "He doesn't eat in the house," he replied at last.

Then she realized his neck was flushed, and not from the sun. From shame? So it should be.

She went to the door. "Come in, Mr. Mathews."

The man didn't move from the seat he had taken on the porch. "No, thank you, ma'am."

"Please, come in and eat."

Josiah Mathews shook his head slowly. "I don't come in the house."

Bronwyn smiled in her most friendly manner. "I am inviting you."

"Mathews eats outside," William Powell repeated behind her.

Bronwyn turned on him indignantly. "I thought this was a free country. Why does he eat outside?"

Josiah Mathews, tall and dignified, looked up at her and spoke in a deep, resonant voice. "I won't come inside a white man's house, not even Mr. Powell's. Not as long as I live, so help me God."

"Oh," Bronwyn said feebly while Josiah resumed his meal.

"Some people think they know everything," Mrs. Murphy muttered. She looked pointedly at Bronwyn.

Who decided that after what had just happened, she had best keep quiet.

When there was barely a crumb left on any of the plates or platters, the men pushed back from the table, gave her a brief nod and walked out.

Mrs. Murphy, who had eaten with even more speed than the men, took Mr. Powell's tray in her ample fists.

William Powell frowned. "My father is still in bed?"

Mrs. Murphy nodded, but there was a genial smile on her wide face as she went toward the hall door. "Aye. Tired he is, poor man. Still, I'm sure he'll be up and about by suppertime. After he eats, I will be going to town with Sam." She paused and looked at William. "Are you sure you don't want me to stay tonight?"

"No, Tiernan will be expecting you. Just leave the tray beside the bed. I will fetch it when I bid my father good-night."

"Sam says he will stay."

"When his son is visiting and staying in the town's finest hotel? Thank him for the offer. I planned to ask Miss Davies if she would mind remaining in the house tonight until I return."

Bronwyn didn't even try to keep the surprise from her face. Neither, apparently, did Mrs. Murphy. Nevertheless, she went out of the room, leaving Bronwyn and William alone with the children.

"There is a meeting in the Town Hall tonight I would like to attend. This is Sam's day off, and Mrs. Murphy's, too, as you know, so I would be grateful if you would wait in case my father— "

"Is it the abolitionist meeting?"

His eyes narrowed slightly, and she suddenly realized she had heard about the meeting when she had eavesdropped on his conversation with James Falconer, so she smiled sweetly—that usually worked with men, and although she doubted it would have any effect at all on William Powell, she tried it anyway—and said, "There was talk of it at church. Of course, I would be happy to look after your father. Owen can mind the girls."

Out of the corner of her eye, she saw Owen's frown. She knew he didn't like being nursemaid, but the abolitionist meeting was important. She was more than willing to stay in the house in order for William Powell to go. James Falconer had said they had evidence of the South's plans. Maybe he could persuade William to care about the abolitionist cause. Once William was involved, surely she could help, too.

"I may not return until quite late, so if you would rather not—"

"It is no trouble."

"Thank you. I should leave as soon as my father has eaten. Oh, and Constance will be here for Sunday dinner."

William went out and she started to tidy the kitchen.

"Am I to put the girls to bed?" Owen asked sullenly.

"Not asking you to cut off a limb, am I?" Bronwyn looked at the girls. "I am expecting Mair and Ula to behave themselves. Now you all can help me clean up."

Working together, they soon had the dishes washed, the kitchen neat and the stove banked for the night.

Then Bronwyn heard young Mr. Powell calling her name. "Go, you, to the cabin. Mind, Owen is in charge, so do as he says, girls. He is to tell me if you do not."

She hurried to the stairs, rather mindful that this was the first time she had been in another part of the house, which was so painfully clean it seemed as if no one really lived there.

She followed the low sounds of voices to the far bedroom and paused, looking inside.

William sat on the bed, gently wiping his father's chin with a cloth. When the older man caught sight of Bronwyn at the door, though, his features lit up with a bright smile and he pushed his son's ministering hand away. "That's what I need, a pretty face, not your frowns, boy!" he exclaimed in Welsh. He shifted to a more upright position. "Why haven't you let her come here sooner?"

William put the cloth on the tray and didn't reply.

Old Mr. Powell pointed to a rocking chair near the foot of the bed. "Sit there, Bronwyn, where I can see you."

She complied.

"Bronwyn! A lovely name for a lovely woman," he replied. "Now I know why Gwilym's been hiding you downstairs." He winked. "Maybe the boy's waking up at last."

She realized William's face was red, but he was bending over the dishes on the tray, so maybe he had not even heard his father's remark.

"Miss Davies will sit with you awhile, Da," he said in English. "I am going to a meeting."

"Meeting, is it?" his father replied in Welsh. "To talk of fighting those Southern braggarts, I hope. I wish I was ten years younger. But better it would be if you were going courting." He grinned roguishly at Bronwyn, and his features reminded her of John Powell. "A pity we're not Catholic, I am thinking sometimes, with my son the monk."

"Good night, Da," William said gravely, still speaking in English as he went toward the door. But for once, his expression was unguarded.

Bronwyn had never seen a man look so grimly resolute.

His father didn't even say good-night. He merely waved dismissively. "Gwilym tells me you've met Evan," he announced.

"Yes, sir," she replied.

"Don't be sirring me, girl. Sounds too bloody English."

"Yes . . . Mr. Powell."

"He's a fine young man, my Evan, isn't he?" Gwilym Powell said, his voice full of pride.

"Yes, he is."

"Handsome, wouldn't you say?"

"Very."

The old man glowed with pleasure. "Can have his pick of any woman he wants, Evan. Reminds me of myself at his age!"

Bronwyn couldn't help smiling and he grinned. It was a pity his older son didn't have at least a little of his father's charm.

"And fight! Sweet Jesus, he'd sooner fight than eat. Wins most times, too. What a son!"

"You must be proud of him."

"What man wouldn't be?"

As the evening progressed, Mr. Powell continued to talk of John and his exploits, many times favorably comparing his younger son to himself. Bronwyn noticed he rarely spoke of William, so finally she felt compelled to mention the son who tended to him. "Your older son—" was all she managed to say before she was interrupted.

"He's a fine lad, of course, but he'll never amount to much." His tone was slightly contemptuous. "A *farmer* he is to the bone. Like his mother's father, solid as a rock and just as dull."

Bronwyn was tempted to disagree. A farmer William Powell was, but dull? No. Stoic. Dutiful. Serious. And passionate, beneath all that—so he was also fascinating and intriguing.

"He hates to fight," the older man said as if revealing an extremely serious character flaw. "Mind, the one time I finally saw him take a man on, I thought he was going to kill the fellow."

"Oh?" Bronwyn leaned forward eagerly.

"Some man claimed to be a federal marshal came one day a year or so ago looking for Josiah Mathews. William told the man he was trespassing, but the fellow wouldn't leave." Mr. Powell shook his head. "No finesse, has William. Just kept hitting the fellow with rights. A good left would have put him out like a light."

So, William Powell *would* fight if he had to—and in defense of a slave. Bronwyn was glad to hear it. But why hadn't he told her about this? She wished he had.

"John, now, he's one for a good fistfight. And knives—I taught him that, too. Comes in handy in those foreign ports..."

Mr. Powell continued to speak of John. Although Bronwyn hoped he would say more about William, he soon grew drowsy and dropped off to sleep.

When all was still and quiet, Bronwyn looked around the room, dimly lit by the light of the rising moon. There was a crayon drawing of a woman on the wall opposite the bed. She didn't look overly young or anything like William and John. She appeared sweet and patient, like the child Constance, so Bronwyn guessed she must be the second Mrs. Powell.

It was so quiet here, with no factories or machinery working through the night, Brownwyn thought as she yawned. She got up and peered out the window toward the cabin. The building was dark, so Owen must have succeeded in getting the girls to sleep. He was certainly a helpful lad. She would be sure to thank him again in the morning. It was always good to be appreciated.

Her gaze returned to old Mr. Powell. He obviously didn't appreciate his eldest son. William Powell didn't seem to need or want any appreciation, but he was only human. How did he feel about his father's blatant preference for John? She knew how she would feel. How she had felt, when the males in her family were listened to and treated better simply because they were men. She had had to wash their clothes, make their meals, clean the house—while they sat and told stories she wasn't always supposed to hear.

She glanced at the closed door across the hallway. That was probably William's room, since it was closest to his father's. With a guilty glance over her shoulder at the slumbering man, she crossed the hall and opened the door, peeking into the dark room and feeling just the way she had when she eavesdropped on her brothers.

She expected a room as neat, tidy and lifeless as the rest of the house. To her surprise, this room was as untidy as any she had ever seen. Obviously Mrs. Murphy did not come in here.

The narrow bed was made, if pulling covers up toward the pillow could be called made. The drawers of a small bureau were half-opened, their contents tumbled about haphazardly. Papers littered the top of it. The floor was bare, as were the walls, and the basin on the commode was filled with dirty, soapy water. She was exceedingly tempted to empty it, but then William Powell might know she had been in his room.

She crept a little farther inside, her curiosity to learn about her reticent employer too great too fight.

Bronwyn's gaze ran over the pile of papers, most of which were bills. The one on top bore a name she recognized. It was from the tailor's. The sum seemed astronomical to her eyes. So much for clothes! John Powell must be a dandy.

Judging by all these other bills, William Powell could ill afford to pay for his brother's vanity.

No, he must not be so badly off. They ate very well. That is, the hired hands, the servants and his father ate very well. She remembered now that William Powell seemed to eat less than Owen.

Maybe it was the worries of financial troubles that always made William Powell so serious and kept the creases in his brow, financial troubles he kept a secret from his much-admired brother and from the father who idolized that brother.

She heard a sound in the elderly man's room and hurriedly went out, a thoughtful expression on her face as she shut the door softly behind her.

William shifted anxiously on the hard wooden bench in the stuffy Town Hall. For the past half hour, James had made an impassioned speech about the evils of slavery and the necessity of stamping it out by any means. He gave every indication of continuing to do so at considerable length, even though it had started to rain and the windows of the hall had been closed. As a result, the room was almost unbearably stuffy.

Jacob Kent, who sat beside William, leaned a little closer during one of James' more voluble moments. William shifted slightly closer to Kent. "The package made it safely to Nova Scotia," Jacob said softly. "We're not expecting any more parcels for a while," he whispered after another few minutes.

"Why not?"

"Too many close calls."

William had to agree. In recent weeks there had been other narrow escapes like that of the lad on the docks.

"Tinkham's offering more money for information."

William frowned but didn't reply. He wouldn't be surprised if somebody sold information to the marshal, despite Reverend Bowman's attempts to give out information only when strictly necessary. The marshal and his men had been too confident they would find a runaway in that crate.

As William's gaze strayed to James at the front of the room, he wondered for the hundredth time if they could trust him. To be sure, James was genuinely eloquent in the abolitionist cause, but William knew his family continued to trade in the South. James had also recently built a new factory on the outskirts of town. A munitions factory. A war would do no harm to that particular business.

Falconer had been a sly child, inciting school-yard disruption without actually participating in it. Rather like he was doing now, although on a larger scale.

Or perhaps he was misjudging James, letting emotions cloud his judgment. Specifically, jealousy.

Lately William had wanted more and more to tell Bronwyn Davies she was wrong about him. He knew she considered him something of a coward for not going to battle in the cause of freedom. She had believed he thought Josiah unfit to sit at his table. Tonight in his father's bedroom he had wanted so much to tell her he was a part of the Underground Railroad and had helped many, many slaves to freedom.

His reasons for wanting Bronwyn to know could only be traced to foolish pride. She admired men who took action in just causes, and in his heart, he wanted her to admire him.

He also wanted her to believe that he was better than James Falconer, who mostly—and merely—talked in the name of abolition. Better, too, than John, who treated fighting like sport. And better than his father, who rebelled because it was glorious and exciting and brought the women to him.

The wind, which had been rising steadily for the past several minutes, threw a sudden torrent of rain against the nearest window, drawing his attention from his unhappy thoughts.

"I must be going," William whispered to Jacob.

He had heard enough and found out what he had wanted to know about the young slave. It was time for the long, wet ride home. He rose as inconspicuously as possible and left the hall while James continued to expound on the conspiracy of wealthy slave owners.

Bronwyn Davies would surely find James Falconer and his words fascinating tonight, William thought grimly as he went out into the dark, rainy night. He pulled up his collar and yanked down his hat before he mounted his horse to begin the lonely journey home.

Bronwyn's eyes snapped open at the sound of footsteps downstairs. She held her breath and wondered how long she had been napping in the rocking chair.

She glanced at the senior Mr. Powell, who still slept peacefully. Outside, rain pelted the house.

Not wasting another moment, she made her way to the darkened hallway and listened carefully. Yes, someone was in the kitchen.

Cautiously she went down the stairs and toward the back of the house. She hoped the sounds she heard were made by William Powell.

She peered into the kitchen. Illuminated by the light of a single dim lamp, William Powell removed his soaking coat. His hat was on a peg and his boots stood near the door.

Thinking himself alone, his features were relaxed. He looked young and handsome in his own lean, hawkish way. His damp shirt stuck to his chest and shoulders, his wet trousers clung to his muscular thighs, and his hair curled about his collar. She hadn't realized how attractive he was. Then he began to unbutton his shirt.

"You will be getting sick," she declared immediately. She went to a cupboard to fetch a towel.

He didn't answer when she held it out to him. She ignored the glimpse of broad chest revealed by his open shirt as he took it and rubbed his hair vigorously, his actions casting strange shadows on the kitchen wall.

"My father?" he inquired, his voice muffled.

"Is sleeping," she replied.

"What?"

"He is sleeping."

He went toward the table and folded the towel slowly before he put it down. "I hope he was no trouble?"

"No, no trouble."

He looked at her steadily, his features unreadable in the darkness. "Good night, Miss Davies."

Miss Davies! Miss Davies! Again that formality! Was he reminding her she was but a servant? A hireling she may be, but at least she had principles! "The meeting—how was it?" she demanded.

"Nobody said anything that hasn't been said many times before."

"Do they think it will come to war?"

"Yes."

"Good."

He faced her. "Would you feel that way if you had a husband to send to fight?"

"I don't have a husband. I don't want one."

"Never?"

"I want to see something of the world first. To have my freedom."

"And a husband would simply be a burden?"

"Yes," she snapped. She told herself she believed it.

He came closer. His dark eyes searched hers, his mouth grim. "But if you *did* have a husband, would you gladly see him go to war?"

"Yes."

For the first time, she saw him smile—but it was a bitter, mocking grin. "I suppose, should he be killed, you would have your precious freedom."

"That is not what I mean. War is not about people."

"It isn't?"

"It's about what is right."

"What do you know of war and fighting and death?"

"I've heard—"

"Yes, you've heard." He took hold of her shoulders in his strong hands. His eyes flared passionately. "Stories told around the hearth from the time you were a baby, as only Welshmen can. Of glory and honor and noble death, of causes and beliefs." His eyes filled with anguish. "Well, I have seen conflict and death. War isn't honorable or glorious. It isn't about causes or beliefs.

"It is about death, and because it is, it is horrible beyond description. Blood. Filth. Men screaming. And dying." He let go of her and sighed raggedly. "Hell could not be worse," he whispered.

Shocked by the raw emotion in his voice, she stood motionless. What did she really know of war?

His expression changed to his usual unruffled calm. "So, since you have no husband and do not want one, let me ask you this. Would you let Owen go to war if he was of an age to fight?"

Had he asked her such a question even that morning, she would have laughed to think there could be any answer other than yes. But now...

"Well, Miss Davies?"

She stepped away from him. "Yes, I would! But I do not think he would ask my permission. He knows a man must fight for what is right! As you did when that man tried to take Josiah Mathews back into slavery."

He recoiled as if she had slapped him. "Who told you about that?"

"Your father."

"He shouldn't have."

"Why not? Proud, you should be."

"Well, I am not!"

"Some things are always wrong and always will be. Like slavery."

"I never said slavery was right. Only that war is wrong."

"But if the South won't listen to reason—"

"Is that what the North is offering, reason? Or threats and hostility?"

"The time for reason may be past."

"So we should do what we only *feel* is right?"

She glared at him. "There is nothing wrong with following your feelings. Provided a man has them, of course."

"I don't, I suppose?" he asked, his tone sardonic. Yet there was a look in his eyes.... "What do you really know about me, Bronwyn Davies?"

"Enough," she answered, telling herself it was the truth.

"Then you should know we are never going to agree on this subject."

Yes, it was hopeless. "I will be leaving now," she said. She marched toward the door.

"It's raining."

"I see that."

"Wait a moment. I'll get you a coat."

"I don't want—"

"Wait." It was an order, plain and simple, so she did. He disappeared down the hallway and returned bearing a greatcoat. It was old and obviously worn. "Put this on."

With a glance at the rain, Bronwyn obeyed. She was not a particularly short woman, but the coat dragged on the ground, and the sleeves hung over her knuckles. It smelled of leather and tobacco and wool. "It's too big," she announced.

"It's the best I can offer."

"I don't need it," she protested. "Good night, Mr. Powell."

"You don't have any boots," he observed coldly.

"It doesn't matter. Anyway, the rain's stopping, so you can have your coat—"

In the next instant, a strong arm went around her shoulders and another under her buttocks and he lifted her up. She swore briefly in Welsh as she found herself held against William Powell. He kicked open the door, carried her across the porch and stepped into the yard.

"What do you think you're doing?" she demanded. She wriggled in his arms and pushed her hands against his chest. It felt like a brick wall.

"Stop that, or I'll drop you," he answered calmly. "I'm taking you home."

"I can walk!"

"You'll ruin your shoes. Or get sick."

"You don't have your hat or coat on."

"I'm already wet."

She knew that and also that his shirt was half-undone. He could catch his death. But by now they were nearly halfway across the yard, so it would be useless to protest anymore.

The smell of wet wool surrounded her, and the rain made the odors of the farmyard strong. Water dripped from the nearby trees. From inside the barn came the soft sounds of the animals in their stalls. The moon struggled to shine through the scudding clouds.

William's foot slipped. Bronwyn's arms tightened around his neck as he quickly righted himself. "You are an awkward burden."

His words should have angered her. But she scarcely heard them. She was too aware of her arms about him. The feel of his hair around her fingertips. The closeness of his clean-shaven cheeks. The strength of him as he carried her.

He stopped in front of the cabin. Her breath caught in her throat as he let her down. Her legs slipped slowly past his hips. When her toes touched the ground, her thighs brushed against him.

Neither of them moved.

"Thank you for the coat," she said finally, her voice nearly a whisper. She began to remove the garment. His hands reached around her, as if to help.

Her own heart beat frantically and she noticed the swift rise and fall of William's chest. Because of her? Because she was close to him in the darkness, her face inches from his? She had but to raise herself on her toes and she would be able to kiss him....

He took the coat—then he let it fall to the ground. He tugged her into his arms. His lips met hers in a fiery, passionate kiss.

Her first impulse was to pull away—but his mouth was warm, firm, insistent. And then all she could remember was the need and loneliness she had seen in the eyes of this son who toiled unappreciated by his father. His quiet, resolute strength. His hunger for fulfillment, which matched her own. She gave in to the yearning of his kiss and let herself revel in the sensation of his lips on hers. His arms held her possessively, and he pushed her back until she was against the wall. She ran her hands over his hard muscles. His hips thrust feverishly against her and his hands cupped her breasts. Her senses reeling, a low moan escaped her lips as her body undulated to match his movements. She kissed his neck and his collarbone, her chin pushing his shirt away.

With a curse, he broke the kiss and stepped back. He looked shocked and dismayed, as if she had been the one to start this.

"It is not wrong to have a moment of pleasure," she said softly, wanting him.

His expression turned scornful, his eyes hostile. "I might have expected that from a Welshwoman."

"What do you mean?"

"I mean that I understand the women of Wales. God knows I knew enough of them. They clustered around my father like a harem in a sultan's palace."

"So, we are all immoral then, because we enjoy what is natural between men and women? Or because your father did?"

He stared at her, dumbfounded. "You have no right—"

"I have every right to defend myself. I don't know what you're trying to do, except deny you have feelings. I kissed you because I wanted to. I am not ashamed of that, or the way I feel. I am not someone pretending to be a Puritan!"

"I am not pretending to be a Puritan."

"American, then," she amended sarcastically.

"I'll tell you what I am trying to be. Anything but Welsh!"

With that, he strode across the yard. Bronwyn threw open the door to the cabin and hurried inside.

I will leave this place, she vowed silently. Just as soon as she earned enough money to start afresh.

She slumped into the ladder-back chair beside the hearth. It had better be soon. Or she would be in love with the man.

Chapter Seven

Cold, wet and ready to collapse from exhaustion, the young mulatto woman struggled through the woods. She dared not venture near the road, for people would surely suspect she was a runaway. Her dress was torn, her hair disheveled and her feet bare.

How many hours had it been since she had eaten? She didn't know. She had lost track long ago.

All she knew was that to stop would be to die, or worse, to be captured and returned to slavery.

"Dear God, I'd rather die!" she whispered as she crept slowly through the woods. She searched desperately for the markings that would lead her to a safe haven. It was nearly morning. Soon the light would make it easier to see. Maybe she could rest awhile.... No. She had to keep going or they would find her.

The last conductor had told her to look for small signs carved in the trees or special formations of rocks. His family had offered her a place to stay and rest before continuing her flight, but she knew the hunters were close on her trail. She wouldn't put their lives at risk.

Was that scratch on the tree a sign?

She fought to see clearly. Hunger made things swim in her vision. She took a deep breath and willed herself to concentrate and focus.

Yes, it was a mark. She had not lost her way. Somewhere, not many miles farther, there would be a small stone church where she could hide.

She stumbled over a tree root and fell heavily to the ground. She lay there for a long time, too weak and hungry to move. Part of her told her to rest. To sleep. If she never woke up again, did it matter?

If only Miss Taylor hadn't died so quick, Ella thought bitterly. Her illness had come on fast and she was dead almost before anyone knew she was sick. For years Miss Taylor had promised to set her servant free in her will—and then died without making one.

And why had Miss Taylor raised her like any other child? To read the Bible, to know right from wrong, to have the same knowledge of moral justice—only to slowly learn that although her skin was as white as her mistress's, the blood that flowed in her veins, the heritage of a great-great-grandmother stolen out of Africa, meant that she was different. Not in her mind or her heart, but in the eyes of the law of the land.

Her body was not hers. Anyone who owned her could do as he wished, legally.

Better if she had been left in ignorance. Perhaps then it would not seem so terrible to be the property of Miss Taylor's nephew, a man she had always avoided. The very look in his eyes when she was in the same room with him made her blood run cold.

Yet now he could beat her. Rape her. Get her with child and sell the baby.

A moan of despair escaped her lips. She had never known her own mother. She had been given to Miss Taylor's family when she was an infant. But she could guess the anguish the seizure of a child would cause. She had heard the tormented sobbing and moans of despair as she had passed the auction place.

She, proud, stupid creature, had dared to feel safe in a world where to have even a drop of African blood was to brand you chattel.

She knew better—much better—now. She would never again put her trust in a white person, no matter how kind or how gentle, not even the white people who helped with the Underground Railroad. She would trust only herself and God.

And she would die before she would let slave catchers find her and take her back.

Then Ella heard the baying of hound dogs and mustered the strength to rise up and run.

Miss Pembrook walked into the parlor of the large house that doubled as her school and started to remove her gloves. Then she noticed William Powell standing in the room, hat in hand. Constance, her cloak on, was beside him.

Miss Pembrook fought to control the irritation she always felt in his presence. He was nothing but a farmer, yet the way he stood and the way he talked, with no proper deference to one of a higher class, even if hard times had forced her to open a school . . . well, it was barely tolerable. It would have been completely intolerable except that he paid, and paid well, for Constance's board and schooling.

The child smiled at her half brother as if they were in league together.

Miss Pembrook cleared her throat. "So, Mr. Powell, Constance tells me you have a new cook."

"Yes."

"Am I to understand that you have seen fit to employ that most unsuitable young woman?" Miss Pembrook made sure her tone was one of surprise, as if she simply couldn't comprehend anyone's motive for hiring Bronwyn Davies.

"Yes. Miss Davies is able to make special dishes for my father."

"She is some kind of culinary expert, then?"

"She is Welsh, Miss Pembrook, and he is eating better than he has in a long time." William cleared his throat before forcing himself to say what he had decided must be said. "Nevertheless, I regret that I may have to let her go. My expenses ..." He hesitated. He didn't want to admit to anyone, and certainly not Miss Pembrook, that he was strapped for funds.

At the mention of money, however, Miss Pembrook's expression of concern became sincere. "I trust we will still have the privilege of Constance's attendance."

"Yes, of course."

Miss Pembrook looked relieved, then obviously realized her selfishness might be a little too apparent, so she knitted her brows in an attempt to appear sympathetic. She didn't fool William for one moment.

"Miss Davies really is an excellent cook," William went on. "I think you should reconsider employing her."

"Really?" Miss Pembrook's eyes gleamed like a fox who has spied its prey. "As much as I would like to oblige you, Mr. Powell, I, too, have had several additional expenses this year. May I ask what wage you are paying her?"

"Five dollars a month."

"That is a sizable sum. I paid the former cook three, which seemed to be more than adequate."

"Miss Davies has her brother and sisters to support."

"Of course, those children. I'm not sure how Mabel will take to them."

"The boy is very helpful around the farm. I suppose he could stay on as a hired hand at my place, if his sister is willing. And the little girls are no trouble." As he said it, he hoped Constance had not mentioned the incident at the pigpen.

"But five dollars! It seems exorbitant. I don't want to have to raise the pupils' tuition—and as you know, I've been thinking I might. If I had to say the raise was partly to pay for a new cook, well . . ."

William knew he was trapped. "I suppose I could pay a little extra each month for Constance."

"Two dollars would be sufficient," Miss Pembrook said smugly. Too smugly.

"Provided Miss Davies is willing to work for you," he shot back.

Miss Pembrook was clearly startled. "Why, why, yes, of course." She smiled thinly.

"I will see if she agrees. Good day, Miss Pembrook."

William took Constance's hand and strode out of the room. He noticed the shabby wallpaper in Miss Pembrook's once fine house, the pitted and scratched Queen Anne table in the hall and the sticking front door. No wonder the woman was so tight with her money. She probably needed every penny.

But then, so did he.

Nor was he convinced that he quite liked the idea of Bronwyn under Miss Pembrook's thumb.

Yet he didn't know how much longer he could allow Bronwyn Davies to live on his farm. He was only human, after all, as last night had amply demonstrated. He had finally given in to the temptation to kiss Bronwyn, and he wished he had not. The touch of her lips, the feel of her body, called forth such passion in him that he thought he would shout with the joy and despair of it.

Because she apparently felt something for him. Perhaps that was the most dangerous thing about her. That, and the fact that despite his harsh condemnation of all things Welsh, he was born Welsh and part of him would always be Welsh. An American like Jane Webster would never understand the thousand little details that made him what he was. Bronwyn Davies recalled to him the best times of his childhood and reminded him of what was good about his countrymen.

He could not think of his own wants. He had responsibilities, and they were the first priority of his life. He would not allow himself to be selfish like his father or John. Besides, he had nothing to offer Bronwyn except his mortgaged farm and responsibilities she didn't want.

So she must leave his house. Before he fell in love with her.

"Willy, I don't think Bronwyn will want to come here."

He glanced at Constance, whom he had almost forgotten.

"And I'm sure Owen and the girls will want to stay on the farm."

They reached the buggy and he bent down to lift Constance onto the seat. He didn't reply as he sat beside her. He was not about to explain his feelings and his reasons to his young half sister.

"I don't want Bronwyn to come here," she announced.

"I thought you would be happy to have her nearby."

Constance gave him a serious, almost adult, look. "I'm not thinking about what I want, really. I'm thinking about Bronwyn. Miss Pembrook doesn't like her."

"Miss Pembrook doesn't have to like her. Bronwyn is a cook. Miss Pembrook won't have to have anything to do with her."

Constance sighed. "I think you should let Bronwyn stay on the farm. Dada likes her cooking. The men like her cooking. You like her cooking, don't you?"

"It would be better if she went to work for Miss Pembrook," he insisted, a trace of impatience in his voice.

"So you can marry Jane Webster?"

"What?"

"Miss Pembrook and her friends think you want to marry Jane Webster."

William sighed. He had suspected gossip credited him with being interested in Jane, and he feared that Jane herself thought so, but now more than ever, he could not marry Jane. "Jane Webster doesn't have anything to do with Bronwyn going to Miss Pembrook's," he replied truthfully.

Constance scrutinized him shrewdly. "Willy, I don't want to go to Miss Pembrook's anymore."

"You need an education."

"Not if it's too expensive."

"It isn't. You let me take care of the money, Constance."

"But who's going to take care of Bronwyn? Miss Pembrook isn't very nice to the servants, Willy."

His eyes narrowed. "What do you mean, not nice?"

"She slaps them sometimes."

"She hasn't hit you, has she?"

"Oh, no! She never strikes any of the students! Just the servants, when she's annoyed."

William stared straight ahead. Bronwyn was sure to be annoying, and he was distinctly uncomfortable with the thought of anyone, even the skinny Miss Pembrook, hitting her. "I'm sure if Bronwyn does her job properly, Miss Pembrook will be kind to her," he said to Constance. And himself. "Look. There's a rabbit. Let's be quiet and maybe we'll see others."

But as they continued on their journey, William's thoughts were far removed from looking for rabbits.

* * *

Bronwyn kneaded bread in the kitchen and glanced out the east window at the dull sky, trying not to wonder why William had not eaten breakfast. She hadn't set eyes on him since the previous night, and she believed she was in no hurry to see him now.

She forced away the memory of William's searing, passionate kiss. She had already wasted enough time thinking about that, and him. She had lain awake for hours, remembering the agony in his voice when he spoke of war and reminding herself she meant what she said about not wanting a husband and her willingness to see her brother go to war. And she had wondered why he was so determined to keep his emotions bottled up inside him like an evil spirit that had to be kept imprisoned.

She reached up and brushed away a dangling lock of hair with the back of her floury hand, then gave the girls a wan smile as they played quietly with their corncob dolls. Owen tinkered with a bit of harness.

Mrs. Murphy stalked into the room. "You are looking gloomy this morning," she observed.

"Thank you," Bronwyn replied ruefully. "Not used to the cold here, me," she said next, lying. She certainly wasn't about to reveal the true reason for her less than joyous demeanor to Mrs. Murphy.

"Huh! Think this is cold, girl? It's not even November. Why, last winter the snow was something terrible—"

"Where's Mr. Powell?"

"Still asleep."

"Oh."

"Or did you mean William?"

"Yes. I was wondering if I should be starting dinner."

"He's gone to fetch Constance."

"He had no breakfast."

"He did the milking," Owen said quietly. "After that he hitched up the wagon."

Bronwyn gave Mrs. Murphy a pointed look. "If he chooses to leave before breakfast, I trust I shall not be held accountable."

Mrs. Murphy didn't reply. She simply sat down in her chair by the window, took out her pipe and started to smoke, for which Bronwyn was grateful. It was no secret that the housekeeper thought highly of William Powell. But he was no saint. Still, let the Irishwoman think what she liked, because they were going to be leaving.

Sam came in from the barn and they proceeded with a very silent meal.

"Can this boy feed chickens?" Mrs. Murphy demanded when they were nearly finished eating. She stared at Owen.

"Of course," Bronwyn replied.

"Good." She addressed Owen. "You'll find a pan and a bag of shelled corn in the little shed behind the henhouse. Mind you don't be using too much or too little. Take the girls with you. They can husk and shell the kernels off some of the cobs in the big crib."

Owen's expression plainly showed what he thought of the woman's overbearing manner. "The chickens have been fed."

"Then I am sure Sam will be able to find a task for you."

It was obvious Mrs. Murphy wanted the children gone, so Owen silently departed, followed by Mair and Ula.

Frowning nearly as deeply as William Powell, Bronwyn tried to disregard Mrs. Murphy as she gathered the ingredients to make soup. She wished the woman would get to her own work, too, or at least leave the kitchen.

"Did you mean what you said about not coming to America to get married?" Mrs. Murphy asked abruptly.

"Yes, I did," Bronwyn replied at once.

The woman didn't appear convinced. "What girl who looks like you don't want a husband?"

Bronwyn frowned. "Not that it's any business of yours," she began, "but I'm not ready to be married. I've spent my whole life caring for my brothers and sisters, and I've decided I want to have some freedom before I die. I won't get that if I'm married."

Mrs. Murphy sniffed derisively. "You'd probably change your mind in a minute if a man asked you."

"Think you I've never been asked?" This time it was Bronwyn's turn to sniff. "Twelve times I have. I refused each one."

"Don't brag to me, girl. I know your kind."

"What kind is that?"

"The kind who teases men, that's what, with coy looks and bright eyes. The kind who's waiting for a well-to-do husband. Say, one with a farm."

"I don't know what you're implying, except that I would prostitute myself," Bronwyn said scornfully. "I would be thinking twice before I said such a thing again, if I were you."

Mrs. Murphy rose slowly. "Are you threatening me, girl?"

"Are you calling me a whore?"

There was a long moment of silence as the two women glared at each other. Mrs. Murphy's gaze faltered first. "No, I am not." Her eyes gleamed with the remainder of anger. "Because lucky for you I have not seen you behave in any way but right."

What would she be thinking now if she had seen Bronwyn in William's embrace? Bronwyn turned away to hide her reddening face, although in her heart she knew she had done nothing wrong. "You will be happy to know I intend to go from here as soon as I've earned enough money."

"What?"

"My family and I will go from here. We would go now, but I have no money."

"We are not good enough for you, is that it?"

"No," Bronwyn replied truthfully. She wished she had not mentioned her plans, because she certainly did not feel like discussing them with Mrs. Murphy.

"Then why?"

"I thought you would be pleased to hear that."

Mrs. Murphy's face softened, and suddenly Bronwyn had a glimpse of the loving, maternal nature hidden behind Mrs. Murphy's rough exterior. "What has happened?"

"Nothing."

"It's William, isn't it? Are you in love with him?"

"No! I can assure you he is the last man on earth I'd ever want to marry."

"Why?" The woman was genuinely puzzled.

"Because he never laughs or even seems glad about anything. Marrying him would be like marrying a grim old man. And even worse, he's ashamed of being Welsh. No, I would never think of him for a husband, not if he were the last man on earth."

"Then it is good for you to go, because if anybody ever breaks that boy's heart, they will have to answer to me."

Bronwyn laughed flippantly. "The man doesn't have a heart to break, I don't think."

"Listen to me good, girl," Mrs. Murphy said harshly, all trace of a loving, maternal nature gone. "The day after his stepmother died, I heard him crying in the cellar, and I never heard crying like that in my life. He's got a heart, all right, and one as fine and loyal and loving as God made. Hurt him, and by all the saints, I'll kill you."

Dumbfounded, Bronwyn stood motionless as Mrs. Murphy hurried out of the room. She had absolutely no intention of marrying William Powell or anyone at all. No, she did not.

Slowly, she went back to her work, although her mind was far removed from making soup. She stared moodily out the window, more determined than ever to leave the Powell farm. It was the only logical course of action.

A sudden movement in the trees caught her attention. An animal, she thought at first, a large one.

Perhaps a deer, although she hadn't seen any near the farm.

She went closer to the window. She could see a bright swatch of fabric among the trees. It was a person in the woods, heading furtively toward the chapel.

Then Bronwyn saw something else down the lane leading to the farm. A group of men, one of them the fat lawman, marched slowly toward the house. They had dogs with them, which strained on their ropes in the direction of the woods. They must be after a runaway slave!

There was no time to be lost. No time to think of consequences. This was a moment Bronwyn Davies had been waiting for all her life.

Chapter Eight

Bronwyn ran out of the kitchen and quickly surveyed the farmyard. No sign of the children or Sam. Mrs. Murphy was in the house. She didn't know when William would return. The fugitive's safety was in her hands.

Lifting her skirts, she dashed toward the woods. There! That flash of fabric again, close to the chapel. A woman, in a torn and muddy gown.

Bronwyn rushed up to her. The poor creature was exhausted, her breathing loud, her lips dry and cracked, her eyes frantic. When she saw Bronwyn, she opened her mouth to scream, but there was no sound.

"I am a friend!" Bronwyn cried softly. She took hold of the young woman and lifted her, putting the limp arms around her shoulders. "You are almost to safety!"

"The dogs," the woman moaned.

"They're tied," Bronwyn answered. Then the baying began. She all but dragged the woman to the chapel porch. She pushed on the latch and shoved the door open, then thrust it closed behind her. The woman collapsed on the floor.

"Your dress—take it off!" Bronwyn ordered.

The woman's dark eyes stared at her blankly when Bronwyn tugged at the fastenings of her own garment. "You must give me your dress," Bronwyn explained hurriedly. "I'll lead the dogs away."

The woman shook her head. "The hounds'll tear you apart."

Bronwyn yanked her dress over her head. "They'll have to catch me first," she said.

The baying dogs were at the door.

With a terrified look, the woman pulled off her dress.

"You'll have to hide." Bronwyn's gaze went to the unusual pews, which appeared to be crates with a back attached. Crates—each about the same size as the one on the pier the other runaway had hidden in. There were small holes in the seat. With a gasp, she pushed at the board on the top and stifled a triumphant cry when it moved, revealing a cavity. "In here, quick."

The woman was too terrified to move.

"You must!"

The woman obeyed. Her heart pounding, Bronwyn grabbed the tattered, soiled gown and shoved open one of the windows. She could hear men's harsh voices coming closer as she climbed on the ledge and jumped onto the ground.

Clad only in her undergarments but unaware of the chill air, she plunged into the woods, dragging the dress behind her and screaming at the top of her lungs.

"Hold on tight, Constance!"

"Willy, what is it?" Constance exclaimed when her

brother uncharacteristically whipped the horse. The animal jolted into a canter. Constance gripped the sides of the vehicle, her eyes wide with fear and surprise. "Willy!"

"Hear the dogs? Somebody's on our farm with hounds." His face grim, William urged the horse to greater speed. Hounds could only mean trouble.

As the wagon careened into the farmyard, the baying stopped. In the sudden eerie silence, a woman's scream pierced the air.

Owen, white to the lips, ran out of the barn. "That's Bron!"

"Stay here!" William shouted. He jumped down and sprinted in the direction of the terrified shrieks. Branches tore at his arms, cheeks and clothing, but he didn't stop. He rushed through the woods, dread and confusion filling him. What was Bronwyn doing in the woods, and what was making her scream like that?

He came to an abrupt halt. A pack of snarling dogs, being restrained—barely—by a motley group of men led by Ed Tinkham, had gathered around the bottom of an oak tree. His gaze followed theirs—to see Bronwyn Davies, clad only in her chemise and drawers, standing on a branch high over their heads.

She didn't seem hurt. She looked terrified—until she saw him. William had never felt so proud, or so necessary, in his life.

"What is going on here?" he demanded. He turned his scrutiny onto the men with the dogs. "You are trespassing on my land."

Marshal Tinkham's expression was truculent, but his son, Frank, edged back, pulling a dog with him. The others slowly followed suit.

"Government business," Tinkham said. He crossed his arms over his chest. "We're after a runaway slave woman and, instead, we treed this—"

"Young lady," William said.

The marshal smiled mockingly. "Yeah, we treed *her.*"

"You are trespassing," William repeated.

The marshal's grin disappeared. "We're the law, Powell, whether you like it or not, so we'll go where we damn well please!"

"I see no runaway here."

"I was just walking to the cabin," Bronwyn said. "Those dogs started to chase me, so I had to run. They tore my dress off!" Her voice wavered, belying her rebellious tone. His heart twisted at her fear and his anger became burning rage. She lowered herself to sit on the branch and swung her bare legs. "And my petticoat. My clothes are ruined."

William's gaze followed her trembling, accusing gesture toward to the shreds of fabric lying on the ground. Some could have been the remains of the petticoat. Others were pieces of a red fabric he had never seen before in his life.

"Aren't they going to take those beasts away so I can get down?" she asked.

The men who held the dogs glanced up at the scantily attired, shapely young woman. Frank averted his eyes, clearly embarrassed, but the others, who were strangers to William, were obviously enjoying the sight.

William's hands balled into fists. "Marshal, tell your men to get the hell off my land."

"And I told you, Powell, we're after a runaway slave. A woman. She's here somewhere."

William's voice was as cold as the rock he stood on. "Are you accusing me of harboring runaway slaves?"

The marshal stepped back a pace. "I'm sayin' that slave gal didn't just up and disappear. And *that* gal knows somethin' about it, I'd bet. Tell her to come down."

"I will when those dogs are gone," Bronwyn said. She would sooner have stepped into a lion's den, and it wasn't the dogs she feared. It was the men below, with their lust-filled faces. If it hadn't been for William's presence, she would still be terrified.

She was frightened enough as it was, despite her bravado. She had managed to climb the tree scant seconds before the dogs reached her. She had thrown the dress on the ground and most of the hounds went for it. Two, however, got hold of her petticoat and nearly succeeded in pulling her off the lower branches. Fortunately, the fabric had torn, so all the dogs had snatched was white cotton.

William Powell looked up at her, a passionate, angry expression in his eyes that both thrilled and frightened her. "Come here," he ordered.

She didn't dare disobey, although she was afraid of falling. Indeed, she had been swinging her legs only to hide the fact they were shaking.

Nonetheless, she slowly made her way down the tree, acutely aware of her near nakedness. Once on the ground, she crossed her arms in a futile attempt at coverage and kept her gaze fastened firmly on her feet.

"Have you seen anyone who might be a runaway slave on my property?" William demanded. His voice lacked any sympathy for her state, her terror or the runaway.

Bronwyn shook her head.

He turned toward the marshal. "Neither have I. Your dogs must have lost the scent and picked up that of my cook, instead."

"Now wait a minute," the marshal said angrily. "These are the finest slave-huntin' dogs there are. They nearly had the gal a few miles ago—they *can't* have lost the scent."

"That is none of my concern."

"*She* knows somethin' about it." The marshal came close to Bronwyn, and her nostrils quivered from his sweaty odor. "How about it, gal? I can stand here all day waitin' and lookin' at your pretty—"

William Powell drew back his arm and struck the marshal. Tinkham bellowed as blood spurted out his nose.

"I'll have you thrown in jail for this, Powell!" Tinkham shouted, his words scarcely audible with his hands over his bleeding nose. He tried to land a blow on William. Which was a mistake.

William, his expression murderous, hit the marshal again, this time on the jaw. Bronwyn heard a sickening crunch of breaking bone. The man fell, and he didn't get up.

"Pa! Jeez, are you all right, Pa?" Frank Tinkham cried, struggling to control his dog. The other men fought to hold on to the straining hounds.

"Frank, take him and get out of here," William growled.

Frank nodded. "I...I'm sorry about this, Mr. Powell."

"Just take him and go."

Frank nodded and gave his dog's leash to one of the other men. He lifted his father and, supporting him, headed back toward the lane.

When they had disappeared through the trees, Bronwyn turned to William excitedly. "A prize-fighter you would have made, with such a right!"

He glared at her as if he would like to take a swing at her, too. "What the hell is going on?"

"When I am dressed I will be telling you," she said defensively, suddenly frightened of the man before her. He was so angry, and yet so controlled in his anger, as he had been controlled when he struck the marshal.

"If you can sit in a tree nearly naked and let a bunch of men stare at you, you can take a moment to explain what happened."

She flushed hotly. "Do you think I *enjoyed* having those men seeing me like this?" she demanded. "They tore my dress to ribbons."

"It was not your dress."

So, he had guessed that much. And he had said nothing. Perhaps, after all, she could trust him with the truth.

"The runaway's in the chapel."

"You traded clothes with her to lead the hunters away?"

"Yes."

He seemed even angrier.

"What else was I supposed to do? Let them take her? I did the only thing I could think of."

"It was a damned *stupid* thing. Those dogs would have killed you if they'd gotten hold of you—and those men might have done worse."

She looked away. He was right—she had seen their faces. "They didn't get me," she said softly.

William studied the stone chapel. "She'll have to remain there for a while. Tinkham's men might watch the farm, if they think the woman's hiding here."

"I will see she gets food and some clothes."

Without warning, William took hold of her shoulders. His piercing gaze locked onto hers. "I would have killed them if they had hurt you."

He pulled her closer. The memory of his craving kiss returned. Her heart beat faster. She lifted her face and closed her eyes, waiting for his lips to meet hers again.

But they did not.

He let go of her abruptly. "Stay here. I'll have Mrs. Murphy bring you some clothes."

William turned away and walked quickly back toward the farmhouse, trying all the while to regain control of his tumultuous emotions.

Dear God, he had wanted to kill that man. He had barely managed to subdue the yearning to put his hands around Tinkham's fat throat and squeeze until the eyes that dared to look upon Bronwyn with undisguised lust bulged from their sockets.

He was his father's son, after all, and the thought was far from pleasing.

He was no better than the marshal, either, for he felt such burning desire for Bronwyn it seemed like a consuming fire. He wondered if that was why he had struck Tinkham, not out of anger at his refusal to leave, but to find some vent for the frustration that had been building in him these several days.

Even now, he could hardly stop envisioning her in her chemise made of thin linen, which did little to hide her perfect round breasts, swelling at the top of the lace, and her shapely legs, naked below the baggy drawers, slender and pale. More than that, she had looked to him—him!—for protection. Perhaps he had reacted from a primitive need to protect someone he loved.

He could no longer deny that he loved Bronwyn Davies desperately. Hopelessly.

He reached the farmyard. The children had stayed right where he had left them, and they looked at him with fear. "She is all right," he said at once. "Some dogs chased her, but she got up a tree."

He saw Mrs. Murphy standing in the door of the kitchen, concern on her brow. He went to the steps. "She is unharmed. Her dress was torn to bits, though. Go to the cabin and take her another, please. She is by the chapel—"

He stopped. Mrs. Murphy, fiery-tempered Mrs. Murphy, was crying. "What is it?" he demanded, dread making him curt.

"It's your father. Sam's gone for the doctor—"

The cold hand of fear touched his heart at her words. Unmindful of the mud on his boots or even Bronwyn waiting in the woods, he ran into the house.

Bronwyn sat in the silent kitchen. Mrs. Murphy was in her chair beside the window, smoking and staring disconsolately out into the yard. Sam had taken the children out to the cabin and offered to see they got to bed.

The doctor was still upstairs.

Mair had brought Bronwyn her second-best dress and told her Sam had gone to fetch Dr. Reed. Bronwyn had dressed quickly, filled with worry for Mr. Powell. She had not forgotten the poor fugitive, hiding and frightened in the chapel. She had gone there as soon as she was dressed and assured her that the hunters had gone for the time being. She told the woman to stay inside and that she would bring her food when she could.

The evening meal had been a silent one. The hired hands had all gone home, leaving only Mrs. Murphy, who had been casting accusing looks at her the whole time, Sam and the children. William did not come downstairs at all.

Bronwyn managed to prepare a basket of food in the pantry for the runaway. She thought of asking Owen to take it, but was not willing to put him at risk, for she had discovered that with assistance in a just but unlawful cause came danger and fear, and maybe even death. She had been terrified of the men and their dogs and knew only William's presence had saved her from them.

There had been no glory or honor when she stood in the tree with the dogs snapping at her. Nothing about the incident matched her wonderful visions of assisting the abolitionists. She was not sorry for her actions, but she knew that she had been incredibly naive. And that William had tried to force her to see the reality, rather than make excuses.

"You should leave," Mrs. Murphy said at last, breaking the long silence. She glared at Bronwyn. "It could be hours yet."

"Wanting some food upstairs, they might be," she said, mindful of the hungry fugitive, yet concerned for William. "I will wait a little while yet."

"I will get it."

"Thought you hated cooking."

Mrs. Murphy shrugged her massive shoulders. "Suit yourself."

"Did the doctor say anything when you took him upstairs?"

"No." She looked pointedly at Bronwyn. "*I* think it's apoplexy."

"Apoplexy?"

"We heard you screamin' like a banshee and next thing I hear is a thump on the floor above. He'd gotten out of bed, probably to see what all the commotion was, and the sudden move and excitement was too much."

Bronwyn could only stare helplessly at the housekeeper. Had she been responsible for this? Oh, surely not! She would never want to the cause the man harm.

What would William think of her if she had?

They heard the murmur of quiet voices at the top of the stairs, and both moved at once to the hall door. The doctor descended. Mrs. Murphy pushed past Bronwyn and confronted the man as he was about to go out the front door. "Well, Doctor?" she asked, wringing her hands.

"As I've told William, he can't last the night. I'm sorry, but there is nothing more to be done except let nature take its course."

Bronwyn gasped and clasped her hands together. "Doctor!"

The middle-aged man, who had fought against death many times, faced the young woman who must be Bronwyn Davies. "Yes?"

"What . . . what happened?"

"It is his heart. It hasn't been strong for some time now. I told William any sudden shock or excitement might do him serious harm."

Bronwyn Davies groaned softly and covered her face with her hands.

"Oh, my dear!" Dr. Reed said kindly. "It was only a matter of time, anyway." He glanced at Mrs. Murphy. "I have been expecting this since my previous visit. I really didn't think he would live past last Christmas. Has anybody sent for the minister?"

Mrs. Murphy shook her head. "Jesus, Mary and Joseph, I never thought . . . I'll send Sam." She hurried out of the house.

"Constance?" Bronwyn asked softly.

"She is sleeping. I would let her rest awhile yet. She was very distraught."

Bronwyn nodded. There was nothing more he could say or do, so the doctor went out the door and closed it gently behind him.

Bronwyn stood for a moment. She stared at the back of the door, waves of guilt washing over her, despite the doctor's words. Her chin trembled as she fought the sobs building in her throat.

She crept silently up the stairs. She didn't know what exactly she intended to say, but she had to tell William she was sorry. If she had known what her screams might do, she would have kept quiet. She would have stayed in the tree until the men grew tired of waiting for her to climb down rather than be the cause of his father's death.

She reached the open bedroom door and listened with anguish to the labored breathing. William sat beside the bed. He watched his father with such an expression of sorrow she wanted to run to him and hold him tight. But that was not her place.

"Evan?" The elder Powell's voice was soft and weak, and he did not open his eyes. "Evan?"

"At sea, Dada," William said gently. In Welsh.

"I want Evan, my son." A plea it was, and all the more heartbreaking to see the countenance of the son who heard it.

"He is at sea, Dada."

"Constance?"

"Dr. Reed thought she should rest," Bronwyn said in a hushed voice. William looked at her as if she was some kind of spirit.

"Let the child sleep," Gwilym Powell whispered. His breathing grew louder. "Wales. I wanted to go home one last... My son?"

"Here, Dada."

"Evan?"

"No, Dada." Patient. Oh, so patient. "Gwilym."

The old man opened his eyes and gazed up at his older son. "Gwilym?" he whispered. Bronwyn leaned closer to hear the weak words. "There's a good boy you are. Steady, like the mountains, with the eyes of your sweet mother."

She heard William's breath catch and hesitated in the doorway. She wondered if she should go, but she wanted to stay. For William's sake.

"I loved her, my son. So much... I wanted to forget... with all those others... and could not. Your face was always before me... to make me remember."

Bronwyn did the only comforting thing she could. Softly she began to sing "Cwm Rhondda," the Welsh hymn of the valleys. She infused the words with all the emotion that filled her heart.

The rich notes carried Gwilym Powell back to the land of his fathers. To the valley where he was born. To the hills where he had fought. To the woman he had loved. Then to the verge of Jordan. And beyond.

"Bronwyn, go away," William whispered. Then he gave a great, choking sob and laid his head beside the body of his father. He wept as she had never heard a man weep before, as if anguish ripped his lonely, tormented soul.

With tears streaming down her cheeks, Bronwyn silently obeyed the request and left William Powell alone with his dead.

Chapter Nine

"You can go now," Mrs. Murphy said several minutes later. She sniffed loudly and glowered at Bronwyn.

Bronwyn turned away from the housekeeper's accusing eyes. Perhaps it would be best if she went to the cabin. She could be of little use here, and deep in her heart she knew she was afraid to see William Powell now. What if he thought she had caused his father's death?

And the cold, frightened and hungry runaway still hid in the chapel. She should not delay taking her food any longer.

Bronwyn picked up the basket she had prepared. It contained some bread and milk, cheese and a piece of pie. She intended to take two of the quilts from her own bed for the woman to sleep upon.

"What's in there?" Mrs. Murphy demanded.

Before Bronwyn could answer, William appeared at the door. He looked from Bronwyn to Mrs. Murphy and back to Bronwyn. "Is something the matter here?" His words were so calm, so cold and so distant Bronwyn would not have believed this was the same man who had cried so stormily only a little while ago if she had not seen him herself.

"*She* is," the housekeeper said tearfully. "I knew she would cause trouble. If it wasn't for her, your dear father would still—"

"No one is to blame for his death. Never say so again." He looked at Bronwyn. "Miss Davies, I wish to speak with you."

Gripping the basket tightly, Bronwyn sidled past him out onto the porch. She tried to regulate her rapid breathing and quiet her wildly beating heart. And she fought to subdue the almost uncontrollable urge to embrace William Powell. Not as a lover, but as a friend who seeks to comfort.

"Away from the house," he said softly behind her.

They walked toward the orchard. The silence stretched between them like the taut string of a harp.

"Sorry I am to the depths of my heart," she said at last, no longer able to wait for him to break the silence. "If I had known what might have happened, I wouldn't have screamed so much. You must believe me."

He stopped near a gnarled apple tree and looked at the ground. "I don't blame you, Bronwyn," he murmured.

She sighed with relief. "Still, if I had known—"

"Do not speak of it anymore," he said, his voice suddenly harsh. "Is the basket for the woman in the chapel?"

Dumbfounded by the change in his tone, she said, "I will see that she is fed and kept warm, and I'll find her something to wear, too."

"Good. Unfortunately, she must remain there, for I don't think even a funeral would stop those hunters from watching the farm. I will get a message to the Underground Railroad somehow."

Her eyes widened. "You know people in the Railroad?"

He inclined his head.

"I didn't know. You should have told me."

"Why?"

"So I could help."

"It is too dangerous. And I would prefer you keep this knowledge to yourself."

"Of course I will keep it secret. But you must let me do more."

"No."

"I understand better why you spoke as you did before. Please, you must try to understand, too. It is why I came to America. Surely there is something I can do—make food or clothing, write letters. Anything!"

"I will tell the conductor. The decision will be up to him."

She gave him a sidelong glance. "Thank you for coming to my rescue. I am sorry for anything I ever said or thought against you."

"Thank you for singing for my father." The matter-of-fact way he said those words might have fooled her once, but now she could hear the pain beneath them.

She could resist no longer. She went to him, put her arms around him and cradled his head against her breasts. He sighed raggedly, then gently pushed her away. "Don't. Don't make this harder."

"I only want you to know you are not alone, William."

"But I am alone, Bronwyn. I am and I always will be. It is . . . it is the way it must be."

"I don't understand."

"I think you do. Because you're alone, too."

"I have Owen and the girls. . . ."

"Everyone who has responsibility for others is always alone. Thinking of them first. Doing your duty by them. Our needs will come later, if at all."

"No," she started to protest, dismayed at his words—and then by the sudden realization of the truth of them.

Ever since her parents and older brothers had died, she *had* been lonely. That was the real reason she had left Wales, because she always felt different and apart even in the midst of her extended family. If she came to America, well, it would not be so unnatural for her to be lonely. When the children were old enough, she would be free of responsibilities and duties, ready to live her life for herself alone.

"After the funeral dinner, you must leave here."

"No!" The word leapt from her throat with no conscious thought. "That is, surely not soon." She did not want to leave here . . . yet. She did not want to go when he needed someone who saw his pain.

He gave her a searching look. "Yes, it might seem suspicious if you left suddenly. So let us say a week afterward. Don't worry, I will see to it no fault is attached to you. I can find you other employment."

His tone was as final as the sounds of clods landing on a coffin lid.

"Do you want me to go?" she asked. She studied his grim face intently. "Answer me with the truth. Do you *want* me to go?"

"Yes!" He pushed past her, but he hesitated. "It would be better for both of us if you did," he said, his voice low and husky with emotion. "Thank you for the song."

And then he was gone.

The next day passed in a blur of activity and mixed emotions. Bronwyn tried not to think about leaving the farm or about her confused feelings for William Powell while she kept herself occupied with making refreshments for the steady stream of visitors who arrived at the house to express their condolences. Sam explained that the minister would direct that the church bell be tolled in a series of notes to announce who had died, or at least enough for people to surmise it was Gwilym Powell, especially when it was common knowledge that he had recently been sick.

As for William, that one tumultuous expression of sorrow seemed to have shut the door on any other emotions. He greeted everyone with quiet stoicism, and Bronwyn suspected there were more than a few who believed William Powell was untouched by his father's demise. She knew better, although he avoided being anywhere near her as he made the arrangements for the funeral and took care of the farm.

True to her word, Bronwyn took food, clothing and blankets to the runaway in the chapel. Instead of showing gratitude, however, the woman remained guarded and suspicious. Bronwyn didn't fault her for that, because it was obvious the woman's journey had been long and hard. She regretted having to tell her she must stay for a while yet in the chapel, but Tinkham and his men had posted a watch on the farm.

Apparently Mrs. Murphy had taken William's words to heart about not blaming Bronwyn. Nonetheless, it had taken some time before the cold anger left the housekeeper's voice.

Constance had cried for a long time when she heard her father was dead. Mrs. Murphy and Sam comforted her, but it was William's soft-spoken words of consolation that dried her eyes. She had not returned to school, and William had asked Owen to take care of her while the adults saw to the arrangements.

Bronwyn had to admit that Owen would have chafed if the request had come from his sister. Since it came from William, he had taken the task as a solemn duty. Constance was clearly pleased by his solicitous company. The other girls, impressed by the gravity of the situation, kept quiet and did as they were told with a minimum of fuss.

The funeral itself was a simple affair, conducted in the house. Most of the townsfolk came, including James Falconer, Jane and Theodore Webster, the Kents, Ma Gibson and her children, Dr. Reed and his wife, and Reverend Bowman and Mrs. Bowman.

When the cortege to the burying ground departed, Bronwyn stayed behind to begin the final preparations for the funeral supper. It was not an elaborate meal, yet everything should be perfect. It seemed the least she could do, and the time passed quickly as she went about her tasks.

She went into the dining room to fetch a platter and glanced toward the parlor where the coffin had stood a short time ago. Her eyes filled with tears, but she blinked them back. No time for crying now.

Still she lingered. She was alone in the house, and for the first time since Gwilym Powell's death, she permitted herself to feel the full weight of grief. She had not known the man long, but for her he had embodied all that was best of the Welsh—the passion and the fierce willingness to act, and the charm.

Yet her grief was not just for Gwilym Powell. It was for her own dead dreams, killed by the knowledge that William Powell was right. Unbridled passion and unthinking actions were fraught with danger and might be no more than the expression of pride or a belief in one's own invulnerability. If William had not arrived, the woman might have been discovered, the sanctuary revealed and she herself . . .

Worst of all, soon she must go from here, from him. Before she came to care too much for a man who would not return her love.

With slow, thoughtful steps she went back to the kitchen.

James Falconer, in a very fine suit, stood in the middle of the room.

"You are not at the burying?" she asked with surprise. She clutched the platter tightly against her chest as if it were a shield.

"It's finished. I see I am the first to arrive for the supper."

"Yes. You can wait in the parlor." She took the platter to the table, hoping he would leave the room.

As before, he came to stand too close to her. This time, she was very tempted to shove him away. "Everything looks very good," he said quietly. *"Everything."*

The hairs on the back of her neck rose at his tone. She kept her attention on the meat she was arranging on the platter. "I think I hear the others coming back now," she lied.

"I understand you are seeking a new job."

"How did you come to know that?" she asked casually. She tried to keep her hands from trembling.

"Oh, I generally hear all the news one way or another. I think *we* need a new cook. We can pay more than William does, I'm sure."

"But she is still employed by me for the time being, so I would appreciate it if you would let her get on with her work."

Bronwyn pivoted quickly to see William come into the kitchen from the hallway. She moved to the stove, away from both of them.

"As you wish, William," Falconer said. "I was merely hoping to assuage the poor girl's fears of being without work."

"She has another job."

"Oh?" Falconer went toward William.

"Miss Pembrook has reconsidered her original offer of employment."

"Miss Pembrook!" Bronwyn cried. They both looked at her with surprise—as if they didn't expect her to have opinion or concern about where she was going to work. She pressed her lips together to still the curses that came to her tongue.

"We will discuss this later," William said. He waited for Falconer to precede him from the room.

"Yes, we will," Bronwyn muttered, sorrow, anger and disappointment waging a battle in her heart.

Three days later, Bronwyn still waited to have her say with William Powell. After the immediate bustle of the funeral, she had expected to have a chance to protest his rather high-handed decision regarding her, but there was still harvesting to be done, especially in the orchard, and every time she even thought of starting such a conversation, William would hurry out, claiming there was too much to be done to talk now.

She would have spoken to him after one of the evening meals, except that by then the man was clearly exhausted. She wouldn't take on a weak opponent.

Finally, when she could no longer stand the uncertainty of her situation and the strain of attempting to decipher William Powell's emotions, she decided she would confront him that very morning before he took Constance back to school, even though she had no clear idea what she intended to say. At least she could let him know *she* would decide where she would go if he was adamant that she leave.

She waited until Sam, Owen and the girls went outside. "Wanting to talk to you, me," she announced. She wiped her wet hands on her apron and stepped in front of the doorway, blocking his escape.

"What about?" he replied coolly. He had been dreading this moment, but he could see the determination gleaming in her bright blue eyes.

He was tempted to run out of the room. Anything, rather than be here with Bronwyn. Otherwise, he was afraid of what he might say to her and terrified he might reveal his love for her.

She would surely scorn him. She had made it abundantly clear she prized her freedom, and he could offer no recompense for that. He did have some pride, and he could not bear the thought of her rejection. She must go before he weakened.

"I will not work for Miss Pembrook."

"She has reconsidered and since her offer was the reason for your coming to Eternity—"

Bronwyn put her hands on her slender hips. Her chest heaved with anger. "That is not important."

"If you do not intend to work for Miss Pembrook, it is none of my business," he said, although it was a torture to him to sound unconcerned.

"Did I *ask* you to be responsible for me? I am a grown woman. *I* decide where I go and where I work. I ask nothing of you."

"And your brother and sisters, they have no say?" A tinge of anger touched his despairing heart. *He* had had no say in his father's plans. He had been treated as if he was no more than a piece of furniture or any other belonging to be moved about at will.

"I will look after them. I have been doing so since they were little more than babes." She came within a pace of him, and her gaze wavered in a way that went straight to his heart. "I will go, but not to that woman's house."

Stay with me, his heart whispered.

She took a deep breath. "You said you did not blame me for your father's death. Was that a lie? Aren't you sending me to Miss Pembrook's for a punishment?"

"No!" His hands balled into fists as he willed himself to keep his true reasons to himself.

She stepped away. "Haven't I done my job well?"

"Yes."

"I know you like Owen, and he is helpful to you. Are you still angry with my sisters?"

"No. I was going to ask if Owen could stay. I will pay him—"

She stared at him. "Think you I will let you destroy my family?"

The words hit him, an echo of his own thoughts when friends of his father's had offered to take care of John. And then Constance.

"Miss Pembrook's is not very far," he forced himself to say.

"Not giving a damn if she lived in the chapel. I have kept my family together this long. I will not see us separated now."

"But you would not have so much responsibility, then. I'm sure Miss Pembrook would let your sisters attend classes with the other girls. You would be at least a little free," he finished quietly.

She gasped. "What is freedom without my family? I love them. There is nothing more important in the world."

His gaze burned into hers. She knew. She understood the one thing that made duty and responsibility no burden.

Love.

He went toward Bronwyn, a passionate intensity in his features such as she had never seen. "Is love more important to you than freedom?" he whispered, drawing her into his arms.

He kissed her. An explosion of sensation rocked her as desire and need fused with the touch of him. She wanted him, in every way, with every particle of her being. She loved him and knew it, so she returned his kiss fervently. His embrace tightened. Her body molded itself to his. Heat flew through her when his tongue slid into the warm confines of her mouth.

His lips left hers to move slowly across her cheek. "Bronwyn, Bronwyn," he pleaded softly. "Stay with me. Marry me."

Although she had been aware of nothing except the exquisite excitement of his touch, his final words jolted her as if she had been shot. She pulled back abruptly. "Marry you?"

He smiled, the first true, warm, loving smile she had ever seen him make. "Please, Bronwyn, be my wife."

She wanted to give in to him. To say yes. But the words stuck in her throat. For so long her life had been focused on her own plans—to get to America, to find a way to participate in the momentous events unfolding there, to raise Owen and the girls until they were old enough to support themselves, and then, at last, to be free herself.

At that moment, they heard the heavy tread of Mrs. Murphy and the lighter steps of Constance on the stairs.

They quickly moved apart.

Bronwyn wanted to run away somewhere, any-where, where she could be alone. She needed to think. His proposal had been so sudden and she didn't know... She wasn't sure...

"Constance is packed and ready to leave," Mrs. Murphy announced. She put down the valise she carried and eyed the couple suspiciously.

Constance, too, looked at William as if sensing she had interrupted something. Bronwyn forced herself to smile.

William said, "Sam should have the wagon hitched." He took hold of Constance's hand and walked past Bronwyn without so much as a glance in her direction. "I will tell Miss Pembrook that I will bring you and the children to the school on Satur-day."

William drained his mug and subtly surveyed the coffeehouse. Since it was a weekday, the place was relatively empty. Nonetheless, he was cautious as he stood up and slipped quietly out the back door. He scanned the nearby alley, then he crossed it swiftly and kept in the shadows as he made his way to Reverend Bowman's house. Because he was a Methodist and well-known as a moderate in the abolitionist discussions, it might seem suspicious if he was seen going openly to the antislavery Episcopalian minister's home.

Reverend Bowman's study was near the back entrance, so he appeared quickly when he heard William's special knock. He beckoned William into the comfortable, book-lined room after he had closed the heavy drapes.

"Have you made plans to move the woman?" William asked quietly.

Reverend Bowman frowned slightly as he sat and beckoned for William to do the same. "The slave hunters have ceased their overt surveillance of your farm, but I think we must assume they have not given up their vigilance just yet."

"It's been days. Surely Tinkham must believe she's moved on."

The reverend leaned back in his chair with a heavy sigh. "I wish that were so, William. Unfortunately, some of us are beginning to think one of my agents is giving information to the slave hunters."

William stared at the minister. "One of us?"

"Perhaps." The reverend shifted uncomfortably. "Or it could be that someone else is finding out our plans somehow and selling them the information. The rewards are no secret. Given a choice, I would rather it were not one of our people, of course. However, the most important thing is that Tinkham is learning too much, by whatever means.

"It is obvious they still believe the woman is in hiding on your farm or nearby. We dare not try to get her out of town."

"I am willing to let her stay in the chapel."

"I know, William, and I am grateful. But I believe we should not keep her there much longer. I have decided one of us will take the woman from the chapel to another place of concealment. After a time, another person will be told where she is, and he will then take her from that place to another safe haven of his choosing, so that no more than two people will know of her whereabouts at any time. We may reuse hiding places to further confuse the hunters, and we must all be prepared for her, so there will be ample choice of refuge.

"And we must move her often, until these hunters weary of searching for her or we can conceive of a plan to get her safely out of town."

"I understand. When and where should I take her first?"

"No, William. We simply cannot take the risk of anyone discovering the extent of your involvement. Tinkham already has his suspicions about you. They may even decide to search the chapel one of these days."

"Not if I'm there."

"As a man of the cloth, naturally I am against physical violence." Reverend Bowman smiled slightly. "And I'm sure Tinkham will reconsider before tempting you to take action. I have heard the poor man is reduced to eating bread soaked in milk."

"I regret hitting him. I . . . I shouldn't have lost my temper."

Reverend Bowman steepled his fingers as he regarded William steadily. "Understandable, I think. You must have been driven to it."

"Yes." William rose. "Is that all you need to tell me about the plans?"

"Yes." The minister stood up. "Miss Davies' act was very courageous. I am certain the slave woman would have been captured otherwise." He raised his eyebrows. "You don't agree?"

"It may have been courageous, but it was too dangerous. She couldn't have been sure she would make the tree before I...someone arrived to help her. Those dogs might have killed her."

"Nonetheless, several people tell me she is a very fine young woman."

William's expression remained unchanged. "Good evening, Reverend."

"Good evening, William."

Reverend Bowman closed the door behind his friend.

It certainly wasn't like William to strike first. The other marshal had punched William twice before he had hit back.

However, Frank Tinkham, who had come to the clergyman with his troubles, was most emphatic on that point.

Protectiveness could be a sign of a deeper emotion, and given William's natural reticence, perhaps the only way one could guess at an attachment.

The minister sat down with a weary sigh. So many young people these days seemed to have such troubles. William took his responsibilities so seriously he might sacrifice himself to them. Frank and Geraldine Gibson, who loved each other in spite of their parents' mutual animosity. Miss Pembrook, who gave vent to her lonely bitterness with gossip. Even James Falconer, who complained about his father's commands. And beneath everything, the growing fear that war would soon be upon them, with its upheavals, changes and death.

Ella watched the fair-haired young woman named Bronwyn set out buttered bread, ham and milk. Bronwyn also pulled a shawl and a bonnet from the basket she used to bring food to the chapel every day.

"There, now," she said quietly in the odd way of talking she had, and she smiled.

Ella looked at her shrewdly. Something was different about her today. She seemed sad or upset, and her eyes had circles under them as if she hadn't slept well in days.

Not that a white woman's feelings mattered. "When am I going on?" she asked.

Bronwyn straightened. "Not knowing, me. Soon, I think. They want to be sure it's safe for you to travel. The marshal still has his men about."

Ella nodded, although she felt rested and anxious to be on her way. She reached for the food and began to eat. "Thanks for helping me," she said somewhat grudgingly.

"What will you do when you get to Canada?"

Ella shrugged. "I'll find work somehow."

When Bronwyn bent to pour the milk from a pitcher into a mug, Ella hid some of the bread in her skirt. This Bronwyn seemed trustworthy, but Ella was taking no chances. If she had to flee suddenly, she would be ready with her own provisions.

At least now she knew she was in Massachusetts. Canada was still a fair piece away, but if she kept her wits about her, she could be in Canada before the snow came. And she would be free.

"Do you have family in the South?"

Ella shook her head.

"I left some behind in Wales."

"Where's that?"

"England, across the ocean."

"Sounds like you miss it," Ella said. Maybe that was what troubled her.

"A little, sometimes."

"I am *never* going to be sorry I ran away."

"I'm not sorry I went away, either," Bronwyn said. "I just wish I could find a place to stay for good."

Ella gave her a surprised look. "Don't you live here?"

Bronwyn's lips became a hard, thin line. "I work here, but not for much longer. Mr. Powell has found a new job for me someplace else."

"You don't want to take it?"

"I don't like the woman I'm supposed to work for."

Ella frowned. "You're a free woman. You don't have to take the job if you don't want to."

"It's not simple as that," Bronwyn replied defensively. "I have a brother and two sisters to take care of."

"You're free. Free to chose. Free to move on. Free."

Bronwyn looked at Ella. Compared to a slave, she *was* free. But not completely. Not with her family to care for.

Maybe she could find another job. James Falconer would probably be able to help her. Given the lust she had seen in his eyes, however, she thought it better not to be beholden to him.

She couldn't stay at William Powell's farm much longer. Ever since she had not responded at once to his surprising proposal, he seemed convinced she had refused him. He gave her no opportunity to speak to him alone, either. To try to explain.

It had taken her a long time to sort out her conflicting emotions. She had been forced to decide if the dreams she had harbored for so long were still worth striving for, or if she should abandon them for what William Powell offered instead.

She loved him. She knew that now. And she was sure he loved her, although he had never said so. Otherwise he would not have asked her to marry him.

He offered her stability and a home when she had always craved adventure, just as she had always known her adventures would have to wait until she no longer had the children to think of. But William had made her see that she would always be tied to them. No matter where she went, they would be in her thoughts and their welfare would be her first concern.

And didn't William offer her adventure of a different sort? He was involved in the Underground Railroad, and if he was not as vocal as some, it didn't lessen the importance of his deeds.

Besides, marriage to William would surely be exciting in other ways....

In the end, she knew if William Powell asked her again to be his wife, she would say yes.

If he asked her again.

There was a sound outside. Bronwyn quickly put her finger to her lips and stood up. Grabbing her bundle, Ella moved toward a window and put her hand on the latch.

Then they heard a voice, the sound muffled by the heavy door. "It's all right. I'm here to help."

The door opened to reveal James Falconer. He smiled charmingly at the two young women. "Good afternoon. Bronwyn, please forgive my rudeness, but this young woman and I must depart with all haste. I am taking her to another hiding place."

Bronwyn paused before she picked up the bonnet and shawl. She didn't feel right entrusting Ella to James Falconer. Perhaps it was only because of his overt interest in *her*. He was, after all, an outspoken abolitionist, so it was perfectly logical to assume that he was an agent for the Railroad.

She handed the items to Ella. "Good luck, Ella," she said quietly.

Ella fixed her gaze steadily on Bronwyn. "You're free. No one can make you do something you don't want to."

"A fine sentiment," Falconer said quickly. "Now we must be on our way." He took Ella's hand and led her outside.

Chapter Ten

"Where the hell is she?"

Tinkham's voice was a barely understandable growl, for he had a bandage of dirty linen wrapped around his head and jaw. He sat huddled in a chair in the kitchen of his small farmhouse located rather too close to the marsh for comfort.

He had sent his wife and children out to the barn before James had arrived, despite the cold. He always banished them from the house when he talked business, especially of this nature.

"I know precisely where she is," James Falconer replied coolly, "and I'll tell you when I get my five hundred dollars."

"I ain't got that much cash on me!"

"If you think I'm going to take a personal check from you, you're sadly mistaken."

"I could throw you in jail for withholdin' information."

"And my father, not to mention most of this town, would make your life a misery if you tried it."

Tinkham scowled—as much as he could with his head bandaged. Falconer had him there, and the young dandy knew it. "I've got two hundred stashed in the cellar. You can have that." It would still be a bargain, a five-thousand-dollar slave for two hundred.

"You must think I've gone simple," Falconer said with his maddening little smile. "I won't tell you a thing for a penny less than the five hundred we agreed on."

"And I'm tellin' you, I ain't got no five hundred dollars. I can get it on Monday."

"She might have been moved by then."

Tinkham grinned slyly. "But you'd know where, wouldn't you?"

"Perhaps, but you've been so clumsy with your searches and watches and questionings, the conductor is getting extremely cautious."

"Well, then why don't you just tell me who the fella is?"

Falconer responded as if addressing a child and as if he had explained all this before, which he had. "If you arrest the conductor, another route will be found and all of his agents will be regarded with suspicion. If I am not considered a trustworthy agent, I will not be able to provide information. No information, no captures, no money."

"You seem to think we couldn't find any runaways without you."

"You couldn't before," Falconer answered, his tone mocking and his expression skeptical.

"Listen to me, you dandified rich boy! I don't give a damn who your daddy is, or about most of this stinkin' town. I want that slave gal and you better tell me what you know, or so help me I'll make sure your dirty little secret ain't no secret. How do you think your daddy and this town's gonna feel when they find out I've been paying you all this time?''

Falconer was out of his chair and had his pistol at Tinkham's throat before the man could blink. "Are you threatening me, Marshal?''

Tinkham's eyes were full of pain and terror, while James continued to smile. "Are you?'' he demanded again.

"No, no,'' Tinkham sputtered.

Falconer let go. The marshal rubbed his throat and moaned softly as he collapsed onto the battered wooden chair in his kitchen. His own kitchen, and this man—

"Don't ever even imply such a thing again, or I might not be so lenient the next time.''

Tinkham nodded grudgingly.

"Where's Frank?''

"Out.''

"Where?''

"How the hell should I know? I just told him to make himself scarce, that's all. Probably wasting his time courtin' that Gibson gal.''

"You're certain he was gone before I arrived? I don't trust him.''

"Don't worry about him,'' Tinkham said placatingly. His jaw ached and his throat was still tender from Falconer's grip. "He knows where his bread's buttered. He wants to get this farm someday, and the only way that'll happen is if he toes the line with me.''

"A man in love is liable to do foolish things.''

Tinkham grunted. "Not Frank. Without me, the boy's got nothin', and he knows it."

"For both your sakes, you'd better be right." Falconer headed for the door.

"Hey!" Tinkham got to his feet. "What about the gal?"

"When I get the five hundred dollars, you get the information."

Tinkham wet his lips nervously. He had the five hundred—and more—buried in different places in his cellar and the yard. But so much just for information...

Suddenly he grinned, although it looked more like a grimace. "Tell you what, Falconer. Seein's how you know just where she's at, you deliver her to me in the flesh, as they say, and I'll give you five hundred dollars, no quibbles."

"It's too much of a risk."

Tinkham had seen the flash of greed on Falconer's face. "You bring her to a place I know, you can have her to yourself awhile."

Think you're so smart, Tinkham thought triumphantly as Falconer's eyes shone with excitement. *I got you figured out.*

"I'll consider it."

Tinkham knew the woman was as good as his. If Falconer wanted to amuse himself with her before he delivered her to her owner, that was fine. Just as long as he didn't damage the goods.

William helped Owen put the last of the bundles onto the wagon. Mrs. Murphy stood ready on the porch for her regular Saturday journey into town. She wore her finest black gown, woolen cape and a large hat she considered the height of stylishness. All that remained was for Bronwyn and the girls to come from the cabin.

"Owen, go and see if they're ready," William said, his voice deceptively calm and his gaze patient while he watched Owen head for the cabin.

Inside, however, William felt as if a hurricane raged.

Like a besotted fool, he had broken his resolve and proposed marriage, only to be rejected. Not in words, but in that terrible, humiliating stretch of silence.

He should have known better. She knew as well as he did that he had little to offer a woman with her dreams. He was nothing but a farmer, as his father had so often reminded him. For a long time, that had made him happy, for it bespoke respectable security.

Then Bronwyn, with her craving for rebellious adventure, had come into his life. Well, he was no hero and he never would be.

"I'm not doing any cooking," Mrs. Murphy suddenly announced, glaring at him.

"I'm not expecting you to."

"Jesus, Mary and Joseph, who, then?" she demanded. "Not you, with the farm to run."

"Sam."

"Letting that fool into the house to cook?" she cried, aghast. "He'll be burning the place down or poisoning us, or both at once."

"I'll hire another cook," William replied, exasperation creeping into his voice.

"Bronwyn's a good cook. You've finally got some meat on those bones of yours."

"She's going and that is the end of it!"

Mrs. Murphy was beside him in an instant. "What is it, boy?" she asked softly, concern in every word.

He turned away. "Nothing. I'm tired, that's all."

Mrs. Murphy put a broad, strong hand on his shoulder and forced him to look at her. "It's her, isn't it?" She frowned. "I knew she'd be trouble, with her face and her spirit and her voice. Good riddance, I say." Then she saw the pain in William's eyes. "Oh, sweet sufferin' Jesus, is it as bad as that?" She sighed, shook her head and put her hands on her hips. "You'd better marry her."

"No."

"Don't trouble yourself about me. Sam and I thought we might finally do the deed and get married ourselves. We can have the cabin and you'll be needin' a housekeeper, because that girl's made for babies—"

"No!" He hesitated a moment. Mrs. Murphy wanted only his happiness, he knew, so he said, "She doesn't want me."

"What!" She stared at him incredulously. "Who in the name of St. Patrick does she think she is?" She enveloped him in a motherly embrace. "Poor boy," she whispered.

William let himself be comforted for a few short minutes, then drew away. "I'll be fine. I have enough to worry about with Constance and the farm."

"You've always got Sam and me to help you, William," Mrs. Murphy said softly. "Never forget we love you almost as much as our own sons."

They heard the sound of the little girls' voices as Bronwyn, Mair, Ula and Owen came out of the cabin.

Despite his efforts, William's gaze was drawn to Bronwyn. She was breathtakingly beautiful in her plain blue gown and woolen cloak, the very same things she had worn that first day. She looked like a queen trying to disguise herself as a commoner and not quite succeeding.

Mrs. Murphy and Sam saw him as a son. Constance relied on him like a father. To the townspeople, he was a quiet, trustworthy neighbor. Maybe Jane Webster cared enough to want to marry him.

Only Bronwyn called forth all the pent-up passion in his lonely soul.

Oh, God, what was he going to do without her?

Bronwyn didn't even look at him as she climbed nimbly onto the back of the wagon with the children. Mrs. Murphy sat on the seat. With his mouth a thin, hard line of perseverance, William joined her there.

It was a very quiet journey. Mrs. Murphy smoked, a thoughtful expression on her face, and the children seemed subdued, which he put down to Mrs. Murphy's presence.

They came to the Tamblyn mansion. It was a huge frame residence, with shutters on its windows, slender chimneys and a widow's walk, a building that instantly conveyed stability, prestige and wealth.

William drove the wagon around to the back entrance, where Mrs. Murphy's son, Tiernan, waited.

The red-haired young man appraised Bronwyn in a slow, leisurely manner while William ignored the sharp stab of jealousy. He was going to have to stop feeling so possessive of her. One day, he might even hear of her marriage to someone else.

Mrs. Murphy climbed down from the wagon. "Tiernan will bring me home on Sunday afternoon," she said. "Goodbye, Bronwyn. Goodbye, Mair. Ula."

"Goodbye," Bronwyn said softly.

The children nodded silently.

Mrs. Murphy looked at William, then Bronwyn, then the children—and then she burst into tears and ran to her son. Tiernan gave William a puzzled frown before he ushered his sobbing mother inside.

"What is it?" Owen asked.

William glanced at Bronwyn and tried not to notice how lovely she was. "She is . . . not well," he lied.

"I am sorry to hear it," the boy replied. "I hope she is feeling better soon."

"Maybe she caught something from Bron," Mair said thoughtfully.

"Hush," Bronwyn hissed.

"Well, you've not been yourself these past few days."

"You look sick, too," Ula added helpfully.

The two adults didn't say a word as the wagon moved on down the main street and past Jane Webster's shop. Jane came to the door and called out a greeting.

William noticed Jane's hopeful smile and the yearning look in her soft brown eyes. Jane did regard him differently from other men. Perhaps he had never noted it before because she had looked at him that way for years, ever since he had lost his temper with James Falconer. Jane Webster was a friend. A good one, to be sure, and a fine young woman who understood the practicalities of life.

Nonetheless, he didn't stop, but simply waved. He didn't think he could make polite conversation today, not with her. All he wanted to do was what he had to do and get back home. To his empty house and his empty life.

They continued slowly through the town. As usual, a group of men stood outside the newspaper office and talked about the latest news from Washington, New York and the Southern states. Teddy Webster was among them, but James Falconer was noticeably absent. Carts loaded with goods from the sloops and other vessels passed them. Usually William enjoyed the activity, but all he could think of was Bronwyn.

They turned along the road to Miss Pembrook's. He heard Bronwyn's little gasp of surprise when she saw the imposing home. There were empty fields nearby, various outbuildings that appeared neglected and a large stand of hardwood trees on one side.

"The Pembrooks used to be very wealthy," he explained unemotionally. "Miss Pembrook's father made some bad investments, so now she runs a school. It was either that, or sell her home."

"Oh."

So, she didn't want to talk to him, either. What did it matter if she said nothing today? He would remember the sound of her voice for the rest of his life.

James Falconer came out the front door of Miss Pembrook's school and watched them drive toward him.

There had been four times in all of William's life when he had been angry enough to hurt someone—when James had made timid little Jane Webster cry by calling her fat in front of all the other children, when the previous marshal had attempted to take Josiah, when Tinkham and his men had looked lustfully at Bronwyn. And now.

A shiver ran through Bronwyn as she regarded James Falconer. How could she ever have been flattered by that man's attentions? He examined her as if she were a horse or a dog he was thinking of buying.

"Good day, Bronwyn!" James Falconer called out jovially. He tipped his fine beaver hat. "William."

Bronwyn inclined her head slightly. She supposed she should at least be polite.

"Miss Pembrook is anticipating your arrival."

"I gather you were, too," William remarked.

Bronwyn couldn't be sure if he was angry or not. She hoped he was—and jealous, too. That might mean he was still cared for her.

The children started to climb down from the wagon, which drew her attention. "Not yet," she admonished. "We should go round to the back door."

James came toward the wagon. "I hope to see you soon, Bronwyn," he said, his voice dripping sweetness like honey. "Miss Pembrook and I are old friends. I often come for a visit."

Bronwyn stifled a groan of frustration. She wanted very much to tell this man in no uncertain terms she had no wish to see him ever again. Yet he was from an important family in this town, and apparently on good terms with Miss Pembrook. It would be unwise to antagonize him. So she smiled with a minimum of warmth and said, "If Miss Pembrook and my duties will allow it."

"Oh, I'm sure she will." He looked at William. "I trust you've had a good harvest, William?"

"Fair."

"Such modesty! I've heard you've had excellent results with that new strain of tobacco. You know, William, if war comes, tobacco will surely be a necessity for our fighting men. It will help to ease the strain—"

"I will not profit from a soldier's anxiety."

For just a moment, James appeared nonplussed. "Well, of course not, William. Of course not. I meant to say, it would be a fine contribution on your part since—" he glanced swiftly at Bronwyn "—I'm sure you will not join the army."

"I will do what I believe is right, James."

Falconer smirked. "I believe we know what that will be."

"Do you?" William asked, the words as cold as words could be—and a sharp stab to Bronwyn's heart. He would fight, if it came to war. She was sure of it. And although part of her knew he would make an excellent soldier and leader of men, part of her cried out that he might die.

So would her heart if he did.

"We must go. Miss Pembrook is expecting Miss Davies."

"Certainly," Falconer said. Bronwyn had completely forgotten James Falconer's presence. Now the man was an annoyance, like a fly in her kitchen. "I wouldn't want to be the cause of any trouble between Bronwyn and her employer."

She didn't speak or look at Falconer when they drove off. She couldn't, or she knew she would tell him to go to the devil, at the very least.

They stopped close to the kitchen door. The children, still silent, waited until Bronwyn got down before joining her on the ground. William unloaded their baggage.

She reminded herself he would come to the school to take Constance home for her Sunday visits. She could see him, then, too, and she would find some way to let him know that she forgave him for sending her away.

"I don't like this place," Mair whispered.

"It's scary," Ula said, near tears.

Bronwyn gulped and managed to smile as her gaze ran over the massive edifice, which didn't look any better up close. "A big house, is all. Remember, it's a school. And Constance is here."

That brought tentative relief to their faces.

A thin woman of indeterminate age appeared at the kitchen door. "You must be Bronwyn Davies. I am Mabel Thomas, the housekeeper. Bring your things and come in."

Bronwyn reached for her basket at the same time William bent down to hand it to her. For a moment their eyes and their hands met.

"I...I wanted to tell you..." Bronwyn began, suddenly desperate to let him know what was in her heart.

Before she could, he snatched his hand away as if her touch burned like a pot on the stove, grabbed the children's valise and went inside.

With a sigh, Bronwyn lifted her basket. "Come." She waited as William came out the door.

"Goodbye," he said. He mounted the wagon and took his seat.

She didn't reply. She couldn't. She didn't even turn around to watch him go as she picked up her basket and led the children into the house.

Because she didn't want him to see the tears in her eyes.

A fortnight later, Penelope Pembrook critically studied her reflection in the mirror over the parlor fireplace. She was looking particularly well tonight. A brisk walk after the evening meal had warmed her and brought a most becoming flush to her cheeks. Her hair was parted and smoothed down, except for the three ringlets on either side of her face. She had wound the curls tightly about the tongs, for she knew loose curls would emphasize her aristocratic nose and she had been sure James Falconer would call this evening. She wore her finest black silk with its multitude of pleats and ruffles. Her students had learned their lessons well, for the stitches were nearly as fine as Emmanuella Silva's or Jane Webster's. She was especially conscious of her mother's best cameo brooch at her neck. With her new lace bertha around the neckline of the bodice—she frowned and pulled the bertha just a little lower—she was really quite attractive this evening. Mabel waited near the door, a man's beaver hat and riding crop in her hand.

Penelope noticed the empty hearth and sighed. It was a cold night and she wanted James to be comfortable, but she had better save the coal for as long as she could.

"Now you may show Mr. Falconer in," she said to Mabel.

The servant went out after placing the hat and whip on a small table near the door.

Penelope reclined gracefully on a sofa and prepared to meet the young, the handsome, the charming James Falconer, the only man in the whole town who was really on a social level with herself. After all, though the Pembrooks had fallen on hard times, they were still one of the founding families of Eternity.

James entered, all smooth manners and flattering attention in his fine clothes. Her gaze strayed to his finely shaped hands so near his slender hips encased in perfectly fitting trousers. "It is always a pleasure to see you, Miss Pembrook."

"It *is* rather late for a *neighborly* visit," Penelope simpered. She smiled slyly and beckoned for him to sit beside her. "How may I help you, Mr. Falconer?"

"I came to make you a business proposition."

"I...I beg your pardon?" James had been visiting so frequently these past two weeks. Surely if he was interested only in business, he would have spoken of it sooner.

Unless he was merely making conversation now.

"Women do not care for business matters."

James gave her a charming, knowing look. "Many women, of course, are not intelligent enough to understand business," he replied. "But you are not of that ilk, I believe, Miss Pembrook. And this is a business matter that I hope will be *mutually* beneficial."

Penelope's heart thumped rapidly, and for a moment she actually felt faint, just like the heroines of the novels she read in secret when the hero was about to propose. Could it be that James was using the language of business as an excuse to comprehend her feelings for him? She would soon leave him with little doubt.

"I came to see if I could persuade you to part with your new cook."

She stared at him, too shocked to be polite. "I...I'm afraid I don't quite understand you."

"I wish to hire Bronwyn Davies. Of course I am more than willing to compensate you for the trouble you will have to replace her, although I am happy to say I have a suitable cook to place at your disposal."

Penelope sat absolutely motionless for a few moments as the dreams she had been harboring crumbled into ashes and dust. No doubt he had been coming so often not to see her, but to see that...that... And maybe more than "seeing." The woman was probably a slut, enticing James with her shapely body, making him forget she was nobody....

"This cook is a free black woman of great repute," James went on. "I'm sure you will find her work more than satisfactory."

Penelope forced herself to think. James Falconer wanted to talk business; she would talk business. She obviously had something he wanted. She would make him pay, and pay dearly.

"I see. I am surprised you don't hire *her,* then. Surely I cannot afford such a *fine* cook. Besides, Bronwyn does a more than adequate job."

James moved closer to her. An hour ago, this action would have pleased Penelope beyond measure, but that was an hour ago, and everything had changed. "You see, Miss Pembrook," he explained glibly, "my father has expressed a desire for an English cook, and you would be doing us a great favor in allowing us to hire Bronwyn."

"I see. Naturally, I wish to be of service to your family." She infused a proper amount of sincerity in her lie. "However, although she has been here only a fortnight, the children like Bronwyn's cooking, and you must trust me when I say that counts for much in a boarding school."

James frowned—until he caught her looking at him. Then he was all pleasantness and charm. "As I said, I am quite willing to compensate you for the inconvenience. And I would take it as a great *personal* favor."

Now she did not doubt Bronwyn Davies had been more than friendly to James Falconer.

What would his father say to such a thing? He had great plans for James. Mr. Falconer made no secret of his belief that James might even be president some day. To do so, he would need an influential wife from an important family.

A wealthy, influential wife from a family whose remaining branch did not have to keep a school to have food in her mouth.

Penelope was suddenly tired. Tired of being polite. Tired of James Falconer. Tired of running a school and worrying about money. Tired of everything. "How much?" she demanded.

He was clearly taken aback by her abruptness, but she didn't care.

"How much will you pay me for the 'inconvenience'?" she asked.

"Fifty dollars."

She barely stifled the gasp that flew to her lips. As much as that! He wanted the slut in his household as much as that! Perhaps she should inform Mr. Falconer.

But then she wouldn't get the fifty dollars. "You are forgetting the brother and sisters. They are useful, too, in their own way."

"Say, seventy-five, then."

She reached for the bellpull and yanked. "I shall summon Bronwyn."

James leaned back on the best sofa like a potentate in his harem. So sure, so confident, so handsome.

Mabel came to the door. "Yes, ma'am?"

"Tell Bronwyn to come here."

"Yes, ma'am."

James Falconer shifted away from her. "I appreciate your sacrifice, Miss Pembrook."

She glanced at him sharply. "Do you?" She got up and went to the window, staring out at the familiar view. There was the pasture where her father had grazed a fine herd of horses, there the fields that had produced abundantly, there the barn that had housed all the livestock. Gone now. If things had not changed, she didn't doubt that James Falconer would have been paying calls to see *her,* not the cook. She hated her father anew for his greed and stupidity, which had cost her so dear. And she would gladly have murdered the banker from Atlanta and the gambler from New Orleans who had duped him.

"You wanted to see me?" Bronwyn Davies stood in the door, her beautiful blond hair and lovely face, perfect complexion and flawless figure an affront to Penelope.

"Yes. You will be working for Mr. Falconer now."

"I ... What?"

"Please remember to whom you are speaking. You will be working for Mr. Falconer as of tomorrow."

"You are ordering me to go? Isn't my work satisfactory?" Bronwyn demanded.

"That is not the point. Mr. Falconer wants you to work for his family, and I have agreed."

"*You* have agreed? You are not my owner!"

"Don't take that tone of voice with *me!* I say you must go, and go you will. And if you are not a *fool,* you will take the job Mr. Falconer offers you and be thankful!''

"I am willing to double your pay," he said. He stood up.

Bronwyn raised her chin stubbornly. "Thank you, but it is better for the children to stay here. I have no wish to move them again."

"Obviously you do not understand," Penelope said coldly. "You are no longer employed here."

Mr. Falconer put on his hat. "Obviously *I* have made a mistake, Miss Pembrook," he said, his lips still smiling charmingly. "Let Bronwyn remain here, since she is so adamant. Now I bid you both a good evening."

With that, he left the room.

Penelope trembled with the force of her anger. To have made such a humiliating mistake about James Falconer and then to have this...this *wench* refuse...

She grabbed the riding crop James had left behind on the table. "You little jade, who do you think you are to stand there and talk to your betters in such an impertinent manner?" she said harshly. "How *dare* you?"

Before Bronwyn could move away, Penelope raised the whip and brought it sharply down on her shoulder.

"You arrogant whore!" Penelope cried. "You should be pleased he wants you!" Bronwyn tried to grab the weapon from the incensed woman, but Penelope moved away with surprising alacrity. She raised the whip and struck Bronwyn's back with all the strength given by her jealousy and frustration. "He wants *you! You! You!*"

As she twisted to escape the slashing whip, Bronwyn stumbled and fell on the floor, striking her head on the andiron.

Penelope gasped and sank to the ground. The crop fell onto the threadbare carpet. "Oh, dear God, what have I done?" she moaned, staring with horrified eyes at Bronwyn's inert body.

Chapter Eleven

Constance's bare feet flew over the threadbare carpet in the upper hall and up the cold wooden stairs to the garret. She banged frantically on the first door. "Owen! Owen! Come quick!"

The sleepy boy opened the door. His brows lifted when he saw Constance in her nightdress, her face wet with tears. "What is it?"

"Miss Pembrook is beating Bronwyn! I heard her—she's hurting her! I don't know what to do!"

Owen's face filled with rage. He grabbed his trousers, but didn't stop to put them on. He pushed past Constance and ran down the stairs, almost stumbling in his haste.

Constance hurried after him, afraid for Bronwyn and afraid for Owen, too.

The boy dashed into the parlor and shouted, "Touch her again, I'll kill you!"

Miss Pembrook turned to him, her eyes wide like a terrified animal's. Owen kicked the whip across the room and leaned over his sister. He shook her gently. "Bron! Bron!"

Miss Pembrook stared at him, then at the bleeding, unconscious figure on the floor. "Oh, God," she moaned, rocking back and forth. "Oh, God." She crawled to the sofa and sat down.

Constance ignored Miss Pembrook and crouched beside him. "Is she . . . is she . . ."

"She's breathing," he replied slowly. "But I don't know . . . We should have the doctor."

"No!" Miss Pembrook half rose from the sofa. "Please! Not the doctor!"

Constance stood up. "I will go for Willy. He'll know what to do."

"You can't. It's night, and it's too cold—" Owen protested.

"I know the way better than you," she said firmly. "I'll get dressed and go right away."

Owen saw the determination in Constance's face. "Wake Mair and Ula first. When your brother comes, he must take us all from here."

Constance nodded, gave her former teacher a swift, accusing glance and hurried out of the room.

Miss Pembrook stared at the prostrate figure in her parlor and the brother who cradled Bronwyn's head in his lap, murder in his eyes. Shame and guilt engulfed her, washing away the burning jealous rage that had consumed her moments ago. How could she have hit the creature so many times, and with such force? It was as if she had been possessed by a demon.

They must not have the doctor here. If Dr. Reed told his wife, soon everyone in Eternity would know what she had done.

Miss Pembrook put her hands over her face. How could she have been so violent? What would happen to her? There would be dishonor and scandal and the parents would take their daughters away. There would be no money at all....

Owen Davies looked at the parlor door. His two sisters stood there, their faces full of surprise and dismay. Before Miss Pembrook could say anything, he spoke swiftly and surely in Welsh. They didn't move, and the boy's voice became softer as he continued.

He changed to English and gave them a small smile. "Bron is strong to take a beating. Go now and pack our things, for we leave this place tonight."

William waited while Ella said her farewells to the Kents, whose farm bordered his own. She had been hiding in a secret cellar beneath the floor of their barn. Now it was his turn to take her to another hiding place. Unbeknownst to William, or anyone else except Reverend Bowman, she had not been here for a day or two. Ella had been at the Kents for nearly ten days.

The young woman looked rested and certainly healthier than she had when she first arrived, he noticed. Perhaps it was also the food that accounted for the new softness in her features. Or perhaps it was the way twenty-two-year-old Rob Kent looked at her.

Ella was very matter-of-fact with her thank-yous until she came to Rob. Her smile seemed warmer when she looked at the young man, and her hand held his somewhat longer than his father's.

Unfortunately, they did not have much time, so William coughed softly. "We must go."

"Of course," Jacob said. "All our prayers are with you, Ella."

She regarded Rob steadily. "I will find a way to let you know when I reach Canada," she whispered.

"The moon'll be out soon," he said, his gaze intent. "Goodbye, Ella. God bless you!"

They cautiously left the barn and William led Ella away from the Kent house through the belt of woodland that connected with his neighboring farm. The going was not easy, for the path he used was tangled with undergrowth. Yet it would not be easy for anyone to follow them, either.

"Are *they* still watching your place?" Ella asked, her voice hushed and her breath white in the cold night air.

"I'm not sure. We haven't seen any sign of Tinkham or any of his men for days, but they may be trying to trick us."

"I don't understand why I'm going back to the chapel, then," she said warily.

"You're going back to the chapel because Reverend Bowman has made arrangements for you to leave for Canada."

"When?"

"Tonight. The hill's the best place to watch the harbor. One of our friends has agreed to take you out of the bay in his boat to a fishing vessel. He will signal us. That's why you should be at the chapel. We can see the wharves quite well from there."

They reached the small stone building. William opened the door. "Don't open this to anyone but me," he cautioned her. "I'll watch for the signal. And don't make any light. I know it's dark—"

"I'm not scared of the dark."

"Good." As he closed the door, a small whisper came.

"Thanks."

After turning up the collar of his coat against the cold night air, William leaned against a tree, prepared to wait for the agreed-upon signal. Skeletal branches with a few remaining leaves clinging precariously moved in the wind. Dry, dead leaves skittered and rustled on the ground like the scurrying of unseen animals.

Hard to believe a woman had once walked with her lover here. Everything seemed dead, and nothing so much as his own happiness.

The beam from the lighthouse that guarded the coast shone bright in the clear air. He hoped Zeke would not be delayed. Or frightened off.

Suddenly he heard the sound of hoofbeats. Galloping hoofbeats coming down his lane. He straightened immediately and scanned the road.

Slave hunters? No, it was only one horse. Nonetheless, he crept cautiously through the woods and reached for the pistol he kept tucked in his jacket.

It was a woman. For a moment, his heart leapt with hope. But no, the person was too small to be Bronwyn.

Constance! Fear gripped William's heart as he ran through the woods. "Constance!" She rode as if her life depended on it, astride a horse she must have taken from Miss Pembrook's stable.

She pulled the horse to a stop and fell into his arms. "You must come! Miss Pembrook beat Bronwyn. She's hurt—"

"Mrs. Murphy!" he bellowed. He lifted Constance in his arms and ran for the kitchen. He kicked open the door and put Constance down in the warm room. "Stay here."

Mrs. Murphy appeared, sleepy-eyed, clad in her voluminous nightgown and nightcap. "Jesus, Mary and Joseph, what—"

"I'm going to town," William said decisively. "I'll be bringing back Bronwyn and the children. Make my bed. Make my father's bed. Bronwyn's been hurt." He paused for a moment on the threshold of the door. "Get Constance to bed, too. Sam!"

Sam came out of the cabin, pulling his trouser suspenders up over his shoulders. "What...?"

"Hitch up the wagon and follow me to Miss Pembrook's as fast as you can," he ordered, dread driving everything from his mind except the need to go to Bronwyn.

"Why?"

William didn't wait to answer. He sprinted to the barn and didn't even stop to put a saddle on his horse, but grabbed the halter and mounted. He spurred the animal into a gallop and rode toward town, his heart beating faster than the hooves of his horse on the road.

Bronwyn hurt—at Miss Pembrook's hand! This was his fault. If he had not sent her away, if he had not sent her there... It was his fault... his fault... his fault....

He halted his horse at Dr. Reed's house and hammered on the front door until a light appeared in one of the upstairs windows. The sash opened and the doctor's nightcapped head emerged. "What is it?"

"Come to Miss Pembrook's right away. Bronwyn's been hurt."

"William? Is that you?"

"Please, Doctor. Immediately."

Doctor Reed nodded and his head disappeared inside.

William galloped onward to Miss Pembrook's. He was off his horse before it stopped and took the front steps two at a time. He burst into the parlor to see Owen seated on the floor, Bronwyn's head cradled in his lap.

"Bronwyn!" He knelt beside Owen and gently touched the bruised bump on her forehead. "Has she opened her eyes?"

Owen shook his head and William realized the boy was trying bravely not to cry.

"Don't worry," he said, although he was filled with dread himself as he began to examine her. Where in hell was Dr. Reed? He looked at the door, as if that action could somehow hurry the man. Then he noticed Mair and Ula standing in the corner. They were dressed, and their faces were full of fear. He forced himself to smile. "She will be all right. Dr. Reed is coming."

He heard a horrified gasp and turned to see Miss Pembrook, white to lips and nearly fainting on the sofa. "Please, please," she moaned. "It . . . it was an accident. She fell . . ."

William turned his pitiless dark eyes on her. "That is not what Constance told me. I know this was no accident."

The woman dropped the whip she had been clutching in her hand and stared at it as if it were a snake. "I . . . it was an accident!"

"Why did you do this?" he demanded mercilessly.

"I . . . She wouldn't . . . He offered her a job. James said he'd give me money . . . She wouldn't . . ." A low groan burst from Miss Pembrook's pale lips as her thin body began to shake with sobs. "He didn't want *me*. Just *her*. And she didn't want to go. . . . What am I going to do?"

"James Falconer wanted Bronwyn to work for him, and she refused?" he asked.

Miss Pembrook nodded, sniffling miserably. "She wouldn't go. He wanted her and she wouldn't go."

Was it possible that Penelope Pembrook had been enraged enough by Bronwyn's refusal to viciously beat her?

"William!" He turned at Owen's call.

Bronwyn's eyelids fluttered open. "William? Owen?"

William took her hand gently in his. "It's all right, Bronwyn. I'm going to take you to my farm."

"Yes," she whispered. She closed her eyes. "I want to go home."

His breath caught in his throat. She called his home *her* home. Maybe all was not lost. . . .

At that moment, Dr. Reed came in the door and hurried to Bronwyn. "Excuse me, William," he said. "Young man."

Owen shifted and gently laid Bronwyn's head on William's hastily rolled coat. Mair and Ula crept closer.

Dr. Reed examined Bronwyn swiftly and confidently. She moaned when he turned her to look at her back. William saw the torn fabric and the blood, and darted a sharp, angry glance at Miss Pembrook. Before he could say anything to the perpetrator of this crime, the doctor said, "She's got a nasty bump. However, I believe she'll be all right if she's kept still and quiet for a few days. She'll have to be awakened every hour for the next twenty-four, just to be sure. These other wounds will have to be treated and her back is going to be sore, but I don't think she'll have much scarring. What happened?"

William glanced over at the sobbing, pathetic heap that was Miss Pembrook. "An accident."

Dr. Reed gave him a skeptical look.

"I said she had an accident," he repeated. "I'm sure Miss Pembrook would agree that it was something that can't possibly happen again."

The woman lifted her tear-streaked face and looked at him with a mixture of surprise and gratitude. Then she nodded her head vigorously. "Yes, oh, yes! I can assure you it won't happen again. You have my word—the word of a Pembrook!"

Dr. Reed reached into his bag. "Use this salve on her back. It'll help. I'll stop by here in the afternoon."

"She won't be here. I'm taking her home."

Dr. Reed gave William a searching look, then nodded. "Fine. I'll come out tomorrow." He went to the door and hesitated. "If you can't get her to wake up, William, come for me at once."

At the doctor's parting words, fear gripped William's heart again, but he kept it from his face as he looked at the children. He noticed the familiar valise and baskets near their feet.

"I told them we would go from this house," Owen said, his voice firm and determined. "Is Constance all right?"

"She should be, with a warm bed and a good night's rest."

"I would have come for you myself, except it is my duty to look after Bronwyn."

"Of course. And Constance knows the road better."

Owen grinned slightly. "That is what she said. But it is a joy to my heart that she will not suffer for her bravery."

William heard the wagon. "Owen, go and fetch some blankets. We shall have to wrap your sister well to take her out."

Owen nodded and did as he was told. He gave Miss Pembrook a black look when he returned with quilts that William drew carefully around Bronwyn.

"Come, girls. We're going home," William said. He lifted Bronwyn and held her gently in his arms as they went toward the door. He halted in front of Miss Pembrook.

"Mr. Powell, I can't thank you—" she sputtered.

"Constance will no longer be attending this school."

Miss Pembrook struggled to her feet. "Please—"

"I will not tell anyone about this," he said, "but I cannot allow my sister to continue here. Please see that her things are packed. I will send Sam for them tomorrow. Goodbye, Miss Pembrook."

"I didn't mean to hurt her," Miss Pembrook whispered helplessly as they walked out the door.

Ella peered outside. The tall, quiet agent was gone. She didn't want to risk calling out, so with trembling hands she cautiously opened the door. She still couldn't see him.

She chewed her lip and wondered if the plans had gone wrong. She had heard the sound of the hoofbeats and the shouts, and the sound of a wagon leaving, and she hoped that had all been a distraction to draw attention away from the chapel. Or perhaps something totally unrelated to her had happened, like a fire in the town, and in all the commotion they had forgotten her. She opened the door a little more and sniffed the air. No sign of trouble, no smell of smoke.

She closed the door. She would just have to wait.

If only Rob would come! He would know what was happening.

But then he might ask her to marry him again. After talking with her and bringing her food for a few days, he claimed that he loved her. That they could have some kind of life together.

She knew he meant what he said. And the look in his eyes, on his face...

Dear Lord, she wanted to believe him. He was so kind and gentle. So understanding. He admired her bravery, he claimed, and she thought he meant it, for she had seen no condescension in his expression.

She heard a wagon rambling down the lane and crept closer to the farmyard. She saw the tall man on the seat beside a shorter, stockier fellow she had never seen before.

The tall man got off and she realized two little girls were also in the wagon, as well as a boy. The man reached into the back and lifted something out.

Some*one*.

A woman, judging by the skirt. Ella moved carefully through the woods as the man went up on the porch where a fat woman waited with a lamp.

"What took you?" the waiting woman asked anxiously.

"That fat fool of a marshal stopped me," the stocky driver of the wagon said. "Thought we had somebody else in the wagon, or so he said."

Ella moaned softly and moved back into the shadow of a thick maple tree. The marshal guessed she was still here!

When the tall man approached the porch, the light from the lamp fell on the face of the woman in his arms. It was Bronwyn.

Ella glanced toward the harbor. She was supposed to go tonight. That marshal suspected she hadn't moved on. She should run now, without waiting to be told. She should take her fate in her own hands once more.

She shouldn't hesitate. Not for Rob, and not for a white woman. It was too risky.

But Bronwyn had saved her life. She didn't want to start a life of freedom with any debt on her conscience.

Taking a deep breath, Ella lifted her head and looked back once more at the bay. "Oh, Miss Taylor, why'd you raise me right?" she muttered as she marched purposefully toward the house.

Mrs. Murphy's thoughts were as murderous as only an irate Irish woman's could be when she hurried to the kitchen to fetch hot water. She mumbled every curse she knew and invented new ones to try to assuage her anger at Miss Pembrook for the beating, William for letting Bronwyn go there, Sam for not driving fast enough and herself for ever having had a single bad thought about the poor injured girl upstairs.

She shoved open the door and came to an abrupt halt. "Sweet sufferin' Christ! Who are you?" she demanded of the strange woman standing in the kitchen.

"Ella."

"Ella who? What are you doing here?"

"What is it, Mrs. Murphy?" William called from upstairs.

"Some woman says her name is Ella is in the kitchen," Mrs. Murphy replied. She moved slowly around the beautiful young woman and eyed her suspiciously, still mindful that she needed to get the hot water.

William rushed into the room. "Ella! I forgot... Come! You must go back to the chapel."

"I saw you carry her inside here," the woman said anxiously, not moving from where she stood. "Is she hurt bad?"

"A bump on the head, and some cuts on her back. Come, it may not be too late."

"I'm not going."

"Who *is* this woman?" Mrs. Murphy demanded.

"I can help. I've done some nursing."

"What in the name of all the blessed saints is going on?" Mrs. Murphy bellowed.

The woman faced the confused housekeeper. "I'm a runaway slave. Bronwyn helped me, and now I want to help her. Like I said, I've done lots of nursing."

"You're a runaway slave? Since when have white people been slaves?"

"It's true," William concurred. There was no point trying to hide the truth now, and he had to convince Ella to go back to the chapel. Dear God, he hoped it wasn't already too late for the signal and her escape. "Much as I appreciate your offer, Ella, you can't stay. You're supposed to leave tonight. The boat—"

Ella gave William a defiant look. "I'm not a slave anymore and you can't order me to. You can take me to Bronwyn."

For once William didn't know what to do. Mrs. Murphy knew little about nursing and most of that was based on old wives' tales, and he knew even less. He couldn't very well drag Ella back to the chapel, and it was obvious she had made up her mind to help. In the end, it was his love for Bronwyn that decided and with a grateful look, William turned and led Ella upstairs.

* * *

James scowled as he waited in the shadows of the alley. The night was damp and cold, and the wind seemed to blow right through his woolen greatcoat. He lit another cheroot, grateful for the smell of the expensive tobacco that disguised the stink of the alley.

Of course, he shouldn't have to skulk about dockside alleys like some thief, but Reverend Bowman had decided to reveal nothing about the various hiding places being used to hide the valuable runaway. It was as if the man no longer trusted any of his agents.

Still, it didn't really matter where the runaway had been, as long as he knew when, and how, she was leaving Eternity. He had guessed that Reverend Bowman wouldn't be planning to keep the runaway there much longer.

Although Reverend Bowman was growing more secretive, his wife was not so cautious and James had long ago realized that Mrs. Bowman was one obvious choice to be involved with the Underground Railroad. After some subtle investigation, he had discovered that Jane Webster also provided food and clothes, so during the past few days, he had thought of several excuses to visit Jane's shop. He knew she didn't really like him, but he was James Falconer, after all. She couldn't exactly throw him out the door, and he flattered himself that she might even appreciate his attention. How often did a plump, homely woman have such a visitor even on the pretense of commerce?

His efforts had paid off. One day he overheard Mrs. Bowman talking about a warm cloak because "it will be very cold out in that little open boat." Mrs. Bowman and Jane Webster certainly wouldn't be going anywhere in such a conveyance; it was surely the slave woman. Unfortunately, James had not ascertained the exact night of departure, so he had spent the past three in the vicinity of the alley that overlooked the wharves.

This slave had better be beautiful, he thought crossly. He deserved some extra recompense for his troubles over her.

The five hundred dollars would allow him to purchase the munitions factory all the sooner. Troops needed weapons, and with his father's connections in Boston and Washington, surely the Falconers would be first in line to supply them. He was doing his very best to bring that day about.

As far as he was concerned, war meant profits, and profits meant power—power that would be his alone to wield. No longer would he be dependent on his father's approval or involvement in any way, nor would he have to listen to his father's grandiose schemes. He would make lots of money, marry a well-connected, wealthy woman and move to Boston. And he would finally be free.

His scornful gaze ran over the harbor and paused appreciatively on the Falconer sloops. If only the old man would listen and build a clipper ship or two, they could really give the Tamblyns some competition.

On the other hand, sloops were smaller and more maneuverable, qualities that would come in handy for smuggling ventures. War would mean embargoes, too, and more money to be made smuggling.

A flash of light caught James' eye and he stared into the darkness. It was Zeke Carter in his dory. The old Newfoundlander, who made his living building ships in nearby Salem, was well-known along the coast for his refusal to use any boat but the dory he had built himself.

James had suspected for a long time that Zeke was involved with smuggling slaves. Now he knew. There could be no other explanation for his presence here tonight.

That bit of information might come in handy if he felt it necessary to compel Zeke to reveal some of his extensive knowledge of the coast, such as caves and inlets where it would be possible to unload goods without being detected.

James watched the dory and wondered where the woman had been hiding for the past few days. He had taken her to the Kents, but she would have been moved several times by now. If only he knew the direction she would be coming from, it would be easier to intercept her and her escort. He didn't expect any trouble convincing whoever was with her that he was supposed to accompany her in the dory.

Zeke was starting to look anxious, too. That was the fourth time he had raised and lowered his lamp in what had to be a signal.

An hour passed, and still there was no sign of the woman. James blew on his numb hands to warm them. His feet were cold, too, but he didn't want to stamp them. It might make too much noise. In his dory, Zeke apprehensively scanned the bay.

Maybe something had happened to prevent the woman from coming.

James noticed that Zeke's attention was most often focused on the hill that was part of William's farm, where the chapel was. Could it be that Reverend Bowman had sent the woman back there? It *would* be the best vantage point to watch the harbor.

He bit back a curse. That was the worst place of all, from his point of view. He hated William Powell—always had—and if the slave was in the chapel, it wouldn't be easy getting her away without William's knowledge. He did have the excuse of going to collect the mortgage payments to explain any visits to the farm. It was unfortunate that Bronwyn wasn't there anymore to add to the excitement of the hunt.

Perhaps Penelope had persuaded Bronwyn to work for him by now. Bronwyn in his house. That was a thought to warm a man. If she was a virgin, that would make the game more challenging. Either way, she was sure to be in his bed one day—like the slave.

James looked back at Zeke, who pushed off from the end of the pier. Obviously Zeke had decided not to wait any longer. James frowned. Zeke would be angry about this unkept rendezvous. Reverend Bowman would have a difficult task persuading the man to risk such a venture again anytime soon. The reverend would probably have to plan a whole new means of escape, which would mean the woman would have to stay in Eternity awhile yet.

There was no point remaining here any longer. With a sharp motion he struck a match for another cheroot. The light briefly illuminated his face in the dark alley before he turned and walked away.

Lost in his thoughts, James didn't see Frank Tinkham, who had come to Wharf Street intending to drown his sorrows with a few pints of ale. But Frank had seen him, and for a long time afterward he wondered what James Falconer was doing in this part of the town with such a self-satisfied look on his face.

Chapter Twelve

Bronwyn woke to searing, burning pain in her back and a dull, throbbing ache in her temple.

Where was she? She was lying facedown on a bed. Whose bed? Where? The last thing she remembered was Miss Pembrook's enraged face. And William's deep, gentle voice.

Where was he? Where were Owen and the girls?

Slowly, she tried to turn over, but her back felt as if the skin was stretched far too tight. With a low moan, she opened her eyes and saw Ella bending over her sympathetically. "What...?"

"Don't try to move right now," Ella ordered quietly. "I'm going to have to take off the bandages to put some more salve on. It'll hurt, but you'll feel better afterward."

"Where am I?"

"Mr. Powell's place."

Now Bronwyn recognized the plain white walls and the simple headboard of the bed. She was in Gwilym Powell's bedroom. From the direction of the weak beam of sunlight coming through the window, it was early morning.

She vaguely recalled Ella's taking care of her, speaking softly, tending to her with gentle hands. And William—he had been in the room, too. "How long have I been here?"

"Two days."

Then Ella pulled on the bandages. The sharp pain made Bronwyn cry out as tears sprang to her eyes. It felt like she was being whipped again.

"That's done," Ella said, by her tone nearly as relieved as Bronwyn. "Does your head hurt very bad?"

"No, not much," Bronwyn answered. "Owen and the girls, where are they?"

"Here on the farm. Mr. Powell brought you all here the other night."

"*He* brought me here? How did he find out?"

"Constance came to fetch him. She heard Miss Pembrook and took a horse."

Bronwyn nodded her understanding. She remembered how Constance spoke of overhearing Miss Pembrook through the chimney. She was grateful there had been no fire in the hearth that night and was impressed that Constance had been brave enough to come for her brother in the dark. "That was a dangerous thing for her to do. She might have been hurt."

"I hear that brother of yours has a voice to raise the roof when he has to. Constance says Miss Pembrook looked like she heard the trump of God when he shouted at her."

"Owen shouted?"

"So she says. And he wouldn't leave you there, neither."

"Owen is a good lad." Bronwyn's heart swelled with pride and happiness to think that her brother cared so much about her, and even more, that William Powell apparently still did, despite the misunderstanding between them.

"Learned it from somewhere, I guess. There. All done. You can roll onto your back now, but take it slow."

Bronwyn did as she was told, carefully shifting to a sitting position. Her back did feel better, she had to admit. "Is Constance all right?"

"She's fine."

"What about Miss Pembrook? Did they send for the law?"

"No. The reverend came by yesterday to see how you were doing. Seems the poor woman's so upset she's had to be put to bed. She told the minister she hoped you'd forgive her."

Bronwyn didn't reply. She had no wish to forgive anyone who had beat her. But the woman had been vicious with jealousy. Poor creature—she seemed more deserving of pity than hate.

Her brow suddenly furrowed with concern. "Sweet Lord in heaven, why are *you* here? Pleased as I am to see you, and grateful, too, shouldn't you be in hiding or gone?"

Ella's face was carefully expressionless. "I've had lots of practice nursing, so I thought I could help. And now we're even."

Bronwyn frowned, puzzled.

"You helped me, so I helped you." She smiled a little. "What harm that Irishwoman might have done, heaven only knows."

"You have my thanks, Ella, but you mustn't stay here. Those men..." Bronwyn tried to suppress a shudder when she remembered the men and their snarling dogs.

"I won't get caught," Ella said with a hint of defiance. "I got this far, didn't I?"

"I would never forgive myself if they found you because of me."

"Don't worry. That won't happen. I'm not stupid."

When Bronwyn remained silent, Ella blushed, the rosy tint making her dusky cheeks even lovelier. "I'm sorry. I'm not angry at you." She smiled self-consciously. "And I had better say right out that if those men has been around the other night, I wouldn't have shown a hair of my head. I mean, I owed you, but I've got to look after myself. Nobody—" she hesitated for a moment, then squared her shoulders "—nobody else cares about me."

"I think you're wrong about that, Ella. Lots of people care enough to risk their lives and safety for you."

Ella's expression was cynical. "Some do. I've met a few fine, caring people. But I think some of them just want some excitement in their lives, or they got a grudge against the South and Southerners." She stared out the window, gazing pensively at the sky. "I don't want to be beholden to anyone. I just want to be free."

"I left Wales because I wanted my freedom and some excitement," Bronwyn confessed. "All that waited for me there was marriage and babies."

Ella's features softened. "That's all I *want*—marriage and a *real* wedding. In a church. Slaves aren't allowed a real church wedding. And if I have children, I want to be where no one can ever take them away from me."

Ella sighed. Then, perhaps wishing to change the direction of her thoughts, she said in a businesslike tone, "Hungry?"

"Yes, starving, I think."

"That's good." Ella went to the door. "Mrs. Murphy!" she called out. "She's awake."

When Ella returned to her seat, she had a pleasant smile. "That woman's been waiting all day to hear that." Her voice lowered to a conspiratorial whisper. "She's been banging around something fierce in that kitchen, too, but she wouldn't say what for."

"The kitchen?"

"Yes."

"Is William there?" Bronwyn attempted to sound unconcerned. She didn't think she was quite successful, judging by Ella's shrewd gaze. Still, she couldn't wait forever to find out about the one person Ella had not mentioned. She wanted to thank him for bringing her here, for one thing. And for another, she wanted to look into his eyes and demand to know how he felt about her.

"I don't know where Mr. Powell is," Ella replied.

Her pipe clenched in her teeth, Mrs. Murphy entered, bearing a covered tray. She gave Bronwyn a huge grin as she ambled toward the bed and set the tray on a nearby table. "Famished you must be, my dear." She drew off the cover with a flourish to reveal a plate of nearly burnt bacon in congealed grease, two runny eggs, black toast and a cup of coffee.

At least the coffee smelled good. Bronwyn smiled weakly. "Thank you, Mrs. Murphy," she said, appreciating the effort if not the result.

Mrs. Murphy started to tuck the napkin around Bronwyn's neck, until Bronwyn winced in pain. She grabbed the tray and placed it on Bronwyn's lap, then stood back with a satisfied smile. "Now eat."

"I'll go wash out these bandages," Ella said. Her lips twitched as she looked at Bronwyn. "Eat hearty."

Bronwyn grinned back wanly and endeavored to comply.

"Where are the children?" she asked as she chewed on the burnt toast.

"Sam's got them out to the cabin putting away their things."

"Oh?"

Mrs. Murphy studied her with a serious expression. "William said you were staying."

"Did he?"

"He did." Her brow lowered. "You remember what I said about breaking that boy's heart? You'd better marry him."

"Is that an order?" Bronwyn inquired. If Mrs. Murphy thought she had the power to break William's heart, maybe he did still care for her. She struggled to subdue her hopeful, yet fearful emotions. What if Mrs. Murphy was wrong about William still wanting her? "Are you proposing for him, by any chance?"

"Don't play me for a fool, girl. You already turned him down—and it's killing him. I want you to tell him you've changed your mind."

"Why don't you tell *him* to ask me again?"

"Again? He's a proud man."

"I'm a proud woman. He never gave me a chance to think last time, so he has only himself to blame if he believes I refused."

The two woman fell silent as Ella came back into the room carrying Bronwyn's clothes.

"Thank you," Bronwyn said sincerely. "Happy I will be to get out of this bed and back to work." She slowly got up.

"I'll leave you to get dressed, then," Mrs. Murphy said. Bronwyn wondered if Mrs. Murphy was going to tell William about this conversation, and half hoped she would. Maybe that would compel William to talk to her.

She glanced down and realized with dismay that she was wearing a man's nightshirt. If this was Gwilym Powell's, surely it was unlucky to be wearing a dead man's clothes.

Then William himself came into the room.

As much as Bronwyn wanted to confront him, she wanted to do so fully clothed, so she moved behind the screen.

William ignored her. "Come with me," he said to Ella.

Ella rose swiftly, her face filled with excitement and fear.

"What is it?" Bronwyn demanded.

Finally William looked at her. "We must go to the chapel. The time has come for Ella to be on her way."

"Now?"

"She should have gone two nights ago. She decided to stay behind because she wanted to help you."

When Bronwyn grasped the full import of William's words, she hurried to Ella and embraced her warmly. "Oh, Ella! You shouldn't have done that for my sake! How can I ever thank you?"

"I told you, now we're even," her friend whispered. "I got notions of duty, too."

Bronwyn pulled back. "God go with you, Ella. My prayers, too."

"And mine for you, Bronwyn."

William cleared his throat. "There is no more time to be lost. Mrs. Murphy has prepared some things for you, Ella. Clothing, mostly. Come, we must leave at once."

Bronwyn wanted to ask more questions and ensure that her friend would be safe, but she knew she must trust to William for that—and that would be enough.

With a farewell glance, Ella left the room.

William lingered a moment. "When you're dressed, leave my nightshirt on the bed. We will talk when I return." Then he, too, went out the door. Slowly Bronwyn began to unbutton the nightshirt.

His nightshirt? It was *his* nightshirt against her naked body? This garment that he wore with nothing underneath....

Suddenly hot and ashamed, she quickly tugged the shirt off. She had to suppress a yelp from the sudden pain. With more care she drew on her undergarments and gingerly put on her dress. As she fastened it, she walked nearer the window. The sun outside promised a fine day, so Bronwyn raised the sash. A sharp, cold breeze full of the scent of dying leaves drifted into the room. The hills nearby were sheathed in mist.

William and Ella came out of the house and disappeared into the woods, hurrying toward the chapel.

How much she hoped Ella would soon be free. Completely free.

As Bronwyn closed the window, she peered along the lane. Between the bare branches of the trees, she could see a group of men riding closer.

She gasped. Tinkham and his men! Thank the Lord Ella had left the house! They didn't have the hounds, so perhaps they were only here to ask questions. She hoped.

In the next moment her heart leapt to her throat. The marshal and his men dismounted a distance from the farmhouse and tied their horses to one of the chestnut trees. Then they made for the wooded hill and the chapel, as if they already knew that Ella would be there.

Bronwyn didn't linger. Ignoring her stiff, sore muscles, she ran down the stairs into the kitchen to confront an astonished Mrs. Murphy. "Find the children and bring them back here!" she ordered. She rushed past her into the yard and on up the hill. The marshal and his men would probably take longer because they would have to be quiet. In a few moments she pushed open the chapel door.

"This is not the time for rash decisions," Reverend Bowman was saying urgently.

"We can't wait—" William began.

"It's too late," she said as loudly as she dared, shoving the heavy door shut. "The marshal and his men are coming now!"

The people paused like a tableau. William looked back at her over his broad shoulder, his features inscrutable as always. Ella stared at her, horrified. Reverend Bowman's brow wrinkled with concern. Jacob Kent was shocked. And Rob Kent's face was that of a man prepared to do murder.

"Quick, Ella, into the pew!" William commanded.

The minister and Jacob Kent pulled the top of the pew bench off. Ella climbed inside.

"Don't be afraid," Rob said softly. "I won't let them take you."

Ella looked up at Rob, and Bronwyn thought that, despite what Ella had said before, there was someone who cared about her very much. But this was no time to think about anything except keeping Ella from the slave hunters.

"I hear them coming," Bronwyn said urgently. "Help me hold the door."

William shook his head. "Move away and let them in. They mustn't think anything unusual is going on here."

Bronwyn hesitated, but she obeyed and went to stand near William. Jacob Kent sat on the pew that concealed Ella. Reverend Bowman reached into his coat and drew out a Bible.

Tinkham, Frank and some of his men crowded through the door, their guns drawn. "Well, well, well, morning, all," the marshal said jovially as he eyed the group before him.

William took a step toward him. "What are you doing here?" he asked without even a vestige of courtesy.

"Looking for a slave, that's what. And I know she's hereabouts, so you can save your breath trying to tell me she isn't."

"I see your jaw is healing nicely," William observed. He took another step toward the marshal. Tinkham backed up. "You have wasted your time again, Marshal," William said calmly. "Please leave."

"Oh, no." The marshal scowled, as much as he was able to. "I know she's on your property and I'm not leaving without her." He regarded them impertinently. "I also know you're all here to help her escape this very morning."

"I don't care what you think you know," William said, apparently still unperturbed. "I'm telling you to leave."

"I'm a federal marshal on government business. I ain't about to go. If you ain't hiding that slave gal, what are you all doing in this place at this time of day? Revival meeting, maybe?"

"Miss Davies and I are getting married."

Bronwyn felt as if her heart had come to a complete stop. She had to fight to keep the shock from her face at William's unexpected announcement, and also to keep from looking at the Kents and Reverend Bowman.

The marshal appeared nonplussed for a moment. "I don't believe it," he said with a sneer. "When?"

"It's perfectly true," Reverend Bowman interjected placatingly. "They had planned to marry before, but Mr. Powell's father's untimely death made for a delay. And obviously after that sad event, a quiet nuptial is in order. Now, if you will excuse us, we would like to finish discussing the order of service. The wedding is today."

Bronwyn risked a glance at William. She thought he was just as surprised as she. Nonetheless he smiled calmly and put his arm around her, pulling her close, and she could feel his heart beating nearly as rapidly as hers.

"What're *they* doin' here then?" the marshal demanded, glaring at the Kents.

"Jacob is the best man. Rob came to assist Mr. Powell with his chores today," the clergyman replied.

"Huh," Tinkham snorted derisively.

"Come on, Pa," Frank said quietly. "Let's go."

"No!" Tinkham regarded the members of the alleged wedding party suspiciously. "That gal's nearby and I ain't about to give up—and I ain't about to let this *farmer* tell me what to do!"

"I have every right—"

"Gentleman, please!" the reverend interrupted. "You're upsetting the bride." Taking her cue, Bronwyn put her face in her hands and wailed piteously.

"Let's go, Pa," Frank pleaded. "Can't you see—"

"Ain't a damn thing wrong with my eyesight, boy," Tinkham growled. Then he grinned slyly. "Well, if there's to be a weddin', we'll just stay right here and help you celebrate." He sat on a pew and crossed his arms.

"Oh, William!" Bronwyn sobbed. "He's going to ruin our wedding!"

William embraced her tenderly. "Don't worry, darling," he murmured. The sensation of his body against hers made her heart race anew. "It doesn't matter if we have one more guest at the ceremony."

Suddenly he bent and kissed her—and it was no chaste, comforting kiss. It was a heated, fierce, demanding kiss that left her completely weak-kneed, breathless and staring up helplessly into his dark, inscrutable eyes.

"Looks like it was time you two *was* gettin' married," Tinkham noted scornfully.

Reverend Bowman cleared his throat. "Yes, well, shall we continue?" He turned to Rob. "I suppose you have to go to milk the cows, Rob?"

"Yes, sir," Rob said slowly. "I'll be within earshot if you need me." He pushed his way through the men at the door.

"Now, then, Bronwyn," Reverend Bowman said as if the marshal and his gang were not there, "I suggest a reading from First Corinthians. Do you agree?"

Bronwyn nodded wordlessly, trying not to stare at the pew containing Ella, the one directly behind Tinkham.

"Good. I believe we have the ceremony well in hand," Reverend Bowman said. He closed the Bible and looked pointedly at the marshal. "The ceremony will not be until noon."

"I'll just sit right here till then."

"Suit yourself," William said nonchalantly.

"But William," Bronwyn protested, "he'll be in the way. How can we decorate the chapel with him here?"

"The ladies will simply have to pretend he isn't there." William raised an eyebrow as he regarded the marshal. "Quite frankly, I'll be very surprised if he can abide that uncomfortable seat for ten minutes, but that is his concern. Come, Bronwyn, let's go back to the house."

He took her elbow and steered her past the marshal, past his men and toward the house. She heard Reverend Bowman and Jacob Kent following.

"Jacob," the minister remarked loudly enough for the men to hear, "you must thank your wife for helping with the wedding supper and her kind offer to decorate the chapel."

They entered the kitchen. Mrs. Murphy stood near the pantry, a hatchet in her raised hand and a fierce look in her eye. The children peeked out from behind her broad body.

"I heard dogs," Owen cried excitedly.

"It's all right," Bronwyn assured them.

Mrs. Murphy lowered the hatchet and the children came around her. "Where's Ella?" she asked.

"Safe in the chapel for the moment," William answered. "But we have to get Tinkham out of there."

"I'll get him out," Mrs. Murphy said grimly, stepping forward.

Reverend Bowman made a slight gesture toward the children. "Surely he could not expect to be invited," he said.

Yes, William thought, they must not know that the wedding was merely a way to fool the slave hunters. There was no telling how long the marshal and his men might linger on his property, but it would certainly be longer if anyone gave any indication that the wedding was a ruse. He could explain all about it later. If he could even explain his sudden hasty idea to himself.

He was also rather surprised that he could think so clearly despite the pounding of his heart. It had been racing ever since Bronwyn had huddled against him, and the moment his mouth had touched hers, desire had surged through him. It was taking a mighty effort to act as if nothing very unusual was happening.

"Invited? Invited to what?" Mrs. Murphy demanded.

"Jacob, you must tell your wife about this," the reverend said. "We will need her help sooner than expected. I shall inform Elizabeth of the necessity of changing our plans."

Sam appeared in the door. "What in the devil is Rob Kent doing milking our cows?"

"There is going to be a wedding," William announced.

The room fell into a hush.

Mrs. Murphy was the first to regain her powers of speech. "Who the hell's gettin' married?"

Constance smiled and clapped her hands together delightedly. "It's William and Bronwyn!"

"*What?*" Mrs. Murphy and Sam exclaimed in unison.

"Yes, Bronwyn and I are getting married," William said sedately. "Today. At noon. We didn't want a lot of fuss." He looked pointedly at the children and Mrs. Murphy nodded with understanding.

"This is all a bit of a rush, isn't it?" asked a still-confused Sam. "Why the hurry?"

"They're in love, fool!" Mrs. Murphy said, giving him a black look.

Reverend Bowman cleared his throat. "Jacob and I must leave you now to attend to other arrangements. We shall return before noon, of course, with our wives and the necessary items for the wedding. In the meantime, I suggest a surfeit of activity to confound the marshal and perhaps even entice him from the chapel entirely."

William walked over to the window. Tinkham's men seemed to be everywhere. But there had to be a way to get Ella away from Eternity. He recalled a deception his father and his fellows had once used, and the commotion of a wedding would make an excellent diversion. If they could get Ella disguised and off the farm, yet convince the marshal that she was still there, Tinkham would stay, too. She could get a good head start before Tinkham realized he had been taken for a fool.

He turned to Mrs. Murphy. "Please get out the good linen and wash the best dishes. The wedding will be in the chapel and the supper in the house."

"Jesus, Mary and Joseph!" Mrs. Murphy cried, apparently in a dither. "Children, help me! Noon! You might warn a body!"

She hurried out of the kitchen, followed by the children. They heard the sound of drawers and doors being opened and banged shut. Owen paused on the threshold and looked back over his shoulder. He smiled warmly and with tremendous approval at his sister. The thought of telling the boy the truth of this deception suddenly filled William with dismay, especially when Bronwyn gave him a shy and awkward sidelong glance—as if she was a real bride.

"What's to be done now?" she asked softly.

He knew what he *wanted* to do. He wanted to go down on one knee and ask her to really be his wife. However, he had already humiliated himself once. He wouldn't do so again.

And even if his heart did win out over his pride, this was hardly the time to declare his love. It *was* time to think about Ella, so he briefly explained his plan to the others.

Sam let out a low whistle. "So, not a real wedding after all, eh? 'Tis a good plan, William. I'll go raise a ruckus in the barn to set them to thinkin'." With a determined expression, he marched from the kitchen.

"We had best be on our way, too," Reverend Bowman noted. "I believe my wife can find the appropriate attire. We shall return as soon as we can."

"Me, too," Jacob said, and he led the reverend out, leaving Bronwyn and William alone.

"Oh, William, there is clever you are!" she said at once. "Tinkham's such a dolt, it will be as simple as child's play."

Admiration glowed in her eyes, and trust, and something more profound that made his heart soar with delight. For him. Not for his father. Not for John. For him alone.

"No game, Bronwyn," he said. He went to her, wanting more than anything to kiss her again. "Ella's life may depend on the success of our . . . marriage."

Chapter Thirteen

A gaggle of female customers stood in Jane Webster's store ostensibly examining the latest styles of dress patterns.

"It must be a very serious illness," Mrs. Sawyer, garbed in a particularly ugly dress of mustard yellow and purple, said with apparent concern.

"My husband saw *Reverend Bowman* going to the school," Mrs. Wormley revealed eagerly. "It must be serious, indeed, if she's had the minister."

Mrs. Sawyer looked at Mrs. Reed. "What does the doctor say?"

Mrs. Reed was a thin, anxious-looking woman who perpetually appeared about to give credence to the proverb about doctors' wives dying young. "Well, you know Nathan doesn't like me to talk about his patients, but—" she leaned conspiratorially closer "— he *said* it was nervous prostration. The *vapors*."

"Ah!" the ladies uttered in unison.

"And what brought on the vapors?" Mrs. Sawyer asked.

Jane, who had so far kept out of the conversation, spoke. "It must be very hard work running a school."

"You're so kind," Mrs. Sawyer said. Her tone, however, plainly indicated she considered Jane's comment to be rather naive. She gave the ladies a look that signified her next words were to be of great import. "Or should I say, *who* has upset her?"

The women gathered closer, even Jane. Unfortunately, at that very moment, Mrs. Bowman entered the store. Since the minister had always made it very clear he considered gossip evil, the ladies quickly began surveying the various dress patterns in earnest.

"Oh, Jane, I wonder if I could have a word," Elizabeth Bowman said. She made a subtle gesture with her hand the women did not see. "I've decided to have the other fabric, after all. Do you still have it?"

"Excuse me, please, ladies." Jane took Elizabeth by the arm to escort her to the back room. When they entered the workroom, Emmanuella smiled at them.

"Could you see if those ladies need any assistance?" Jane asked. She gestured toward the store. Emmanuella got up and left the room.

"I need a wedding dress," Elizabeth said with no preamble. "Today. By noon."

Jane gaped at her, completely bewildered. She was used to Elizabeth's sudden requests for clothing or fabric, but this was the first time she had asked for a wedding dress.

"William Powell and Bronwyn Davies are getting married."

Jane sat down heavily in the nearest chair. *"What?"*

"I know it's unexpected..."

Jane blinked rapidly. She willed away the tears that sprang to her eyes.

Elizabeth came close so that no one could possibly overhear. "William is involved in the Underground Railroad. He has an escaped slave, a young woman, hiding in the chapel. Tinkham and his gang found out somehow, and they came to take her this morning. Fortunately, Ephram and the Kents and William were there with her. William told them they were at the chapel to discuss a wedding."

"It's a trick?" Jane tried to stifle the hope that blossomed anew at Elizabeth's words.

"Yes."

"But... today?"

"That was my husband's doing. Apparently, he had hoped it would compel the marshal to leave the chapel. Unfortunately, the man insists on staying to see the ceremony. Ephram feels sure that once the ceremony starts, Tinkham won't linger. So, you see, Jane, we must have a wedding gown. If you don't have one, anything white will do. And some fabric for a veil."

Jane rose rather shakily. The whole notion of William's marriage to someone else, although a deception, shocked her. Even now, her first instinct was to refuse. It would be like helping Bronwyn Davies steal William's affections. Or would it really? She had seen the way William looked at Bronwyn at church, and there was no denying he never regarded *her* with anything other than benign affection.

She stared at the worn floor. What had she felt for William all this time? Romantic love? Or respect, admiration and some kind of hope that he wouldn't care she wasn't pretty? That he would like her enough to

free her from her life as a shopkeeper and seamstress?

It didn't matter now, when a runaway's life was at
stake. Tinkham wasn't a pleasant man, but he wasn't
stupid, either. If he was going to believe the story of
the wedding, it would have to look as if there really
was a wedding. And if the dress that had once been the
embodiment of her hopes—and might finally prove to
be the evidence of her self-delusion—could help to
save a poor woman from a life of misery, there could
be no other recourse but to give it, and gladly.

"I do have a gown," she said. She went to the cupboard and opened it to reveal a white dress of such in-
tricacy and beauty that Elizabeth gasped with sheer
delight. The bodice was cut low and off the shoulders, with lace that served to cap the layered sleeves.
The skirt was flounced in three broad rows and
trimmed with more wide lace. Delicate embroidered
flowers decorated it. It must have taken hours to
make.

Jane drew out a long veil attached to a circlet of tiny
embroidered silk flowers.

"Oh, Jane, this is wonderful," Elizabeth said, her
tone reverential. "Whose is it?"

She caught a glimpse of Jane's face before she
turned away and wisely refrained from repeating her
question when Jane remained silent. Obviously Jane
intended this garment for herself, and with a sudden
burst of intuition, Elizabeth realized who Jane hoped
the groom would be. "This wedding is only a ploy,"
she said. "Perhaps you have another dress that would
suit our purposes."

Her features composed, Jane faced Elizabeth. "No, take it with my blessings. If I know Tinkham, the ruse will depend on authenticity to be successful. The dress will help, and I'm sure William and Bronwyn will make a most convincing couple."

Elizabeth gave Jane a brief, motherly embrace. "Thank you, Jane."

Jane nodded, then spoke in a businesslike tone. "The gown will have to be altered. The waist, the bodice, the length. I will need Emmanuella's help."

"What about the store?"

Jane waved her hand dismissively. "Teddy can mind it for a while. He does the books, so he'll at least know the prices."

"I was planning to stop at Ma Gibson's. Nobody else could make a wedding cake in such a short time. Maybe I could ask her to send Geraldine to help in the shop."

"Fine." Jane carefully lifted down the heavy garment. "Emmanuella!"

"Thank you," Elizabeth repeated sincerely as she hurried out of the room, making way for Emmanuella to get by. Elizabeth paused in the shop when another idea occurred to her, and she smiled at the women. "I am so happy you're all here," she exclaimed. "I suppose you're wondering what I had to see Jane about?"

Mrs. Sawyer's eyes gleamed like those of a miser who'd spotted a dropped penny. Elizabeth suddenly decided that if she was going to lie, she might as well do a thorough job. She just hoped Ephram would understand. "Ladies, I have just learned of the most sad business," she proclaimed somewhat despondently. "It seems William Powell and Bronwyn Davies were not unknown to each other before she arrived from Boston."

"Really?" Mrs. Wormley gasped.

"Yes. I don't know the details, but you remember when William went to Boston several months ago and he told my husband it was about some cows?"

Mrs. Sawyer's garish hat bobbed with her enthusiastic nods.

"Well, apparently he met her then. They fell deeply in love—"

"William Powell?" Mrs. Reed asked in stunned tones.

"Yes. But the poor, dear girl wouldn't leave her—" Elizabeth remembered the woman who had raised Mrs. Sawyer when her parents had died, and whom Mrs. Sawyer had tended devotedly for years after she fell ill "—sick aunt."

Mrs. Sawyer beamed with approval.

"Her aunt recently passed away. Bronwyn and her brother and sisters were all alone in Boston, so naturally William asked her to come here. They planned to marry right away. Then his father passed away. Well, they decided the wedding would have to be postponed, and they knew Bronwyn couldn't stay on the farm even though she and the children were living in the little cabin, not the house."

"*That's* why she went to Miss Pembrook's school!" Mrs. Sawyer crowed triumphantly.

"Yes. A few days ago, my husband went to see William, and the poor man was terribly upset over everything. So, Ephram suggested they get married."

"But his father's only been dead—" Mrs. Reed began.

"I know and naturally I agree. Still, Ephram didn't see anything wrong as long as it was a quiet affair. William and Bronwyn were delighted, and they chose today. However—" she sighed in exasperation "—William thought Ephram meant *absolutely* quiet. No guests at all. Well, imagine how I felt when I learned that! Ephram meant no dancing or spirits, and only William's closest friends and associates. Poor William was all set to postpone the ceremony yet again, until I assured him that I would invite his friends. And I'm sure you'll all do your best to show William we *are* his closest friends. Can I count on you to let his other good friends know, since I must attend to some parish business for the rest of the morning?"

More enthusiastic nods and smiles.

"The wedding is at noon on his farm. I had to speak to Jane about the dress. Imagine, Jane doing all that work and not a peep about it! You simply must see the gown. It's the best thing she's ever done. In fact, it's the most beautiful wedding gown I've ever seen."

The women's attention strayed toward the back room.

"Jane's got it all boxed up ready to deliver. Now, I must be on way. Good morning, ladies. I trust I'll see you at the Powell farm."

Well satisfied, Elizabeth hurried out of the shop and mounted her buggy. Those women would be at the Powell farm by noon even if a hurricane blew in. The romantic story, the curiosity about the gown, the conviction that they must be good friends of William Powell's—yes, they would be there.

Elizabeth drove through the town at a leisurely pace, but once on the deserted road, she gave the mare a flick of the whip that sent her trotting swiftly onward.

In a little while, she turned down the lane to the Gibson farm, and as always, she could hear the happy sounds of children's voices.

Elizabeth smiled. She and Ephram had wanted children very much. They had almost given up when God blessed them and Elizabeth discovered she was expecting. Little David had not been overly strong. Nevertheless, he had managed to survive the perils of early childhood and seemed to be growing healthier every day.

Her smile disappeared. With a civil war almost a certainty, she was relieved David was still far too young to be involved.

Ma's boys were old enough, though, and if war came, surely her two eldest would sign up. Ma had had enough trouble in her life. Her husband had died two years ago and left her with nothing except a small, poor farm and her children. It was a credit to them all that they managed, and even more, that they could be counted on to share what little they had in the anti-slavery cause.

Elizabeth waved to the children running about the farmyard and got down from the buggy. She called to one of the boys to take a large burlap bag full of flour into the kitchen and went inside.

The room seemed filled with more children, dogs and the aroma of the six loaves of bread Ma Gibson baked every day.

Ma looked up from the applesauce she was serenely stirring. "G'day, Mrs. Reverend. What's the flour for? Geraldine, fill the kettle. Rosco, wipe yer nose and get off that chair. Have a seat, Mrs. Rev."

"No, thank you. I haven't time. I need your help." Elizabeth made the same gesture with her hand she had in Jane's shop.

"Oh?" Ma put down her spoon. "Kids, clear out."

At once, the commotion spilled out the door and into the yard.

"There's going to be a wedding," Elizabeth said. "William Powell and Bronwyn Davies."

Ma raised her eyebrows. "William Powell's gettin' hitched? Whew, I can't hardly believe it."

"Yes, there's been a problem with the package. We hope to get it out during the ceremony. There isn't much time. We need a wedding cake."

"When?"

"Today."

"My Lord in heaven above!"

"Nothing fancy, of course."

Ma had already grabbed her mixing bowl. "Rest easy, Mrs. Rev. A wedding cake you shall have."

"We need it by three o'clock."

"Well then, it ain't gonna be no fruitcake. Geraldine!"

"Jane's taking Bronwyn a wedding dress, so we wondered if Geraldine could help with the shop. I'll drive her there."

"Of course. Jemima!"

Geraldine drifted into the kitchen. "Go with Mrs. Reverend here," her mother commanded. "You're getting to work in Jane Webster's shop."

Geraldine smiled as her younger sister Jemima came through the door.

"Well, Geraldine, don't just stand there. Go. Now, Jemima, fetch the flour. And the raisins. And anything else comes to mind that'll stretch a cake recipe. Maybe this here applesauce..."

Already forgotten, Elizabeth and Geraldine slipped quietly away.

"I think it's an excellent plan, William, considering how quickly we've had to act. I have made arrangements for a hiding place elsewhere for Ella. If we can dress her as a wedding guest and let her mingle with the others, it might enable us to get her away unnoticed. We'll have to ensure that someone keeps Tinkham occupied."

"Rob's volunteered to act as a decoy if Tinkham doesn't leave before the ceremony. Rob'll head off with the wagon—and with a cargo that looks as if it could be hiding someone. Hopefully, Tinkham and his men will follow him, while Ella stays behind."

"Excellent."

William gazed at the minister, his expression placid. "If Tinkham doesn't leave until after the ceremony, the marriage won't be legal, will it?"

As always, Ephram Bowman was amazed at William Powell's cool composure. There wasn't another man in a thousand who could come up with a plan on such short notice without showing the least sign of agitation. And then to stand here asking about the exact legal status of the ceremony as if he were discussing the weather... "William, it all depends when—and if—we stop the ceremony. I'll have to ready the proper documents, just to be prepared. And obviously the ceremony will have to be authentic. However—" he eyed William carefully, seeking some idea of the man's emotional state "—if we are forced to go through the entire ceremony, you could have the marriage annulled afterward."

"Would that be difficult?"

"Well, um—" Reverend Bowman cleared his throat "—you would simply not consummate the relationship."

William nodded, and never had Ephram Bowman found the man's inscrutability more annoying. As an agent of the Railroad, a man with a poker face was a definite asset, but as a friend, he could be intensely frustrating. Especially in a matter such as this.

In his heart, Ephram thought he had never seen a couple more suited than Bronwyn Davies and William Powell, with their joint heritage and, if that kiss in the chapel was anything to judge by, mutual passion. Unfortunately, William would have made an excellent medieval monk, with his lean, hawklike

features and notions of duty, devotion and martyr-
dom.

Instead, he was a Massachusetts farmer who deserved a wife who loved him. Ephram hoped there
would be no need to annul the marriage, so much so
that he was almost ashamed of himself.

Almost.

The marshal and his men did not leave the farm.
Bronwyn, not knowing what else to do, commenced
baking things that would be appropriate for a wedding supper. Nonetheless, she kept looking out the
windows and wondering where William was. And how
Ella was faring. And poor Rob.

Tinkham's men walked about, obviously keeping
their eyes open for signs of a runaway. Tinkham himself hovered near the chapel and smoked.

What were they going to do if Marshal Tinkham
insisted on staying for the ceremony? She supposed a
wedding would have to be performed. Ella's safety
depended on them, and if it took a wedding, so be it.
There were many worse things she could think of than
marrying William. Fraudulent though the marriage
might be.

What if the marshal stayed for the wedding supper? What if he wouldn't leave afterward? How far
could she and William be expected to maintain the il-
lusion of a newly married couple? Surely Tinkham
wouldn't insist on following them inside... and upstairs... maybe even to the bedroom....

She was so very warm. The oven. It had to be the
oven.

Mrs. Murphy strode into the kitchen. "What the devil are you doing here?"

"Baking."

"Fine thing for the bride to be doing."

"I have to do *something*."

"You should be actin' like a bride, all nerves and tears," Mrs. Murphy declared. "And William better start actin' like a groom, although he'd likely be behavin' just the same if he really was gettin' married."

Bronwyn didn't reply as she gazed unseeingly at the dough in the bowl on the table. She wished this was not a feigned ceremony, but a real one. If only she could be sure of William's feelings! "The children?" she inquired as Mrs. Murphy continued to stare at her.

"Washed and dressed and sitting in the parlor. I told them I'd tan their hides if they moved an inch."

Mrs. Bowman, Mrs. Kent, the rest of the Kent family and the Gibson clan crowded into the kitchen, mercifully preventing Bronwyn from having to speak.

"Go upstairs," Mrs. Murphy ordered her abruptly. "The bride shouldn't be doing all this work."

Bronwyn sighed thankfully and left the hot kitchen. Once on the landing, she sat down on the top step to think. This was becoming more complicated all the time and she was worried sick. *Why* wouldn't the marshal go? Had Ella gotten out of the pew? Surely it would be cramped and hard to breathe inside it. What had possessed William to come up with such an outlandish idea? Would his plan work?

The front door to the house opened. Jane Webster and Emmanuella Silva entered, bearing two enormous boxes. They spotted Bronwyn and came up the steps toward her. "We've got the dress," Jane said softly.

"Dress?" Bronwyn inquired.

"Wedding dress."

"Oh."

"Come. It's nearly noon. Which room?" Jane asked.

Bronwyn hesitated. Which room, indeed?

She paused outside William's—and noticed Mrs. Murphy had made the narrow bed with clean linens and put on a quilt.

She blushed hotly, and led the women into the room that had been his father's.

They closed the door and set the boxes on the bed, then opened the first to reveal the most beautiful garment Bronwyn had ever seen. As she examined it, she felt another pang of intense regret that this was not to be her real wedding dress. Or her real wedding to her real groom.

"We don't have much time to do the alterations," Jane said worriedly. Emmanuella took pins and thread from a small sewing basket she carried.

Bronwyn nodded and began to undo her dress.

Then they heard another sound. Bronwyn recognized it at once as William's deliberate tread on the stairs.

Of course, she thought, he would not get married in his working clothes.

Jane lifted a pair of embroidered pantalettes made of linen so fine it was almost sheer, a thin chemise and a corset out of the second box. "These first."

"I don't think . . ." Bronwyn demurred.

"The dress won't look right without the proper undergarments," Jane said matter-of-factly. "We're going to have enough sewing to do as it is."

Bronwyn gulped and quickly stepped into the fine undergarments. "It's a lovely gown," she said as Jane prepared to lift it over Bronwyn's head.

"For the beautiful bride William deserves," Jane replied faintly, putting aside her dreams about William Powell once and for all.

William pulled on the fine wool jacket. It fit, and very well, too. John would undoubtedly be annoyed that his brother had worn it first, but William didn't care. For once in his life, he was going to dress as well as John. After all, it was his wedding day.

His wedding day.

How he wished it truly was, and not just a scheme to help a runaway slave, worthy though that was.

With quick, aggressive strokes he brushed his hair. Well, what other explanation could he have given in such circumstances? What other reason could he and the others offer for being in the chapel on a weekday? Tinkham hadn't even believed the plausible lie, which had probably been planted in William's imagination by the sight of Ella and Rob Kent standing in front of Reverend Bowman.

Or it could have been his own desire that made him speak.

He swore eloquently and sat down with a sigh on his narrow bed. There was no use denying his feelings, at least to himself.

He wanted to marry Bronwyn Davies so much it was like a physical hunger. He wanted to live with her, work with her, sleep with her. Make love with her. He wished with all his heart this was a real wedding.

But that was not to be. Bronwyn Davies didn't want a husband, and certainly not a farmer. She wanted freedom and adventure. John was the type of man she yearned for, with his roguish, carefree ways and his seafaring life.

William had fought the urge to seek her out all morning, wanting to explain... what? That he had come up with his plan with no real thought, but hoped they could make it a legal ceremony? That he had meant to bestow only a chaste kiss in the chapel, but his desire became nearly uncontrollable the moment his lips met hers? That he had realized she had yielded, but not responded as before? That he feared that whatever she had felt for him once, he had destroyed when he made her go to Miss Pembrook's school?

He reached into the top drawer of his bureau and drew out a small wooden box. Inside was a carved wooden spoon and a plain gold band that had been his mother's. He looked at the ring a long moment, then tucked it into his pocket.

A soft rap sounded on the door.

"William?" It was Rob Kent. "All set?"

William opened the door. Rob shook his hand fervently, but there was a sorrow in his eyes that William, given his own feelings, thought he recognized. Rob Kent loved Ella, and she was going away. "Thanks, William. I won't ever forget what you've done for Ella. Do you think Tinkham'll go when Reverend Bowman gets started?"

"Probably."

The door to his father's bedroom opened, and William saw Bronwyn standing by the window in a lovely white gown. He swallowed hard and turned away, for the gown only served to accentuate her beauty.

Jane came out of the room first. He smiled at her, realizing it must have been she who provided the wedding gown on such short notice. Jane didn't look at him and he felt a twinge of regret. It wasn't Jane's fault that he didn't love her; he just didn't.

Bronwyn didn't say a word as they went down the stairs. Neither did he, although he did take her hand as they joined Mrs. Murphy, Sam and the children and went out of the house. After all, if Marshal Tinkham and his men were watching, they would expect to see a jovial wedding party.

They crossed the yard, which was filled with people who joined the procession toward the chapel, including Tinkham who stubbed out a cheroot and moved closer, surveying the gathering. A woman Bronwyn recognized from town wearing a hideous yellow and purple gown pressed a lace handkerchief to her watery eyes. A thin, sickly-looking woman studied her with frank curiosity.

It seemed Reverend Bowman was a resourceful man, for she was amazed at the number of people waiting. She barely had time to acknowledge any of them before they entered the chapel. Sprays of late-blooming flowers and bright autumn leaves decorated the windowsills. Near the front, Bronwyn noticed a woman dressed in black and heavily veiled. Although the widow stooped like an old woman and had white hair, she thought it must be Ella in disguise, and breathed a sigh of relief that William's plan was working so far.

Reverend Bowman was already in the chapel, wearing his robes and with his prayer book open. She and William were Methodists, so an Episcopalian ceremony wasn't...

But this wasn't a real wedding, she reminded herself.

Reverend Bowman cleared his throat expectantly, and everyone grew quiet. "Dearly beloved brethren..."

Bronwyn glanced back over her shoulder and glared at the marshal. *Why didn't the man leave?* She was in a wedding dress, William was in a fine suit of clothes and looking very handsome in them, the minister was in his proper garments, he was saying the service...

Bronwyn wondered how long Reverend Bowman would go on with this fraud. Surely he would have to stop soon or the wedding would be legal.

"...let him speak now, or forever hold his peace."

Tinkham strode forward, his face full of scorn. "This ain't no real wedding."

"I beg your pardon?" Reverend Bowman asked.

"You ain't announced any official intentions that I heard."

"No, we haven't," William replied stonily.

"I have the proper documents, Marshal." The reverend reached into his pocket underneath his robes and pulled out a piece of paper. "As you can see, it's all filled out quite legally. And I *am* an ordained minister. So unless you have some other objection, I must insist that the ceremony proceed.''

Surprised, Bronwyn stared at the paper. Proper documents? Legally filled out? They had thought of everything.

Tinkham pushed his way past her and grabbed the paper. "I don't give a damn."

William slowly turned to face him, and in his eyes was such a violent anger that he almost frightened her.

The marshal wisely went back to his place, but he did not leave the chapel.

William took Bronwyn's hand and started to repeat the marriage vows. She could only gaze hopelessly at his large work-worn hand holding her own and remind herself this was a fraud.

A complete fraud. There had not been one traditional Welsh thing done today. No poetry at the bride's door, no feigned kidnapping of the bride, no race to the chapel. If she were really getting married, she would want all that.

Then it was time for her to speak. Reverend Bowman waited for her to repeat his words.

If she refused, there would be no marriage, legal or otherwise.

At that moment, someone shifted in their seat, drawing her attention. Ella. It had to be Ella sitting there dressed in black, her head covered by a veil.

The marshal's head began to turn in Ella's direction.

"I, Bronwyn Cordelia, take you, Gwilym..." she began, but she had to pause. Although she had caught everyone's attention, including Tinkham's, by using the Welsh version of William's name as she had intended, she didn't know William's second name.

"Cyfartha," he whispered.

"Take thee, Gwilym Cyfartha." She proceeded with the rest of the vow. William slipped a plain gold wedding band on her finger and the ceremony continued.

"I now pronounce you man and wife," Reverend Bowman said at last.

Then William leaned down to kiss her and what she saw in his eyes drove everything else from her mind. His anger was gone, replaced by the same yearning, hopeful expression she had seen before. To tell him of her own feelings, she rose on her toes and kissed him. When she pulled back, his eyes widened with undisguised surprise, and then unconcealed joy.

Before either of them could move or speak, Reverend Bowman said, "Now you can sign the document, and then we can celebrate your wedding."

Chapter Fourteen

The wedding supper proceeded with a dreamlike reality to Bronwyn. Food came and went as if by enchantment. People she had never met admired her dress and offered their congratulations. Mrs. Murphy's state alternated between weeping and smiling. Children ran in and out among the adults and ate such an astonishing array of baked goods they would surely be ill. Sam and some of the other men disappeared every so often, and each time they returned, they were a little less able to walk without stumbling. William seemed to have vanished from the face of the earth, along with Reverend Bowman, Jacob Kent and Josiah Mathews. Only Ma remained her own vital self, admonishing her children and producing a large wedding cake that Bronwyn would have found delicious if she had been able to notice the taste of anything.

"Mrs. Powell!"

Bronwyn came out of her reverie with a start and smiled tentatively at Ma Gibson. "Yes?"

"Alvin! Jemima, where's Geraldine? We got to be going now or the kids are gonna be sick. They've et enough to ruin their digestion for a week. I'd better get

'em home and dosed. So, thanks for a good time.''
Ma's eyes twinkled mischievously. ''You got yourself
some man there. If I'd been twenty years younger, you
woulda had to work real hard to get him, I'll tell ya.''
She embraced Bronwyn tightly. ''Best wishes and
every happiness.''

She let go and Bronwyn drew a long breath. ''Thank
you very much for the beautiful cake.''

Ma gleamed with delight. ''Turned out not bad,
didn't it?''

Geraldine glided into the room. Her cheeks were
noticeably pink, and Bronwyn realized Geraldine was
really a very pretty young woman. Perhaps Ma's hopes
for her daughter had not been so outrageous.

''Where have you been?'' Ma asked ominously.

''Outside,'' Geraldine replied innocently. A little too
innocently.

''With Frank Tinkham?'' Ma demanded.

''I believe Frank left some time ago, Mrs. Gibson,'' Reverend Bowman said as he entered the dining room. ''With his father.''

''Good.'' Nonetheless, Ma's expression was not very
amiable when she looked at her daughter. Bronwyn
felt sorry for Geraldine—until she caught a good look
at the girl's face. There was defiance there, as well as
pain, and suddenly Bronwyn thought Geraldine and
Frank would find happiness if their parents would
only leave them alone.

Reverend Bowman sighed as the Gibsons swarmed
out of the room. ''It is so unfortunate she blames Ed
Tinkham for her husband's death.'' He saw Bron-

wyn's quizzical look. "It was an accident, really. One of Tinkham's dogs spooked Dan's horse and he fell."

"Frank doesn't appear to agree with his father's line of work," Bronwyn offered.

"No."

"Why does he help him, then?" she asked quietly.

Reverend Bowman drew her aside. "Because of his mother and his brothers and sisters. He thinks it better for them if he...cooperates. Or if he is around to be the object of his father's ire."

Bronwyn sighed. Frank was not a dashing figure, or even brave, but there was nobility in him. She regretted thinking so poorly of him before. It seemed she had been misjudging many people. She gave the minister a shy sidelong glance. "Where is William?"

Reverend Bowman surveyed the dining room, which was nearly empty. "He will be here shortly."

"The widow woman?" she whispered.

"Safely away."

The reverend cleared his throat. "William is a reticent man."

"I know, Reverend."

"Nor is he demonstrative of his feelings."

"Yes, Reverend."

"I just wanted to say—"

William himself came into the room. "Ah, here's the happy groom!" Reverend Bowman said jovially.

"Marshal Tinkham and his men have finally gone," the happy groom noted coolly.

Bronwyn regarded William steadily and tried not to look dismayed. Or upset. Or disappointed. All of which she was, despite her firm resolve to accept that this marriage was basically a fraud. Later the minister would tell them how to... undo it.

Reverend Bowman's tone grew businesslike. "I think we should assume that Tinkham has left one or two of his men keeping a watch on the farm."

Bronwyn told herself she should not feel so happy, but the ruse would have to be maintained awhile yet.

The minister signaled his wife. "I believe it is almost time to go."

"Very well." Elizabeth smiled at Bronwyn. "Jane and I will help you with the gown." Before Bronwyn could protest, Elizabeth Bowman had hurried over to Jane and Emmanuella, who led Bronwyn from the room. She wanted to protest, but she didn't dare. She wasn't sure she could get out of the elaborate gown by herself.

Upstairs in the bedroom, the women were silent as Jane and Emmanuella undid the tiny hooks along the back of the gown. Jane, Elizabeth and Emmanuella carefully lifted the garment from Bronwyn. She stepped quickly behind the screen and began to remove the delicate undergarments.

"Please, accept them as my wedding gift," Jane said when Bronwyn put the camisole over the top of the screen.

Bronwyn hesitated. The things were so lovely and she had never had anything like them. "You've already done too much. I couldn't," she protested.

"I insist." Jane's tone brooked no further argument.

"I can't thank you enough, then. For everything."

"It is in a good cause."

Bronwyn reached for her old underclothes, then stopped. She would let herself wear the new ones a little longer. She put her usual blue calico dress on over them, but was very aware of the finery beneath.

"You can keep the wedding dress, too," Jane announced.

Bronwyn came out from behind the screen. "Oh, no! It wouldn't be right! You've worked so hard on it—"

"I won't ever wear it."

"What of your own wedding day?" Elizabeth Bowman observed. She carefully folded the wedding dress and put it into the box with the veil.

"If I ever do get married, I will make another dress," Jane replied with a tone of finality. She lowered her voice and looked at Elizabeth. "Has Ella gone?"

"We made sure Tinkham was otherwise occupied near the chapel, then William and Sam took her in our buggy to a safe place."

Bronwyn said a silent prayer of thanks that they had not been discovered.

Then Elizabeth said, "I can hear Sam singing in the kitchen." She closed the lid of the box. "I think just about all the guests have gone. We should be on our way, too."

Jane nodded. "You made a lovely bride, Bronwyn," she murmured.

Emmanuella said something in Portuguese that Bronwyn took to be congratulations. Bronwyn gave her a wan smile and led the women out of the bedroom. The voices of William and Sam joined in the song Bronwyn had heard William sing the other day in the barn. As they joined the remaining guests in the kitchen, William gazed at her and softly sang:

But when your soul has drunk its fill
When the tide has lost its pull
Then, my love, please turn for shore
Safe in my arms forevermore.

His deep, strong voice filled the room, making Bronwyn forget the wedding was a sham. She forgot the other people nearby. All she was aware of was William, the look of love in his eyes and the sound of love in his voice.

Until Mrs. Murphy sniffed loudly and said, "Lovely, just lovely. Now it's late and I'm tired. We should see if Owen's gotten the girls to bed. Come, Sam, get up."

Reverend Bowman also rose. "It *is* growing late, and it certainly has been a very busy day. Good night, everyone."

Bronwyn's gaze moved uncertainly from the children to Sam and Mrs. Murphy and then to the reverend. They weren't leaving William alone in the house with her, as if this wedding was real. Were they?

Elizabeth and Jane said their goodbyes. They were! In a moment, only William and Bronwyn stood in the kitchen.

William cleared his throat. "Mrs. Murphy insisted on sleeping in the cabin with the children."

"And Constance?"

"Her, too." William shifted uncomfortably. The sleeping arrangements had not been his idea. He should have protested. But he hadn't.

Bronwyn's fingertips brushed the table, moving back and forth slowly. "So we are to spend the night alone here?"

She wasn't looking at him, which made it easier for him to speak. "It would be a strange wedding night if we didn't. As Reverend Bowman pointed out, the marshal probably has men keeping watch."

"How can you be so sure?"

"That is what I would do."

"At least Ella is safe," she said after a strained silence.

"For the present."

"Yes."

He wanted very much to see her face, but he couldn't in the dim light while she stood with her head bowed.

"It was good there is no Welshman among them to see what there was not," she added quietly.

"What do you mean?"

"Not one Welsh thing about it, was there? No bidding, no poetry at the bride's door, no race to the church. Nothing of home in it at all."

"This *is* America."

"I know—and you are an American."

There was another long moment of quiet between them because he could not bring himself to agree at once. He, too, had missed those traditions, although it had taken her mention of them to make him understand what he had felt was missing. She brought back the good memories of things he had seen in his boyhood that had long been buried beneath the bad.

"William," she whispered, "why did you think of a wedding?"

Every part of his being was acutely aware of her. Of the nearness of her hand to his. Of the scent her hair, the rise and fall of her chest, the lashes covering her splendid eyes. He came around the table and stood next to her. "Bronwyn, I..."

She looked at him questioningly. "Yes?"

This might be the closest he ever came to marrying for love. Tomorrow and forever after he might find the memory of today nearly unbearable. But for now, he was content with what he had tasted.

No. Not content. He would never be content with the pretense of this marriage. Yet what could he offer her except poverty and responsibility? She had made it very clear she wanted none of that.

She reached out, put her fingertips on his chin and forced him to look at her, her gaze searching his face. "Why?" she whispered with such longing and desire he could scarcely believe the evidence of his senses. He had to take her in his arms and hold her close. He put his lips to her warm, willing mouth. Her body arched against him in a way that was not merely yielding, but expressing a desire that drove him nearly mad. Responding fiercely, he cupped her cheeks with both hands and kissed her long and hard.

He knew he had to possess her. Totally.

She moaned softly and caressed his back. Then she whispered the one word that could free him from his self-imposed restraint. She said, "Yes."

Yes, Bronwyn wanted him. She desired him, needed him, craved him in every possible way. She would give up—no, give away gladly—whatever freedom she had ever possessed or wanted to be William Powell's wife.

His fingers moved to her bodice and feverishly undid the few buttons at the top until her warm soft flesh was exposed. He pressed burning kisses there. His thumbs brushed her hardened nipples instinctively, and her knees weakened as if turned to hot liquid. She moaned again, her fingers digging into his shoulders.

He swept her up in his arms and, holding her against his chest, carried her through the hall and up the darkened stairway of the empty house, taking the steps two at a time.

Happy in his arms, Bronwyn kissed his chin, his cheek, his neck. She wanted to taste every part of him. To have him taste her.

He set her down—she didn't notice or care where—and, with a low groan, kissed her passionately again.

He felt so good in her arms. So right. Her husband. He wanted her as much as she wanted him. She knew it. She had seen it his eyes, felt it in his touch.

She wanted nothing more than him, and he was everything. He was adventure. He was excitement. He was familiar and yet different. He was hers, and she was his, and that was enough.

Her fingers went to his shirt buttons, scrambling to undo them. At last she succeeded, and she could move her lips over his strong, hard chest.

His lean fingers gripped her arms and pushed her back. Something hit her legs. The bed. She sat on it and pulled him down with her.

Her breathing quickened as he caressed her, every movement of his fingers increasing her excitement. Impatiently she shoved the shirt from his magnificent torso. He lifted her legs up onto the bed, then lay beside her and reached inside her bodice to stroke her breasts, his breath hot on her cheeks. She responded freely to his touch, for his desire inflamed her even more. He rolled her onto her back. Then he was there above her, his face mirroring the hot, hungry need she felt.

He pushed her skirt and petticoat up, and with one swift tug tore off her pantalettes.

She knew what he was going to do—what she wanted him to do. She pulled him down and her tongue intertwined with his as she wrapped her legs around him.

And then he was inside her. For an instant there was pain, but it was a moment soon forgotten as he began to thrust, his movements wild and savage.

Her response was equally primitive, equally untamed. He called to a part of her that was instinctive and basic and free.

Their breathing grew hard and erratic, their caresses desperate. Their bodies throbbed and thrust together with swift, pulsating motions until the intense, blissful moment of completion.

When his heartbeat returned to normal, William moved slowly away from Bronwyn. Their breathing grew quieter. He looked at her, his wife, lying beside him still wearing her dress, her pantalettes nothing but a torn piece of fabric on the floor.

He stood up and fastened the breeches he hadn't even bothered to remove completely. He turned away and flushed with shame. He had behaved like an animal, and certainly not like a gentleman.

He had taken advantage of her. He hadn't told her about the possibility of an annulment. He had thought—if that word could be used to describe the surge of emotion that had overwhelmed him—only of his own selfish desire to possess her.

He was no better than his father, after all.

And yet . . . and yet, he loved Bronwyn. With all his heart and with all his soul. Even the mere idea of losing her now, to another man or death, gave him pain. If she were gone . . .

Would he try to forget her by marrying again? By seeking unthinking release in another woman's caress?

Perhaps. His attention wandered to the hill outside, to the woods and the chapel and his father's grave. No, never.

Bronwyn stirred and raised herself on one elbow to look at him. Despite the knowledge that what he felt for her was love, he was ashamed to meet her steadfast gaze. "I . . . I had better see to the cattle," he said.

"Mrs. Murphy told me Sam and Rob had taken care of everything."

"Oh."

Bronwyn got off the bed. She suddenly realized she hadn't even bothered to take off her dress. The lovely, delicate, finely embroidered pantalettes lay on the floor, ruined, a casualty of their frenzied passion. It was a pity, of course, yet she was too happy to be truly upset at the loss.

But something *was* wrong. William wouldn't look at her. He acted as if they had done something they shouldn't have.

"What's the matter?" she asked. She hadn't done anything to be ashamed of. Although the wedding had started out as a sham, there could be no mistaking how they felt about each other. He loved her, and she loved him.

William bent down to pick up his shirt from the floor, and for the first time she realized they were in his father's bedroom. Maybe that was what bothered him.

He pulled on his shirt. "I'm going to make sure everything is all right," he muttered.

Before she could reply, he went out of the room.

In a dark room in the back of the waterfront tavern, James Falconer stared at Ed Tinkham with disbelief. "A wedding? What are you talking about?"

"I tell you, it was a wedding. William Powell and that good-looking cook of his. We heard the slave gal was there so—"

"How? From whom did you hear this?"

Tinkham shrugged dismissively. "I got other ways of findin' things out than waitin' for you to tell me. Don't matter now, anyway. We went there and found Bowman, those Kents and Powell in the chapel. No woman there 'cept that Welsh witch. And they says, 'we're here 'cause they're gettin' married.'"

"It had to be a lie."

"I thought so, too, so I waited there the whole damn morning," Tinkham replied with a scowl. "They got married, all right. They had a marriage document and a ceremony. She had a wedding dress. He had a ring. Lots of the townsfolk showed up.

"Course I figured the gal might still be there, so when Rob Kent drove off in a wagon, we followed him. Thought we had him, too, till he took the wagon into the marsh."

"Did you follow him?"

"I'm no fool. It's too dangerous. And too damn cold for anybody to stay in the marsh overnight, anyways. I put men on the road and we waited for him to come out. Wasted the rest of the day, just waitin'."

"Didn't Rob drive out?"

"He did—but the damned wagon was empty. If the gal *is* in the swamp, she'll catch her death for sure. I left men standin' guard, just in case."

Falconer thought a moment. "Who was at this supposed wedding?"

"I told you. Powell's friends. The Kents, Ma Gibson and her brood, Jane Webster, folks from the Methodist church. Reverend Bowman and his wife and just about anybody else from the town you can think of. Even Josiah Mathews and his kids."

"Reverend Bowman?"

"He was the one married 'em."

"Oh," James said. He hid his interest. Surely a Methodist like William would want the Methodist minister. If Reverend Bowman had been involved, it must mean this unexpected wedding had something to do with the Railroad and perhaps even the escape of the slave.

The wedding itself didn't matter anymore, although James was sorry he had been at the site of the factory all day. If he had been in town, he would have heard of this business and could probably have located the slave.

That couldn't be helped. What mattered now was finding the valuable runaway. James agreed with Tinkham that the marsh was no place for a woman to hide this time of year. But where else could she be? Who else had had a visit from Reverend Bowman recently?

He recalled something he had heard the other day about Miss Pembrook's being so ill Reverend Bowman had called on her.

"What? You thought of something?" Tinkham demanded.

"Perhaps," James replied coldly. "But since you didn't see fit to tell me what you had learned, I think I will keep my surmises to myself for the present."

Bronwyn woke up and opened her eyes slowly. The bedroom was dim in the dawn's first light.

She was alone. Nothing had been disturbed. Not the linen by the washstand. Not her petticoat hanging over the chair, still damp where she had washed the small stains of blood from it before she put on her nightdress. Not the other pillow beside her. She had lain awake a long time, wondering when William would come back, but she had fallen asleep, tired from the excitement of the wedding and the tension and...other things. Apparently William had never returned.

She could hear people moving and speaking below as she got out of bed. Mrs. Murphy and the children, she thought, although she listened for William's deeper tones while she dressed and washed.

She sat on the bed. As far as she was concerned, she and William were husband and wife. She was sure she loved him, and she thought he loved her. If not, he wouldn't have made love to her last night, and then the marriage could have been annulled.

She smiled grimly. If there was any man in all of Massachusetts who could control his desire, it had to be William.

But he hadn't. He had been uninhibited and free, and it had been wonderful. Surely he had felt that way, too.

Could it be he thought her behavior too wanton for a virgin? If so, he should have lingered long enough to see the evidence.

What else might make that troubled look come to his face? Ella's plight? Perhaps he had gone to make certain she was all right. His absence might have nothing to do with her or their marriage or their wedding night.

She had to believe that, because the alternative—that he was sorry to be married to her—was simply too agonizing to contemplate.

Anxious to see her husband and assure herself she had guessed correctly, she hurried downstairs. "Where's William?" she asked Mrs. Murphy when she entered the kitchen, trying to sound unconcerned.

"He's gone to town," she replied. "Owen, too. Left after he helped Sam with the milking. Didn't he tell you?"

"I was . . . asleep."

Mrs. Murphy grinned slyly. "Of course you were."

Bronwyn turned toward the girls, who eyed her with frank curiosity. Although they smiled happily, they had dark circles under their eyes. There would be quarrels and tears from the lack of sleep as the day progressed. "You were very late going to sleep last night. A nap later, is it?"

They frowned, but they recognized Bronwyn's commanding tone too well to complain.

"You look tired, too," Constance observed innocently. "And William could hardly stop yawning. You both should take a nap."

Mrs. Murphy put her hand over her mouth to stifle a laugh and Bronwyn knew her face was red. "Maybe," she muttered. She started to fix the breakfast as if nothing out of the ordinary had happened yesterday.

As the day passed, Bronwyn felt anything but happy, especially when William did not return for the noon meal. Then she began to worry. What if something had happened? Perhaps Ella had been discovered. Maybe William had been arrested. He had taken Owen with him. He shouldn't have if there was any danger at all.

She tried to convince herself she would have heard if something serious had happened, and though her anxiety grew with each passing hour, she didn't want to ask Mrs. Murphy where they had gone. How would it look if she had to confess to the housekeeper that William had walked out of the room last night without telling her anything?

As she fretted, she remembered what William had told her of his childhood, about the waiting and the uncertainty. It must have been like this for him often. She could understand why he might come to believe it was better to remain aloof than to care about someone.

When William and Owen didn't come home for supper, she decided it would be better to reveal her ignorance than live with the worry. "Did William say when they would be coming back?" she asked before anyone started to eat.

As she had expected, Mrs. Murphy looked at her with surprise, but her answer was totally unexpected. "They've been back since noon."

To think she had been so worried, and all for nothing! "Why aren't they here for supper, then?"

"He said he had something to make and Owen should learn how to do it," Sam replied. "I wasn't to disturb him."

"Oh." Bronwyn suddenly felt as if she would cry with frustration. Which was ridiculous. And annoying. If her husband—and he was that, after all—couldn't give her the simple courtesy of coming to dinner...

The meal in the Powell kitchen was a short and silent one. The children were tired, Mrs. Murphy seemed content to eat and smoke her pipe, and Sam looked too sick to speak, probably because of all the eating and drinking yesterday.

Bronwyn went to look out the window again. There was still no sign of William and Owen. Finally Sam went out to the barn. Mrs. Murphy began to mend an apron, and the girls helped Bronwyn with the dishes.

As Bronwyn washed, it occurred to her this marriage might already be turning into the very thing she had always wanted to avoid. She was still the cook, only now she wasn't free to leave because she was William Powell's wife. She loved him, but he didn't even come home for supper. Overwhelmed by fatigue and self-pity, she sniffled and wiped her nose with the back of her hand.

"The children and I will go to the cabin now," Mrs. Murphy said, giving her a puzzled look.

"We're not finished," Bronwyn said crossly.

"Good enough."

"Can I sleep in the cabin again?" Constance asked hopefully. "I like being with the girls. I'm not used to sleeping by myself after living at school."

Mrs. Murphy took the pipe out of her mouth. "Of course you can, Constance. They need a honeymoon."

The girls started to giggle.

"I am mistress of this house," Bronwyn snapped. When she saw the surprised and hurt expressions on the faces of the others, she regretted her hasty words. "I'm sorry. Tired I am."

To her chagrin, Mrs. Murphy smirked knowingly. "You're right, *Mrs. Powell*. And exhausted after yesterday, too, I'm sure, so no offense taken."

At that moment, Owen sauntered through the door. "Hello, Bron," he said cheerfully.

"Where have you been?"

"In the woodshed."

"Where is William?"

"Here." He came inside. A smile sprang to her lips, but then she remembered how worried she had been. "Where were you? Your supper is cold."

He took something out of his pocket and laid it at her place at the table. "Making you this."

They all stared at the intricately carved wooden spoon, but none so reverentially as Bronwyn. William had made her a love spoon, a traditional token of affection.

A thing of beauty it was, with its smooth polish, the shapes of leaves on its handle, the warm glow of the wood. Nevertheless its beauty was not nearly as important as its meaning.

"Teaching me to make one," Owen said proudly. He put down his own effort. "Not as good, of course."

"It's wonderful," Bronwyn said while she looked lovingly at William's.

"It's only a *spoon*," Mrs. Murphy said, both surprised and dismayed.

"A special one," Bronwyn replied softly.

Constance picked up Owen's spoon.

"You can keep it," he said in an offhand manner.

She smiled happily, until he said, "I need more practice before I make a really good one."

Although a disappointed expression crossed her face, Constance didn't put it back down.

Mrs. Murphy rose to her feet. "'Good night' is what we should all be saying. So, good night, William. Good night, *Mrs. Powell.*"

Owen and the girls didn't protest. They left at once, Owen grabbing a thick slice of bread and butter as he went.

When everyone was gone, Bronwyn lifted the spoon and examined it, marveling at the delicate workmanship. Obviously William had a talent and eye for detail she had not had a chance to notice before.

"I wanted you to have one tradition," he said awkwardly, overwhelmed by her pleasure. He had made it hoping to give her something to appease the haste of their wedding, and to show her that he did care for her, very much.

"You taught Owen, too."

He nodded. "He might want to make one someday."

"Where were you this morning?"

"We had to go to the mill. I had no wood fine enough here."

She put down the spoon gently. "Why did you leave me last night?"

He shrugged and looked away, not ready to admit his failing.

"I haven't been with another man."

"Oh, God," he groaned, even more ashamed he had made her think she was to blame. "I know."

She sighed with relief and her expression grew softer. "Good, is that." She came another step closer, and he wanted to back away, afraid of her proximity. Afraid of his reaction to her, which even now sent the blood throbbing through his veins and filled his mind with memories of last night.

"Then, were you troubled about Ella?"

"No. I trust Reverend Bowman to keep her safe."

She gave him a strange, searching look. "Then why did you look at me as if you were ashamed and sorry for what we had done? I know what you think of Welshwomen, but you've said you could tell I was a virgin. Do you regret what happened between us? Are you sorry we are married?"

He took her gently by the shoulders. "No, Bronwyn. I was ashamed of myself. I acted like...like an animal. And I never told you..."

She waited breathlessly for him to say he loved her. He sighed raggedly. "I should have told you that according to Reverend Bowman, the marriage could be annulled if it wasn't consummated."

Bronwyn frowned in disappointment. "Not stupid, me, William Powell. I supposed the marriage could be annulled if we didn't make love." She put her hand up to touch his cheek. "If I had asked you to stop, you would have. But that is not what I wanted. I wanted to be your wife. I wanted *you*. I love you, William Powell."

"You said you wanted to be free. Not to marry." He spoke as if he was afraid to believe her.

"I know what I said. At the time, I meant it. Just as you meant what you said about not being married." She gave him a hopeful glance. "I changed my mind."

He pulled her into his arms. "Bronwyn, Bronwyn," he whispered hoarsely. "I love you! I want you for my wife. But I have nothing to offer—"

"Except yourself, and that is more than enough for me."

He gazed into her eyes, his own filled with so much love she could hardly breathe. Then he bent to kiss her tenderly, his lips merely brushing hers.

As always, his touch inflamed her with desire. And now, knowing he did love her, she felt all her fears and doubts slip away. She returned his kiss and wrapped her arms around him, holding him close. Her breathing quickened as his kiss grew more passionate and swept her into the warmth of his love.

Together they went upstairs and, without a word between them, to the bedroom where they had first made love.

Chapter Fifteen

Tonight, William enticed Bronwyn with gentle, lingering kisses. He kissed her cheeks, her earlobes, her neck, as he loosened her gown.

With a sigh, she slipped her hands beneath his soft, worn shirt to caress his hard, firm chest. She wanted to enjoy his body in a way she had not last night. To see, taste, feel, discover every little part of him.

And he, her. They undressed each other with delightful, excruciating slowness in the light of the moon. This time, there was no primitive frenzy, but learning and lingering. They murmured tender endearments in the language they both knew best, William's words coming awkwardly at first, then swiftly when he saw the happiness in her eyes.

Tonight, they came together with the knowledge that they were husband and wife, newlyweds embarking on what they hoped would be a long journey together.

The tempo increased, for their passion would brook no long delay. In moments, they both cried out, sated and satisfied.

William smiled warmly as he held her in his arms. "I think I have loved you since I first set eyes on you," he whispered.

The wind moaned softly outside, and a cloud passed over the moon. He glanced outside and rolled away. "Oh, God, Bronwyn, I have to leave."

"What? Now? Why?"

"Reverend Bowman asked me to take Ella on the first part of the journey north. I said I would."

"Tonight?"

"We don't dare let her stay here any longer. Tinkham's so angry and determined to find her we can't keep her hidden much longer."

"It's too dangerous. I won't let you."

"You won't let me? Who was it accused me of not doing enough?"

"Well, that was before." She brightened suddenly. "Go then—but I'm going with you."

"I can't allow it."

She grabbed her clothing and started to dress. "I didn't ask your permission." She became serious. "William, I can't stay here and wait. You know what that is like. Better for me if I share in this."

Because he did know, he nodded his head in agreement.

James looked at the sleeping, naked Penelope Pembrook with barely disguised loathing. She was too thin to be enticing, too desperate to be interesting and too inexperienced to be exciting.

She would probably expect him to marry her now. Stupid creature! He already had what he wanted of her. He was sure the runaway was here in the school, but he would never have been able to search during the day. There were too many people around then.

So he had decided to come courting. The servant had told him Miss Pembrook wasn't seeing anyone. He had persuaded her to tell her mistress who was waiting.

Then Penelope had come down to the parlor. She looked pale and wan, but he didn't think she was very ill. When he spoke of his worry for her, she seemed to get healthier by the minute. And when he told her about the marriage of Bronwyn Davies and how it was obviously a good thing he hadn't hired a woman who must have a reason to marry with such indecent haste, she had positively glowed.

Then he had begun the all-too-easy wooing. He had told her that he was so very concerned for her welfare and that the founding families needed to look after one another. Surely she had to agree with him, and she did. Eagerly. He went on to say how easy it was to overlook the tender beauty of the tea rose—he had kissed her hand—when a peony bloomed nearby.

And so he had gone on until he had cajoled his way into her bed. Their lovemaking had been heated, but mercifully brief. Now, while she slept, he could look around the school undetected.

James got out of bed and slipped on his clothes. He felt for the small revolver he had tucked in his jacket pocket. The moon was bright, which pleased him because he didn't want to risk a candle. He opened the bedroom door and slipped into the hall.

The runaway was probably in the garret. It was warmer than the cellar and a better vantage point to watch for slave hunters. He would have to be careful, though, for the housekeeper probably slept there, too.

With cautious steps, James made his way up the narrow wooden stairs. He opened the first door to find an empty room. The next was vacant, too. In the third, he could detect the sleeping form of the housekeeper, wrapped in quilts.

He opened the fourth door and saw a man and woman sitting together on a bed, fully clothed and holding each other with their heads bowed in an attitude of tenderness and despair.

Rob Kent jumped to his feet. "Falconer! What are you doing here?"

"I've come to help her escape."

A woman of astonishing beauty rose slowly to her feet and clung to Rob. If he hadn't known she was a slave, he would never have suspected she was anything but a well-born white woman. "Now?" she whispered.

James nodded his head.

"Where's William?"

"He couldn't come," James said quickly. "Tinkham's watching the farm."

Rob gave him a strange look. "You've come for Ella. Nobody else?"

"You're not here to help Ella."

James spun around to see Penelope standing in the doorway. In her trembling hands she held a rifle and it was pointed at his head. "What are you doing?" he demanded.

"I am making sure Ella and Rob get away safely," she said. A sob escaped her thin lips. "You're a scoundrel and a liar, James Falconer."

"Penelope! You know I'm an abolitionist," he protested, going toward her with his hands held out in supplication. "You can trust me, especially after—"

She didn't lower the rifle. "You're so fine and clever and charming—and always so sly! I was a fool to believe anything you ever said to me, and I won't believe you again. Not about love. Not about anything. I should have known you were after something. I should have known it wasn't me. But I wanted you so much...." Her words trailed off into another sob.

Incredulous, James stared at her and then cursed his own stupidity. He had underestimated Penelope Pembrook, and perhaps overestimated the force of his charm. Still, if they were alone, he could probably reason with her. It might mean letting that slave escape, but he could find out the next stop on the route, and there was still a chance he could give Tinkham enough information to lead to her recapture. "Penelope." He lowered his hands, the right one close to his jacket pocket where his gun was. "Penelope, my dear, you must believe that I am here to help."

"Keep your hands up," she said. "I suppose you'll spread it all over town that I'm a loose woman. Won't you?"

"Heaven forbid—"

"Heaven will have nothing to do with the likes of you, if there's any justice at the gates," she said, scorn and sorrow both in her voice. "Back away, James."

Startled, he turned to Rob. "You don't believe her, do you? She's just upset because I said I wouldn't marry her after she practically threw herself into my arms. You believe me, don't you, Rob?"

"No, I don't," Rob said coldly. "Because Ella's not going anywhere without me, and Reverend Bowman knows that. If you were supposed to come tonight, you'd know it, too."

"There was no time for him to tell me much," James answered glibly. "Tinkham knows about tonight's plans, the same way he knew about Ella's hiding in the chapel."

"That's impossible," Penelope said. "Rob, Ella, you'd better hurry. The others will be here soon."

"Penelope, if you know anything about the Underground Railroad in these parts, you'll understand that I could very well have been called upon—"

"Be quiet, James." She gestured with the rifle. "Come. You're leaving, too."

James shrugged his shoulders. "You don't understand, Penelope," he said sorrowfully. The rifle wavered in her hands. "I care about you. I don't want to see you in any danger. What if you're caught?" he went on, moving closer. "You'll be jailed, and your school closed. Even if everyone around here agrees with your actions, they might think twice about sending their precious daughters to be schooled by such a radical woman."

Penelope hesitated a moment, then gripped the rifle more tightly. "Do that, and I'll tell the whole town you're in league with Tinkham," she countered. "We both have appearances to maintain, and you have your father's opinion to worry about. You'll do anything to keep your name out of the mud. So you will leave now, quietly."

She stepped out into the hall and gestured for him to go by. He began to pass her, then suddenly lunged for the rifle, grabbing it away from her as she fell. "Don't!" he warned Rob when the young man rushed into the hall holding a revolver. "Give it to me!"

Rob stared down at Penelope, now weeping on the floor, then glanced back at Ella cowering inside the room. He drew himself up. "No."

"I don't want you to shoot me by mistake. You still believe I'm not to be trusted?" James asked calmly. "I've been an abolitionist for years. Penelope's just upset because I hesitated when she spoke of marriage."

"I didn't..." Penelope protested feebly.

"I never said I wouldn't, did I?" Penelope's eyes widened as he reached down to help her up. "But the important thing now is to get Ella safely away. Forgive me for being so rough, my dear. Come, now, there isn't much time."

He turned and hurried down the stairs. The others hesitated, but had little choice except to follow him. They reached the front door and everyone paused when they heard the rattle of a wagon. Still eyeing James skeptically, Rob stepped forward and opened the door a crack, then further. "It's William."

Rob and Ella went out through the door and James could hear their muted greetings. Bowing slightly toward Penelope, he said, "After you, my dear." Her glance at him as she passed told him she was obviously wavering in her mistrust of his motives. What a gullible, desperate creature she was!

Outside it was cold and windy, and the moon provided some natural light. A lantern swaying on the waiting wagon also illuminated the area in front of the school.

James saw at once that William wasn't alone. Bronwyn sat beside him on the seat. "Good evening, James," William said coldly, his expression one of surprise and barely disguised dislike. Bronwyn looked at James as if he were some kind of wicked beast.

Suddenly James was filled with fury. These…these *immigrants,* these *lawbreaking* immigrants, had no right to look at him in such a manner. Before he could speak, however, Tinkham's voice shattered the quietness. "Hold it right there, everybody."

Bronwyn gasped and reached for the gun William had hidden under the seat while Ella held on to Rob. William put his hand gently on Bronwyn's and shook his head.

Tinkham stepped out from the shadow of the house and came to stand beside the wagon, on his face a triumphant smirk and in his hand a gun. "Not going to try and tell me this is a weddin', are you?"

"No," William replied calmly. "We are going for a drive. Where are all your men, Tinkham? Don't tell me you didn't bring reinforcements?"

"You're all under arrest for aidin' a runaway. And I don't need more men with the likes of you." He glanced at the schoolmistress, then looked at Falconer. "You'd have done better to tell me what you were up to. Good thing I knew enough to follow you, eh?"

Miss Pembrook gave a stifled cry. "I knew I shouldn't have believed you! I'm going to tell—"

"Who?" Falconer replied mockingly. "Who will you *dare* to tell, my dear? Who will believe a woman who acts no better than a common whore?"

Concerned as she was for Ella, Bronwyn's heart filled with pity for the poor woman who ran sobbing into the house. Until James Falconer strode boldly toward them. "I always knew you'd end up in jail someday, William. Welshmen are all thieves and cheats, aren't they?"

Bronwyn half rose off the seat, but again, William laid a detaining hand on her arm.

Pointing the rifle at Rob, James moved toward Ella. "You're coming with me, my beauty."

"You'll have to kill me before I let you take Ella!" Rob cried, pulling her close and raising his chin defiantly.

James shrugged his shoulders with his usual nonchalant grace. "If that's the way you want it."

Ella looked at Rob with frightened, yet adoring eyes. "No, Rob, don't—"

William jumped from the wagon. He grabbed the rifle, pulling James to the ground.

"Run, Ella!" Rob yelled. The rifle skittered to a stop a few feet from him, but he ignored it and ran at Tinkham while William and James wrestled for possession of the weapon.

"I won't leave you!" Ella screamed as Bronwyn felt for William's gun. Her fingers closed on the cold metal.

Suddenly and with more speed than she expected the heavy man to possess, Tinkham reached out and grabbed her arm. He wrenched the gun from her hands and tossed it onto the ground. Then he pulled her from the wagon and held her in front of him. "Stop right there, Kent!" he shouted harshly. "Falconer, grab the gal. You two, get the hell up, or she'll be sorry!"

William rose slowly to his feet and glared at the marshal. Bronwyn saw the primal anger in his face, and fear, too—for her. "Let her go, Tinkham," he growled.

James grabbed hold of Ella. "You should have run when you had the chance. Too late now." He pulled Ella past William. "Well, William, it seems you're bound for jail, after all." He paused in front of Bronwyn. "It's a pity, Bronwyn, that you'll be joining him there. Perhaps if you're nice to me, I'll see what other arrangements we can make."

"I'd rather die than take any favors from you."

"She's a very pretty bride, William," James said, ignoring her outburst. "Since you didn't invite me to the wedding, I'm sure you won't mind if I give her a congratulatory kiss now." With one hand still clutching Ella, he took hold of Bronwyn with the other while his mouth crushed hers.

Anger consumed her. How *dare* he! He was worse than the mud beneath her feet or the fox who tears the heads from lambs for no purpose. She gave a mighty twist and managed to half turn herself away. Then she cursed him vehemently.

James thrust his face inches from hers. "You might as well save your breath, my dear. I don't care what you're saying in that gibberish of a language—unless you want to ask me to let you go. Nicely."

"What about the others?" Bronwyn demanded.

"You'll have to ask me *very* nicely."

"I'll kill you, James," William said coldly and deliberately. He took a step toward them.

"Aren't you forgetting who has the guns?" James remarked, letting go of Bronwyn. "And it won't be you I shoot." He pulled out his pistol and pointed the weapon at Bronwyn.

William halted and her heart contracted at the anguish in his face.

"Quit playin' your little games, Falconer," Tinkham said uneasily. "Let's take the woman and get out of here."

"Shut up, Tinkham. I'm busy."

"What will it take for you to let William and the others leave?" Bronwyn asked.

"What are you offering?"

Bronwyn knew what he wanted. She had met men like him before and beaten them at their own game, thanks to her brothers.

She bowed her head and said sorrowfully, "Myself."

"Bronwyn, no!" William cried hoarsely.

"Hey!" Tinkham growled. "I ain't lettin' that gal go."

"It's the only way, William," Bronwyn pleaded softly, staring at William and willing him to stay where he was. She hoped he would see she had a plan. "Will that satisfy you, Mr. Falconer?"

James' eyes gleamed rapaciously. "Yes." He let go of Ella, who immediately dashed toward the woods. Tinkham roared with anger and let go of Bronwyn just as she kicked James in the shin with all her might. William tackled James, and Rob ran into the woods after Ella.

The unexpected sound of horses coming down the lane made them all freeze. Reverend Bowman, followed by other men from the town, galloped toward them.

"Everybody stand still!" Tinkham shouted, waving his gun menacingly as the riders pulled their horses to a halt. "My men are all around here! You fellows get down and drop your guns, or I'll shoot!"

Reverend Bowman surveyed the scene before him. "As you wish." He dismounted, followed by the others. Their guns thudded on the dirt.

Tinkham grabbed William by the shirt collar, pulling him off Falconer. "Go stand over there with the rest of your friends," he sneered. "Get up, Falconer. We gotta go after that gal. Find some rope. We don't want anybody following us." James moved to obey.

Then Frank Tinkham stepped around the side of the house, his gun drawn. "Pa, I can't let you do this."

"The hell you can't, boy. If you don't like it, clear out."

"This is wrong, Pa. I won't be a part of it anymore."

"Then you ain't gettin' another thing from me."

"I don't want anything from you."

"Good. Get the hell out of here now, before my men think you're in with these rebels."

"You don't have any men. I dug up most of your money and paid them to clear out. You'll never see them again."

"You *what?*" Tinkham's face turned purple with rage.

"Give up, Pa. You aren't goin' tell me what to do anymore."

"Are you crazy, boy?"

"Tinkham, forget him," James said angrily. "We've got to get the girl."

"No, Mr. Falconer," Frank said. "I won't let you."

Falconer hesitated and glanced at the weapon in Frank's hand. Then he smiled. "You wouldn't dare hurt me, Frank. I'm James Falconer. Harm me, and my family will see that you rue it for the rest of your life. What of your darling Geraldine then, Frank?"

Frank's face was as pale as the moonlight, but his expression was grim. "Don't move, Mr. Falconer."

James made a derisive sound and turned toward the woods. A shot rang out. James dropped his rifle and spun around, his hand clutching his left sleeve where a red stain grew. "You shot me!" he cried in disbelief.

"That was a damn stupid thing to do, boy," Tinkham said, advancing on his son. "Give me that gun!"

"No, Pa." Frank's face was full of terror and determination. "Stay back!" he warned James, who was also moving toward him.

"I'm a marshal, you fool. And that gal's worth five thousand dollars. I'll split it with you. Then you can marry Geraldine."

"No, Pa. I won't take that kinda money, and I won't take any more orders." Frank's hand began to tremble.

"Tinkham!" William called out. He saw the anger and hate and hurt in Frank's eyes. He knew exactly what Frank was feeling now and could guess what Frank might be capable of. "Forget it! Let her go!"

"I will not!" the marshal growled. "Frank, do as I say. You're breakin' the law and—"

Frank's finger tightened on the trigger. William dove at Tinkham.

There was pandemonium as James joined William and the marshal in a struggle for his pistol. Bronwyn ran to retrieve the fallen rifle. Reverend Bowman and his men hurried to pick up their weapons. Miss Pembrook peered out from the doorway. A gun fired. Tinkham gaped at his son, and slowly toppled over into the dust.

"Pa!" Frank cried, sinking to his knees beside his father. Bronwyn hurried to the wounded man's side, but it was already too late.

"He's dead!" Frank muttered, staring at them with wide, wild eyes. "Dead!" He stood up and his face was ashen in the moonlight. Without saying another word, he stumbled off into the night, his arm across his face and his shoulders shaking with sobs.

James struggled to his feet and saw several loaded weapons trained on him. "*He* did it! William Powell! He shot Tinkham."

Nobody's expression changed. James pointed at William, and his voice was nearly hysterical. "You did it! I saw you! I'll see that you hang for murder!"

"Will you?" Reverend Bowman asked softly.

"I will! And I'll have the law on Frank Tinkham, too, for attempted murder."

"I don't think that would be wise, James," Reverend Bowman said. "It could have been your hand on the gun when it fired. And it would be the word of all of us here against yours."

The men behind him nodded their agreement. James stared, aghast. "You can't threaten me! I can have you all arrested for breaking the Fugitive Slave Law."

"You wouldn't dare!" Bronwyn cried.

Miss Pembrook stepped outside. She eyed the guns anxiously, then turned her attention to James. "As you were so quick to point out to me, James, gossip can be a terrible weapon against you. Who do you think the townsfolk will believe—you, or all of us?"

"*Me*. They would believe *me*. I have plenty of evidence."

Reverend Bowman frowned and looked at James with undisguised loathing. "I am afraid he may be telling the truth this time. And I believe we must also assume that he will do what he says he will. A new marshal will surely be sent to replace poor Mr. Tinkham. Perhaps a misguided but enthusiastic one might even track down some of Tinkham's men to corroborate James' testimony. But it looks bad for you, too, James, with so many witnesses willing to testify against you."

"My father will believe me, too," James said, becoming more confident. "He won't listen to people who break the law."

William stepped forward. "Are you sure, James?"

"Absolutely."

"Your father finances us," William replied quietly.

James shook his head even as the reverend nodded an acknowledgment. "As much as I hate to suggest this, gentlemen and ladies, perhaps it would be best to let James go—with the provision that he leave town at once and never speak of what he knows about the Railroad. If he does, we will expose him as the liar and scoundrel he is and have him charged with murder."

"I'd never be convicted!" James protested, but now his voice was full of bravado, not confidence.

"Maybe not, but your reputation will be ruined, and your father will surely disown you. I think that should be enough to compel you to go to Boston or far away from here, and soon."

Bronwyn joined William and reached for his hand. "Reverend Bowman's right," she said. "As Miss Pembrook says, people like Mrs. Sawyer and Mrs. Wormley will be only too fascinated to hear what we might have to tell them."

James' eyes darted from one grim, determined face to another. Then his own expression hardened. "Very well, I'll go. But not because I'm afraid of you or what you might say. War is coming, and I intend to be in Boston when that happens. I'm going to make a lot of money, and then I'll come back here and make you all pay!" He spun on his heel and, still clutching his bleeding arm, marched toward the stable.

Bronwyn looked at William. "Do you think he will come back someday?"

"Unfortunately, I do. But let's hope that day is a long way off."

As they watched James gallop down the road, Reverend Bowman moved to stand beside them. "I wish we didn't have to let him go, but he knows too much. If we had him arrested, I'm certain he would tell the authorities everything."

"Snake," Bronwyn said vehemently.

"Forget him," William said, pulling her into his embrace. "We're all safe, at least for the time being, but this is the last time I let you convince me to bring you along on something like this."

Bronwyn wanted to protest, but she didn't. Her presence had been too distracting for William, and while the thought of sitting at home and waiting was terrible to contemplate, she knew her own comfort was less important than the job William and his friends had to do.

Two figures appeared at the edge of the woods. "We couldn't go without knowing you were all right," Rob explained when he and Ella drew near. "I guess we can be on our way now."

"There's no hurry," Reverend Bowman said. "Zeke Carter's probably left by now." He sighed wearily. "I'm never going to be able to convince him to wait with his dory again, I'm sure!"

"Then, please, everyone, come in for some tea. Or if you gentlemen would prefer, I do have some of father's brandy hidden in the pantry," Miss Pembrook offered.

The waiting men nodded. After asking two of the men to carry the marshal's body to the undertaker, Reverend Bowman led the way into Miss Pembrook's parlor.

Once inside, Penelope drew Bronwyn aside. "I want to apologize for everything I've said, and especially how I hurt you."

"That's all in the past, Miss Pembrook," Bronwyn said sincerely. "I hope we can be friends."

"Please, call me Penelope."

"I will, and gladly."

Soon everyone was seated or standing in the parlor. Bronwyn sat beside William, and Ella was enthroned on Rob's lap.

As Rob accepted some brandy, he said, "Miss Pembrook, how did you know that Falconer was lying when he said Tinkham knew about our escape the same way he knew about Ella hiding in the chapel?"

The woman's face reddened. "Because I was the one who told Marshal Tinkham about Ella's concealment in the chapel."

"On my orders," Reverend Bowman added hastily.

Miss Pembrook's blush deepened. "I was only too happy to be of assistance," she answered, flustered. "I'll go see if the kettle's boiling." She hurried from the room.

"I knew Tinkham would keep raising the reward until he got some information," the reverend explained, "so I decided it was better to provide the information myself. Or rather, send someone who would benefit from the reward money."

"But we almost got caught!" Rob said indignantly.

"Which would never have happened if you had let us take Ella when we wanted to. We spent too long trying to persuade you not to go with her. I blame myself for underestimating the strength of your passion, Rob. And something good did come of it, after all." The minister looked pointedly at William and Bronwyn, who blushed nearly as much as Miss Pembrook had.

"Miss Pembrook was anxious to help because of her family history," he continued. He saw Bronwyn's and Ella's puzzled faces. "It was two Southerners who persuaded her father to make his unfortunate investments. She was quite amenable to robbing another Southern gentleman of his 'property.'"

Rob's arms tightened around Ella, and he looked from William to Reverend Bowman. "Since we don't have to leave tonight, we have a favor we'd like to ask."

In William and Bronwyn's bedroom, Ella smiled shyly. She was a vision of bridal beauty in a gown of plain white satin with a fitted bodice and long, tight sleeves. The same veil that Bronwyn had worn hung about her like a white mist. The simplicity of the ensemble accentuated Ella's natural loveliness. "Do I look all right?"

Bronwyn adjusted the veil a little. "You are beautiful. Everyone will think so, especially Rob."

"I can't thank you enough. And this veil..."

"Jane says it should bring you luck."

"They're all good people. I hope they'll be happy—although nobody could be as happy as me. Married to Rob and with a real church wedding!"

"Well, a chapel, anyway."

Ella's brow wrinkled with concern. "I hope staying here for the wedding isn't going to get any of you in trouble."

"One more day should be safe enough."

"Is Falconer really gone?"

"Yes. He stayed only long enough to let Dr. Reed see to his arm. Apparently he told the doctor his gun misfired while he was cleaning it."

"Are you ever going to tell people what he did?"

Bronwyn sighed. "James Falconer *does* speak eloquently against slavery. He could still be helpful in the abolitionist cause."

"I guess we'll just have to believe he will, but I'll be glad to get to Canada. Then I know we'll be safe. Is Frank all right?"

"William asked Reverend Bowman about him. Terribly upset he is, poor fellow, but he says he couldn't stand what his father was doing for another moment. He didn't want anyone to be hurt, though. Reverend Bowman thinks Frank will be all right, with Geraldine's love and help."

"I wish I could speak to him, but we daren't stay any longer."

"I wish you didn't have to go at all, Ella."

"So do I. At least I've got Rob." She blushed prettily. "He says he doesn't mind where he is as long as we're together. He'll miss his family, of course. Canada's a long way off. That's why it's so kind of you to let us get married here before we go, so they can be with us. And maybe we'll be able to come back someday. Rob's sure we will. He says slavery's days are numbered in the United States.''

Bronwyn nodded. Although she agreed with Rob, she feared more men would have to die before slavery would be ended. And she knew now that violent death was horrible, whatever the cause.

There was a knock on the door. "It's time to go," William called.

"Are you sure I look all right?" Ella repeated nervously.

"Fine," Bronwyn replied. She opened the door and let Ella precede her.

William joined her, and they followed Ella down the stairs. When they went outside, William took Bronwyn's hand and walked beside her as they went to the chapel.

"Isn't Ella beautiful?" Bronwyn whispered. "It's so wonderful she and Rob found each other, and so sad that they have to go so far away to live."

William squeezed Bronwyn's hand and looked into her eyes. "She's not as pretty as my bride," he replied softly. "And I wonder if Rob can possibly love his wife as much as I love mine."

"Perhaps this chapel's blessed. But hush now. The ceremony's starting."

Rob stood by the altar. He looked nervous, but just as happy as his bride. Reverend Bowman smiled warmly. The other guests, including the rest of the Kent family, Mrs. Bowman, the Gibsons, the Websters, Mrs. Murphy, Sam and the children, all turned expectantly to watch Ella take her place beside the man she loved.

As the ceremony began, brilliant sunlight streamed through the chapel's narrow windows. It rested upon Rob and Ella like a blessing of hope and happiness, or the last lingering benediction of summer before the winter begins.

* * * * *

Maura Seger's
BELLE HAVEN

Four books. Four generations. Four indomitable females.

You met the Belle Haven women who started it all in Harlequin Historicals. Now meet descendant Nora Delaney in the emotional contemporary conclusion to the Belle Haven saga:

THE SURRENDER OF NORA

When Nora's inheritance brings her home to Belle Haven, she finds more than she bargained for. Deadly accidents prove someone wants her out of town—fast. But the real problem is the prime suspect—handsome Hamilton Fletcher. His quiet smile awakens the passion all Belle Haven women are famous for. But does he want her heart...or her life?

Don't miss THE SURRENDER OF NORA
Silhouette Intimate Moments #617
Available in January!

On the most romantic day of the year, capture the thrill of falling in love all over again—with

Harlequin's

Bachelors

They're three sexy and *very single* men who run very special personal ads to find the women of their fantasies by Valentine's Day. These exciting, passion-filled stories are written by bestselling Harlequin authors.

Your Heart's Desire by Elise Title
Mr. Romance by Pamela Bauer
Sleepless in St. Louis by Tiffany White

Be sure not to miss Harlequin's Valentine Bachelors, available in February wherever Harlequin books are sold.

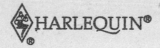

VB

This holiday, join four hunky heroes under the mistletoe for

Christmas Kisses

Cuddle under a fluffy quilt, with a cup of hot chocolate and these romances sure to warm you up:

#561 HE'S A REBEL (also a Studs title)
Linda Randall Wisdom

#562 THE BABY AND THE BODYGUARD
Jule McBride

#563 THE GIFT-WRAPPED GROOM
M.J. Rodgers

#564 A TIMELESS CHRISTMAS
Pat Chandler

Celebrate the season with all four holiday books sealed with a Christmas kiss—coming to you in December, only from Harlequin American Romance!

CHRISTMAS STALKINGS

All wrapped up in spine-tingling packages, here are
three books guaranteed to chill your spine...and
warm your hearts this holiday season!

#302 THE KID WHO STOLE CHRISTMAS
Linda Stevens

#303 I'LL BE HOME FOR CHRISTMAS
Dawn Stewardson

#304 BEARING GIFTS
Aimée Thurlo

This December, fill your stockings with the
"Christmas Stalkings"—for the best in romantic
suspense. Only from

HARLEQUIN®

INTRIGUE®

If you are looking for more titles by

BARBARA BRETTON

Don't miss these fabulous stories by one of
Harlequin's most renowned authors:

Harlequin American Romance®

#16393	BUNDLE OF JOY	$3.25	☐
#16493	RENEGADE LOVER	$3.50	☐

Harlequin® Promotional Titles

#83246	SOMEWHERE IN TIME	$4.99	☐
#83238	TO HAVE AND TO HOLD	$4.99	☐

(short-story collection also featuring Rita Clay Estrada,
Sandra James, Debbie Macomber)

(limited quantities available on certain titles)

TOTAL AMOUNT	$
POSTAGE & HANDLING	$
($1.00 for one book, 50¢ for each additional)	
APPLICABLE TAXES*	$_____
TOTAL PAYABLE	$_____
(check or money order—please do not send cash)	

To order, complete this form and send it, along with a check or money order
for the total above, payable to Harlequin Books, to: In the U.S.: 3010 Walden
Avenue, P.O. Box 9047, Buffalo, NY 14269-9047; In Canada: P.O. Box 613,
Fort Erie, Ontario, L2A 5X3.

Name: _____

Address: _____ City: _____

State/Prov.: _____ Zip/Postal Code: _____

*New York residents remit applicable sales taxes.
Canadian residents remit applicable GST and provincial taxes.   HBBBACK2